Surfaces

ANN DENTON

Le Rue
Publishing

Le Rue Publishing
320 South Boston Avenue, Suite 1030
Tulsa, OK 74103
www.LeRuePublishing.com

ISBN: 978-1-951714-22-2

If you ever had a wish go wrong, this one's for you...

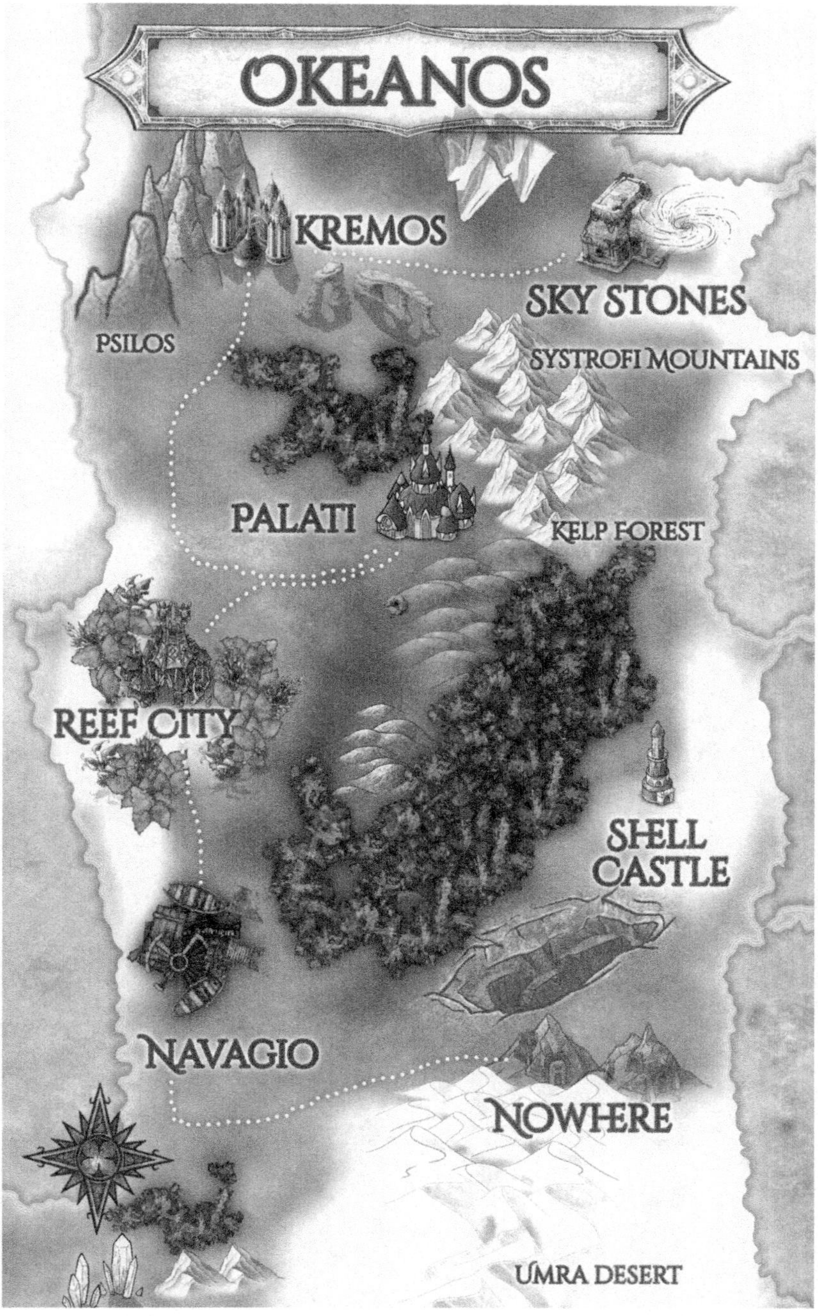
OKEANOS
KREMOS
SKY STONES
PSILOS
SYSTROFI MOUNTAINS
PALATI
KELP FOREST
REEF CITY
SHELL
CASTLE
NAVAGIO
NOWHERE
UMRA DESERT

PROLOGUE

Raj

I think I've had a heart palpitation, I decided as I rubbed dolefully at my chest, trying to soothe the uncomfortable ache inside. I'd heard of such things, seen older men at my court in Cheryn struck down by a sudden illness of the heart, sometimes even dropping dead.

Unease slithered through my ears and down the back of my neck.

Illness wouldn't do.

I was the unending king, the sultan of Cheryn. Temporarily deposed but I'd regain my crown—once I'd finished here, that was. Once I'd destroyed the Queen of Okeanos and her pathetic little sister.

I tapped at the offending organ in warning.

It had better heed that warning. Or I'd find a replacement.

Could a heart be replaced? It had never been done that I was aware of. But I'd performed wish magic that no djinni before me had ever seen. And I didn't mind sacrificing a few hundred men to experiment and see if it was possible.

I tapped my fingers against my thumb one by one as I pondered where that odd palpitation had come from. Was it turning myself into an underwater being? Perhaps. I was used to djinni shape, the loose twist of smoke instead of limbs on my lower half. Was having a fully corporeal body all the time making my heart work too hard? It seemed unlikely. I'd given myself human legs on land before ... but never for quite this long.

Perhaps.

Or perhaps it's the excitement of destruction. It's been a bit since my fight with Bloss. I was used to a regular routine of bloodshed. Maybe my heart was out of shape, not as desensitized as normal.

Or maybe it's water pressure. The sea pressing down on me.

I'd have to deduce the source of this irritation and get rid of it.

After all, I had plans. I'd lived over a thousand years and planned to live at least another millennium. I had revenge to complete and a kingdom to regain, then a world to conquer—that left no time for petty mortal matters.

I chewed my lip and wondered where the chink in my magical weave of wishes was. What had I forgotten to wish for that had allowed disease to slither in? Was disease even possible?

Deftly, I sought out the black ring on my finger and twisted it as I lay on my sea sponge bedroll in the dark, not bothering to relight my lantern. This heart issue was far more pressing and besides, I wasn't a fool scared of darkness.

I *was* darkness.

I let my mind roll through the various wishes I'd forced Cheryn's citizens to make for me through the years; wishes to strengthen my body, to renew it, wishes to magically reinforce it. There had to be at least five hundred wishes made for my skin alone ... trying to recall ones made for my heart would be impossible.

A wish couldn't restore a prior state, it was one of the limitations of wish magic, so I couldn't erase whatever damage had been done by this palpitation.

Drat and dust.

However ... I might be able to get around that. Wishes were all in the wording. If I couldn't wish for something that *was*, I could wish for something that had never been in the history of the world.

Most djinn didn't understand that, weren't creative enough to conceive of it.

That was why I'd risen above them to rule the most magical country in all the kingdoms of Sedara.

I carefully composed my wishes inside my mind. Then I twisted my ring and whispered, "I wish this shuddering heart inside my chest was strong and bright, powerful, and long-lasting as the sun."

I felt the organ heat and swell a bit inside my ribcage as the magic took hold. A little sliver of satisfied excitement ran through me before suddenly, for no sarding reason, I burst into tears.

What the sard?

1

Avia Hale

A shaft of moonlight pierced the ocean and drifted down through the coral reef, gently caressing my face as though soothing me. It wasn't. All the moonlight in the sky couldn't ease the raw torment inside me. Still, I stared up at the moon through a skylight in my borrowed bedroom in Reef City as tears filled my eyes, and my hands clenched into fists so that I wouldn't touch my chest, that empty cavern, and realize the magnitude of what I'd just done. I'd given up my heart. Literally.

There should be a rule, some sort of limit to the number of horrors a soul can endure.

My tears erupted in a fountain despite my effort to maintain control and blink them away. Too much had happened today, and I'd had to hold back for hours. A queen had to remain calm in any crisis.

I'd had to shovel aside cold, unmoving rock after the tournament arena collapsed in upon itself, its rainbow benches disintegrating into a mountain of debris. I'd helped move bodies. Lifeless bodies. And I'd carefully had to bite my tongue—but never hard enough to draw blood and scent the water for the shark shifters. The mask of calm, collected control I'd worn all day had grown too heavy and now that I was in my room, it fell from my face as tears slid from my cheeks into the seawater.

Up on land, tears didn't dance. But under the ocean, your tears mocked you by trailing from your skin and spiraling gorgeously down toward your feet. Sadness turned into this beautiful wisp. It didn't fall and plop with a splat, breaking apart just like you did. Tears under the ocean were wrong. Just wrong.

In my private quarters in Mayor Deacon's home, away from the aftermath of the rebel attack, with the spell to transfer my heart to my enemy complete—I couldn't staunch the flow.

The emotions that swept me up and leaked out of my eyes varied from one second to the next because I was overwrought. First, I remembered the lifeless eyes of two people dragged from the rubble with a dull sort of regret and self-loathing. Then I pictured my advisor,

Sahar, sobbing over her son, Keelan, the sweetest, funniest man competing for my hand in this shite tournament. I catapulted into a turbulent sorrow that rocked me like a boat in a storm. I had to remind myself Keelan would live. His arm was ruined, his life forever changed. But he was alive. The next emotion that tugged at me wasn't driven by a visual memory. It was just a red-hot bolt of anger.

I was a mess, and my chest ached horribly with all these chaotic feelings. It was almost as if giving up my heart had doubled my ability to feel, which was absolutely wretched. I tried to breathe and calm myself, not to let the sensations take over my good sense, but it was so difficult—my feelings were wild, and I'd leashed them for so long that now they bolted around inside of me bucking and trilling some wordless lament.

"Avia." Lizza, the undead witch who'd just performed her spell on me, spoke my name.

I stayed turned away, not wanting her to see my pain. I was crying too hard to respond anyway, though her voice made me start and then grow embarrassed. I'd nearly forgotten she was there, caught up in this whirlwind of emotions. I swiped at my eyes and took a deep breath, before I turned toward her rotting face, spotting a flap of skin that hung loose on her cheek.

Wallowing won't do. Buck up, Avia. I scolded myself firmly as I searched my head for solutions because I needed to ground myself before these abysmal sobs bruised my ribs and scalded my throat. I decided to use a physical distraction to center myself. It was a technique one of my fathers had taught me when I'd been four years old and prone to fits. I used to have a stuffed toy mouse and I would stroke his tail to calm down.

I grabbed at one of the ribbons on the skirt of my ruined dress, trying to ignore the rips and frayed spots from the day's disaster. I stroked the material while I took slow deep breaths, trying to focus on the external instead of the internal. I let my fingers travel over the silk and noted the smooth texture, the ripple of the hem. I focused on the steadiness of my own breath. It worked a bit differently underwater than it had when I'd thought I was human. Though the ocean felt like air to me, it didn't act like air, and when I blew out a steady breath, a tiny little current traveled through my room and jangled a small bedside sconce hung with crystals.

I tried to focus on what I could do now rather than everything that had happened. I could access my power. I could prevent things like today's terror.

A sea sprite was meant to control the sea itself with her magic. I was half-sprite, one of maybe a dozen in the entire world. The entire ocean was at my beck and call. Or would be, once I learned to control it.

I squinted my eyes as I attempted to envision myself bending water to my will. Naturally, I imagined stopping the arena's collapse by shoving a huge wave across the rainbow-colored coral seats, a wave that swept the crowd safely away, gently suspending the rocks in water while those in the tunnels beneath swam off. If I could do such things, surely there'd be no more protests. No more shouts of sky-breather. No one carrying *Forsake the Crown* banners.

I felt light-headed at the prospect that I'd be able to do so much. But there was also a growing sense of foreboding in my belly. It was like the little bursts of smoke and lava that preceded a volcanic eruption. Because there was a price to that kind of power. To access such power, a half-human sea sprite like myself had to give up her humanity—her emotions.

The first step: magically giving away her heart, which I'd just done. The organ had been magically plucked from my body and placed inside the body of my greatest enemy—so that I could access my powers and protect my kingdom from violent rebellions like the one today.

I still had emotions because I hadn't used my powers yet. But soon, I'd be forced to do so, I was certain. The rebels wouldn't stop. There'd been two attacks in a short period of time. There was certain to be a third.

One I'd have to react to, and then…who kew who I'd become…

I'm slowly going to turn into a monster because of Watkins and his fucking rebels. But if I was going to suffer, then so was he.

That bastard.

The shark shifter had taken advantage of my hospitality and used it to feed information to them so they could attack the jousting arena—no one but an insider could have done it.

Keelan had nearly been killed in that strike. Other innocent people had died today. Two that I knew of but more were with healers, their outlooks uncertain. It was the kind of horror I would not stand for. It would end, I'd make certain of it.

I gritted my teeth together. "Get it together," I chastised myself softly.

"What was that?" Lizza asked from across the room. "One of my eardrums is about rotted out, you know? Speak up."

I shook my head and said, "Nothing," but my tone was harsh, and my face was grim as I thought about the rebel who was responsible for all of this.

"I don't like that expression at all," Lizza retorted while she fiddled with some of her magical knick-knacks, things I didn't know the name of. "You look as wild as the Queen of Gitmore."

I turned my violet eyes toward her, my mind still swirling with furious thoughts of revenge as I stared at the mage that I had been loaned by my sister, Bloss. I swiped at my tears one more time and finally managed to stifle them. "I do not. She's ancient." I was only eighteen.

Lizza cackled as she gazed back at me, the greenish tone of her undead skin highlighted by the floating lanterns that bobbed around the bedroom. One of her eyes was starting to get a bit of a grey film over it. It was disorienting to look at—but the undead always were. Their bodies rotted even as they lived on endlessly, and Lizza had lived for quite some time. Her jawbone peeked out from beneath her skin as she said, "She's a babe in swaddling as far as I'm concerned. In any case, the vengeful look doesn't suit you any more than crying does. And I won't do a spell for that wrinkle between your brows—best not to encourage it."

I stuck my tongue out at my mage, embracing her levity because it was better than the other emotions tugging at me. Those were all much darker monsters, ones better wrestled in private. I tried to relax my face though my stomach still fizzed fearfully. I was too impulsive. I knew that. But I'd just given in to impulse in the most terrifying of ways, trusting it with my magic—my future.

Mayi, my birth mother, had had terrible luck giving her own heart to a lover and then her unwitting child. I wasn't repeating her mistake, wasn't trusting someone with mine. In fact, I'd done the opposite by giving mine to the man I trusted least in the world, one I hated. It took the saying, *Keep your friends close and enemies closer,* to another level. But I still wasn't certain that my decision wasn't a huge mistake.

It was risky.

Unlike my sister, I didn't enjoy risk.

Ugh. My chest lurched uncomfortably, and even though my heart wasn't present, my emotions still erupted from that spot like a phantom limb, spreading over my body and prickling. I rubbed at my chest bone, trying to get the sensation to die down. "I thought I wasn't supposed to have feelings once I gave my heart away."

"Let me grab the x-ray fish and we'll just confirm that my spell actually worked, and your heart is gone," Lizza said before turning back to her bag. She dug into the battered black leather, and an alarming number of sounds erupted from within—including a wail that sounded much like a small child.

"You mean you're not sure it's gone?" I sat forward on the bed in a panic.

“I meant what I said. I want to check,” the crotchety old mage shot back as her hand dug into the bag.

Oh, well then. That’s reassuring. Thanks, Lizza, I spat back. But only inside my head.

Lizza pulled out a small glass jar, the lid sealed on with wax. Inside, layered and tightly packed, were at least forty x-ray fish. Their translucent bodies revealed their backbones and bits of organs. Lizza deftly broke the seal with a large knife and then pried off the lid. Immediately, the charming scent of dead fish floated around the room, carried by the current.

My nose wrinkled and my stomach jumped in rebellion as Lizza stomped forward with the jar, eyes set grimly on me.

“That looks disgusting.”

“Probably tastes worse than it looks,” she replied. “Now, head back, mouth open,” she ordered gruffly.

My stomach sank, though as soon as I’d seen the jar, I’d been expecting bad news. Lizza’s magic always seemed to involve eating something horrid. I had a feeling she was secretly a sadist and enjoyed a bit of torture alongside her magic. “Only one, right?”

“Just swallow,” the mage replied, holding the rim near my lips.

Not the answer I wanted.

Suddenly, my tongue was coated in a thick slime interrupted by the occasional scratch of a fish scale. But, to my utter shock and amazement, once I got past the strange texture, the taste was ... strawberries and cinnamon. I could almost imagine it was jam if I ignored some of the textures. It was surprisingly sweet, almost delicious even. I swallowed once, trying not to inhale through my nose so that the scents couldn't call my taste buds liars. If these fish didn't taste like strawberry jam, I really didn't want to know. I couldn't hurl. I was certain that if I puked these nasty creatures up Lizza would have a fit and then make me eat them second-hand off the floor.

The undead woman did *not* mess around when it came to magic.

The second swallow I took was even worse than the first because the scent of decay finally hit me when I had to breathe. Immediately, I gagged and had to fist my hands in my golden hair as I swallowed.

"Please," I begged after the third swallow.

"Anything. My kingdom. You can have it. Just no more."

But Lizza was relentless. Perhaps her heart had rotted along with her skin. She made me finish the *entire jar*.

By the time I felt the last little fin flop down my throat, I desperately shoved past her for the pitcher of bubble that perched on my nightstand. It was supposed to be for washing, but I grabbed the glazed clay handle and tilted it back to chug down all of the contents trying desperately to rid my mouth of the awful film coating it.

When I set down the pitcher and stared into the mirror, I gave a startled cry. I hadn't looked at myself thoroughly since I'd returned to my quarters. I was expecting to look a fright. What I was not expecting was for Lizza's spell to work instantly. Eating the enchanted x-ray fish had turned my pale skin translucent from the waist up. My gold hair seemed to float eerily just above my skull. My wide violet eyes now blinked oddly in their eye sockets, pink muscles flexing each time my gaze changed direction. I reached up to touch the cartilage of my nose only to be distracted by the muscles and veins in my hands. My skin was as clear as the tips of the betta fish fins that sprouted like fairy wings on my back.

"Holy sarding shite," I whispered. "This is scary."

Lizza rolled her eyes. Or attempted to. It appeared as though one of her eye muscles no longer worked properly, and so one eye just bounced from side to side eerily for a second before popping back into focus. "You need to see a bit more of the world if you still think body parts are scary."

I turned a little to my right, staring down at my left pectoral muscle and trying to see if I could tell if my heart still lay underneath. I couldn't, though I could see the steady surge in my veins. My blood was pumping ... where was the source? I turned further and leaned forward as I tried to gaze between my ribs.

"Is it really gone?" I asked as Lizza bent down near me.

She only hummed in reply. But then her fingers prodded at my ribs as she shoved aside my slinky top to get a better look.

"Ack, too many muscles in the way," she muttered before turning away and shuffling back to her bag of doom.

"I'm full. Stuffed. I can't eat anything else," I called out futilely.

"Only a man's testicle, no big deal this time," she replied.

I clenched my teeth together, uncertain if she was joking.

A second later, Lizza was back with a tiny vial. One second she held it and the next she'd dumped it onto her palm and was rubbing black powder on the left side of my chest. To my horror, not only did my translucent skin seem to disappear—but my muscles started to rot away making the bones beneath visible.

I shrieked.

The door to my room flew open and my personal guard, Felipe, peered inside.

I waved my translucent hands frantically to stop him. "Go away! I'm fine! I'm fine!"

The handsome merman cocked a dark blue brow as he stared at me in utter shock. "Shite."

My other regular guard, Ugo, poked his head in as well, the tip of his spear appearing around the door. "What's going—oh my sarding hell!" The orange-haired merman burst into the room, spear pointed right at Lizza.

"Get out!" I screeched, trying to cover my chest out of habit, though if they saw anything there other than nightmarish bone and half-rotted muscles and tendons, I didn't know.

"Are you sure?" Felipe asked, raising his scarred eyebrow and sounding disinclined to listen to my request. "This isn't harming you?"

"Yes, I'm fine. Leave."

"You don't look fine. You look see-through." Ugo couldn't help but point out the obvious.

"Out." I hissed the word from between my teeth.

"Magic stuff going on in here. Lady things. About monthly cycles and nipple circulation; all that fun stuff." Lizza turned to them with a grin that showcased her decaying lip.

I wasn't certain if it was Lizza—or what she said—but Ugo shuddered and the two mermen exited in a flurry of bubbles, the door closing behind them with a definite *thump.*

I let out a massive sigh of relief and a half-sobbing laugh followed. "Well. That was … traumatic all around."

Lizza didn't respond. She was too busy bent over and prodding at me, rubbing in little bits of leftover powder. "Ah! There it is! It worked! You have a hole where your heart used to be ... kind of odd to see all those arteries just disappearing into midair."

I glanced down, and sure enough, even the bone seemed to disappear underneath Lizza's black powder. The left side of my chest appeared to hold only a lung and a couple veins that dangled like vines. But the thing that made my stomach lurch was … well seeing my own stomach and the snaking pink of my intestines.

I fought against the lurch of disgust that went through my system at the knowledge that this freakish sight was my own body. But I couldn't quite fight off the lightheadedness. My still-translucent hands grabbed onto the dressing table in front of me and I leaned into it for support.

"How long until this wears off?" I asked, trying to avoid looking at my face in the mirror or my hands or my feet. It didn't really leave me with a lot of options. I ended up glancing upward at the ceiling of my coral room, back at the skylight that mocked me.

"Scare powder lasts about an hour."

“Scare powder?”

Lizza answered, “Yes. The undead army used to use it to intimidate their foes. Not many men can stand to see someone’s innards—even soldiers. Rub a little on. Show off an intestine or two and they flinch away—easy targets. Chop their heads off fast as chickens at supper.”

My nose wrinkled but I couldn’t argue with the truth of her words. I’d never been in battle myself—not unless one counted the attack on my carriage as we traveled here to Reef City.

But neither I nor my guards were able to handle the sight of me right now. I could only imagine the vision that would have faced soldiers squaring off against the undead army. Too bad they’d mostly disbanded, many desiring the afterlife. I had a few left in Okeanos. Posey, a half-flower sprite. Lizza. Not too many remained.

Lizza continued on, "I haven't used the x-ray fish before; that's something I picked up visiting some of the local healers in your capital city, Palati. Not sure about that one. It could last longer or shorter."

"This stuff lasts about an hour? I have meetings ..." I brought my palm toward my face but stopped short, distracted by the stretch of muscle and vein. Lizza was right. It was so disorienting. I closed my eyes in frustration.

Of course, a knock came on my door at that very moment. I turned to see Felipe open the door and quickly lower his eyes to the floor. He tried to hide a shudder but failed. "Majesty, I'm sorry to interrupt, but there are several competitors here to see you." He chewed his lip, an unusually nervous sign from my normally stoic guard was normally so stoic. "There are at least four men out there. And they all wish to withdraw from the tournament."

Withdraw? Well... isn't that the golden topper to this shitecake of a day?

2

Lizza helped me dress because I refused to terrorize my poor mermaid, Gita, with the sight of her mistress as a ghastly … gross … well, nearly undead figure because my muscles were still exposed beneath my skin. For Lizza, dressing me wasn't much worse than looking in the mirror during her own daily routine. Or so she told me as she walked to the dressing room to select something for me to wear.

"I didn't know the undead got dressed," I said stupidly. What I didn't say was that I very much had *wanted* to believe that Lizza's clothes had melded with her rotting body and were never ever removed. Anything else was just too horrid to imagine.

I dug into a box on top of my dressing table full of jewelry and carefully selected and put on three choker necklaces to hide my neck from sight before even finding a new outfit. Without the broad strips of black ribbon and jewels, the muscles and tendons moved clearly with every word I spoke. And I was certain that if rumor of such a sight spread, *all* the men competing for my hand would quit.

I sighed, wondering how long I could put them off.

"Please, you and I aren't all that different," Lizza scoffed as she yanked out and rejected various revealing dresses from the rack. "Just a bit of sag here and rotting flesh there, but really, we're basically the same."

I pressed my lips together, trying to remain diplomatic, but then Lizza added, "I mean, between the sheets, let me tell you, a man can't tell one broad from another. Shoot, half have no idea what they're doing. One time, I was with a man who was rather drunk and he kept prodding his dick at a little decayed bit near my thigh and ripped right through—"

Images far worse than the sight of my own innards poured over me like hot tar. "Found a dress yet?" I asked, my voice a desperate screech as I tried to wipe my mind clean, though the effort was as futile as trying to swipe away thick mud … it just ended up spreading. I spent a few horribly torturous moments stuck inside my own mind with Lizza's love life weaving a tawdry picture before I calmed myself with images of Evaness … my old bedroom and its tapestries, running through the hallways and hiding behind suits of armor, squatting with a servant girl behind the orchestra and making fart noises as they practiced for some ball. Those were the days. My life used to be simple and easy. Now each day seemed to compete to come with a challenge worse than yesterday.

Lizza hummed as she quested for the perfect dress until she finally stopped on a gauzy golden silk piece that was layered and draped to resemble petals. She pulled it out. “Hmmm. How’s this?”

The dress was one of my favorites. I’d tried to describe a rose to one of the seamstresses and she’d come up with this dress that resembled a chrysanthemum more than a rose, with long slender golden petals that puffed out into a short but wide skirt. And while my legs would be on display, my entire torso would be covered because the neckline was straight from shoulder to shoulder. It was definitely one of the most modest gowns I had, one I’d requested before trying to embrace the “freer” nature of Okeanos residents, where mer women and sirens often went topless. But it would perfectly suit my needs today since my upper half could not be seen for at least another thirty minutes.

I nodded at her, and she walked back over, laying the dress over the chair near my dressing table before she helped me strip off the old gown with fingers as rough as tree bark.

I'd drunk all the bubble in my pitcher, so had no means to wash off the dirt from the rubble that stained my translucent arms here and there. I was going to just dismiss it—dirt was the least of my worries—but Lizza went to her bag and got out two pink crystals. When she returned, she held them decisively near my chest and tapped them together once, making a tiny white spark alight inside them. The dirt floated instantly away from my skin as I watched in awe.

"Don't move or that muck will get right back on you," she warned.

I froze and let the little particles drift slowly to the floor while I tried to think about what to say to these men who wanted to quit.

What could I say, really? I wouldn't force anyone—other than Watkins—to continue the competition. That bastard could rot in a tower room in my castle for all I cared. No, actually, he couldn't. Because that would be too easy.

But if these other men wanted to leave, I would let them, even though the thought created a hollow void in my chest.

The tournament had already been reduced to twenty men from the joust—or would be tomorrow morning when standings were announced. Those who'd competed already knew their basic rank.

While there were three more rounds to complete in the open ocean tomorrow morning, it was pretty well-known which men would make it through those, other than Keelan, whom I wasn't certain could compete with his ruined arm. I didn't know if the challenge would be too much for him because I had no idea what it was.

Those who'd already lost or known their elimination was certain had no reason to come announce their intention to quit. That meant these four were competitors that were supposed to make it through to the next round.

We'd be down to sixteen instead of twenty if they left.

"What will people think if men abandon the tournament?" I asked, grabbing at the emerald on one of my choker necklaces. It wasn't really a question for Lizza since she was as much a foreigner to Okeanos as I was. It was a question for Sahar, my adviser. But I'd insisted the siren take the rest of the day off to be with her injured son. And I couldn't walk into that room to face those men without knowing what to say.

"They're cowards," Lizza retorted as she set her crystals down and helped me wrangle the dress over my head and get it set in place.

"Perhaps, but they're practical. We've been attacked twice now." I fussed with the bottom hem of my underskirt as I ruefully tried to consider things from a competitor's perspective. They'd signed up for a bit of adventure but gotten quite a lot of trouble instead.

I wasn't worth all this danger, obviously. I mean, I'd have thought the same of nearly any man. Well, except for Mateo. Perhaps Felipe. *All in all, they're just being prudent,* I decided. Then I smoothed the silk petals of my skirt and grabbing a brush so that I could deal with the tangle of my hair. I could appreciate caution.

"Meh, open attacks are easy to deal with. It's stealthy ones you have to worry about," Lizza shrugged as she went back to her bag and began to deftly reorganize the contents and pack it up. "If these fools can't handle open attacks, then you're better off without them. They wouldn't be able to handle the pressure of court life long-term."

I tried to convince myself that was true as I set down the brush and had my fingers work a particularly nasty snarl. But my gut didn't believe her.

My gut told me that these men had lost confidence in me and my position as queen. They thought these attacks were too much for me and didn't think I could keep them safe. The fact that I'd simply watched as my carriage was waylaid and been carried off like some fainting ninny didn't bode well.

What if Humberto was in the group that wanted to leave? The great hero who'd saved so many? He'd been forced to use his power because I hadn't had access to mine.

Or Valdez? He'd shifted and attacked a shark.

My stomach got as knotted as my hair when I realized how they might feel. That guilt transformed into fear as I thought about how many people they'd tell. What they'd say.

Queen Avia just stood there. Didn't even lift a finger. She made her guards fight for their lives and let her own household be attacked. Watched it all like it was a game of hammer-throwing.

The news of their choice would spread as quickly as a disease and infect the ears of many.

Shite. What could I do to minimize the damage?

"Should I make a formal announcement that I'll allow any man to withdraw?" I chewed my lip uncertainly. What if there were more than four who wanted to leave? Could I really host three more rounds of the tournament with only twelve men? Or ten? What if only five stayed? Faith in the crown would plummet.

A desperate desire to speak to Bloss or have Queen Gela alive and well rose up inside of me. I wanted someone to hug me and tell me how to fix this.

Declan had been right. I should have called off this foolish tournament from the start. I was arrogant denying my brother-in-law and flippantly thinking that I was ready to handle a crown.

"They must feel unsafe if they're leaving," I said aloud, mostly thinking to myself as I dug out the last of the snarls.

Lizza *tsked* before saying, "I don't know about that. If you want to know how men feel, ask a man. No magic in the world can make me understand those idiots."

I barked out a laugh before I could fully suppress it, but then I pressed my lips together while I plaited my hair, running through options, each one seeming more foolish than the last.

Lizza stood to leave. I quickly fluttered over to my dressing room, snagging a furry sapphire cloak from the rack and tossing it over myself. Felipe and Ugo had been traumatized enough by the sight of me and there was no reason for them to continue to suffer. "Thank you, Lizza. You're a treasure." I told her as I pulled the cloak carefully down over my forehead so that my face was thrown into shadow. Hopefully, that would conceal the worst of it.

She gave a grin. "Yes, well, I wish I could say the same about your own castle mages. I'm off to talk the bumpkins through some basic healing spells."

"I appreciate that. And then, maybe soon, we can test out your theories about using my power and retaining my humanity at the same time." I retained hope, perhaps a bit more hope than was reasonable, that the undead witch could prevent me from turning into a cold-hearted beast the first time I activated my sea sprite magic.

"What's the rush on that?" Lizza looked genuinely confused as though my request had taken her off-guard.

What's the rush?

Fury lanced me and part of me wanted to drag her back out to the arena and show her the chaos because to me the need to use magic burnt like a wildfire—it was urgent and obvious. I was going to have to use power soon to stop this rebellion. But Lizza was old and had seen hundreds of battlefields. Today probably only registered as a blip on her scale while it weighed my soul down heavily. I licked my lips and smiled carefully before saying, "I want to be the queen the people of Okeanos deserve. And they deserve to be safe and well-treated."

Lizza didn't argue, though she did sigh. "Always more work to do. I'll look over my notes on the matter."

She pulled open the door and I was going to pace my room a bit, draw out the time before the impending conversation with the four men abandoning ship, but I saw Felipe lean in to check on me. Impulsively, I beckoned him in.

“Felipe, can I speak with you for a moment?” I asked.

The burly merman swam aside to let Lizza out first before he came into my room. I nodded toward the door, and he closed it with a gentle thump.

My hands fingered the hem of my cloak nervously, plucking at the threads. “Lizza says this spell she did to check on me should wear off shortly. But … there’s so much to do. I didn’t want to delay. Is the horror sufficiently hidden?”

His mouth quirked up in a half-smile and said, “Never a horror, Majesty.”

“Liar,” I retorted.

“Careful. Those who insult my honor have to face a duel.”

“You’d point your sword at me?”

“I’d do more than point.”

Ugo’s head popped in through the door. “I couldn’t help overhearing. Do I need to swim off a bit and give you two some privacy so you can stick her with your sword?”

“UGO!” Felipe bellowed.

"We were just teasing," I chastised, the heat of embarrassment rising on my cheeks.

"Just checking. I do not want to be on duty for any... sultry business."

I rolled my eyes.

"Get out." Felipe ordered his fellow guard around as though he was a captain.

Ugo shut the door with a click and Felipe turned hesitantly back to me. "Sorry. We seem to have gotten off track."

I cleared my throat. "Yes. Um. The men who want to withdraw... Are they still just outside?" I couldn't hide my hesitance, not only about meeting them while I looked like this but about meeting these men at all.

It was one thing to have one man reject you. Or for a couple to simply decide they were incompatible. But to have four men shove me aside at once ... even if it was because of an attack, it was going to be a painful experience, because even if I didn't feel anything for them, all of them had decided that I wasn't good enough. I wasn't worth it—and that stung because it hit on every insecurity I had.

But Felipe shook his head and relief flooded my veins as he said, "I had them move down the hall to a small meeting room."

“Good. Good.” I nodded and paced, the cloak rubbing my betta fish fins uncomfortably. I second-guessed my decision to invite Felipe in but I had no one else to ask.

“Is … is everything alright?” Felipe asked softly, tilting his head, his blue eyes studying me, or what little he could see. He floated gently just above the ground, tail fin swishing lightly. Normally, he took a potion that gave him legs so he could walk beside me and make me more comfortable, but his potion had long ago worn off in the aftermath of the attack. The dark blue scales of his tail glinted in the lantern light as my eyes focused on them and I tried to find the words I needed.

“Majesty?” he asked again, dragging my gaze up his torso, over his leather and tortoise shell armor, which had been dented and damaged. There was even a bit of coral stuck on one side that I had the urge to grab and remove. But I didn’t.

I looked up at his face again and I was glad for the cloak, so he couldn’t see the nervousness that stopped my question in my throat and drove me to pace.

Much of the time, Felipe faded into the background, fulfilling his role as my bodyguard perfectly. But sometimes, he was as perceptively sharp as a spear, usually when he worried about me. My problem was that his concern always felt like something more than a simple desire to keep me alive. Or perhaps I just *wished* it did because I'd been smitten from the moment he was assigned to me. The surly merman with the heart of gold—the romantic, girlish side of me just couldn't resist those traits. The soft look he'd just given me made me blush and derailed my thoughts with desperate imaginings.

He didn't feel the same. There'd been one moment… but it was probably all projection on my part. Felipe was quite a bit older than me—in his mid-thirties. He was already graying at his temples, his dark blue hair fading slowly.

I took a second to study the lines on his face, the few crevices in his forehead that I thought made him look distinguished. The crow's feet around his eyes were hardly there though as if he didn't quite laugh enough, which was a shame. He was an extraordinarily handsome merman. And he was thoughtful. He deserved to smile more. I tried to hope one day he'd find a woman who made him smile, but I was actually too selfish to hope for that.

I swallowed hard to force my mind to the topic I wanted to address and shoved aside the tender hope that his softer looks brought out because they were foolishness, plain and simple.

"I need to know what to say to those men who want to withdraw," I told him, hoping my tone didn't come across as too brisk because I was overcompensating. "I don't know enough of Okeanos's customs. Sahar's gone right now. I just … how should I address it?"

His grip on his spear grew tighter and his reply was quick. "You'll ask them what size shackle they prefer."

His response startled me. It couldn't have been further from what I was thinking than the sun was from the moon. I froze and stared at him. "What?"

"Those sea scum deserve to be locked up. They signed up to risk life and limb for tournament competitions but they're going to turn tail at the first sign of true danger? Sarding fools don't deserve your hand or to be anywhere near the throne."

A delighted, almost giddy sense of satisfaction rose up inside of me at his brutal defense and his scorn for the men outside. I absolutely adored his indignation on my behalf. It showcased his loyalty, which was something I had in short supply as a foreign queen. I refused to let myself hold on to the wistful thought that his anger signified anything more. Or, I tried to. "Well, I agree about the cowardice. But taking them prisoner—"

"You don't have a choice."

"No?" My eyebrows shot up nearly to my hair.

"The stability of Okeanos depends on people having faith in the strength of the crown. Letting those dimwits swim off would admit you have no belief in your own magic. It would say you don't think you'll be able to end these attacks. That's not true. Is it?"

A long moment passed where Felipe and I stared at one another, tension mounting, at least on my end. My secrets sat on the edge of my lips and the urge to trust him welled up, his warm gaze as intoxicating as whiskey—and twice as likely to loosen my tongue. I craved that look he gave me, that intense stare. His brow was straight, and his features were relaxed and anyone else might not have noticed. But his eyes burned. They were a deep blue fire; I could feel their heat from across the room and it stoked something low inside my belly.

I took a step toward him.

My lips opened.

But I forced myself to glance away.

Queen Gela, Bloss, and Lizza would all skin me alive if I spoke.

Magical secrets were a queen's undoing.

"Queen Avia..." His tone was soft, nearly breathless, as if he might be just as affected as me.

No. It couldn't be, could it?

Not when I looked like this ... I glanced over at the mirror and saw that my cheeks and forehead had nearly returned to normal. But a glance down at my hands told me to keep my fingers covered. The transparency spell was fading but not gone. Which meant his look … might have been …

I glanced back.

Shite.

He was even closer than before, having swum up further into the space between us.

He inhaled but then held his breath, almost as if he was fighting back a confession.

Just like me.

My eyes caressed his jawline. He'd proved his loyalty time and again. And I'd thought more than once that he'd guessed at my issue—my failing heart.

Without meaning to, I stepped forward, so close that I could feel the heat of his body warming the water between us. I had to tilt my head up to gaze into his eyes, which had grown hooded.

Desire swirled inside my veins and nudged me up onto my tiptoes.

"Is it an issue?" he whispered, his tone promising that he'd keep it between us. "Are those attacks too much?"

Gah! I wanted to tell him. I wanted to tell him and then kiss him.

But . . . he wasn't part of the tournament.

And I'd bound myself—sworn an oath before this tournament started only to marry the competitors who were declared winners.

Felipe and I could never be.

Shite! It was so damned ironically unfair that the man I was falling for happened to be the one who wasn't competing for my hand. Over thirty competitors, but I swooned over my guard!

Torture.

It was torture.

I dropped down onto my feet and turned away so that the physical pull broke.

Just as I'd have to break the emotional pull.

I couldn't let this happen.

"It's not an issue. My magic will be able to stop them." *But I want to ensure no one has to stop me afterward.* I couldn't help a glance backward at him.

His eyes studied me sadly, as if he knew exactly why I'd walked away.

I was also certain my sharp guard had heard the unspoken "but" in the tone of my voice.

"Avia."

His use of my first name made me clench my fists and the silence drew on. I struggled not to confide in him while his eyes dared me to. For a moment, I was brought back to the way he'd held me in the tunnel, when I'd given into my emotions and been simply a girl instead of a queen.

But that wasn't our reality.

And my lips stayed sealed.

Eventually, Felipe gave a brief but firm shake of his head, breaking the moment and leaving me relieved. "I didn't think it would be a problem. But you can't let these men go. It *cannot* happen."

"Could I make it seem like these four got cut during this round?" I hedged. "The crowd won't know any different." I didn't like the idea of locking men up simply for being cowards because then I was certain almost half the kingdom would be in chains.

"And keep the weakest for the throne? No," Felipe's expression was grim and downtrodden. "Believe me, Your Majesty, this isn't something I like suggesting. It's not something I say lightly. You don't have to lock them up if you don't want to. You can release these four after the next round if they're the worst performers, but they *need to compete*. When they signed up for this tournament, they put their names on a magically binding document."

Sarding hell, of course they did. My stomach sank. I knew all about magical contracts because Evaness had one for any men who married their queen. "What happens if they try to leave on their own?"

Felipe shrugged. "That was up to the castle mages. I was just told what documents to use for sign-ups and that I wasn't allowed to use any other paper, to flip the scroll over and use the back if I had to."

My stomach felt like a rock that had been skipped across the surface of a pond only to sink. I had no idea of the depths of the rules of this tournament. I'd declared it needed to happen and Sahar and my staff had taken care of the details while I tried to learn other things—like the history, the accounting, the current state of politics in Okeanos. Dammit all.

"Well, we're not shackling innocent men." I sighed bleakly and nearly reached to rub my forehead, where a tension headache threatened. But I remembered my transparent state when my hand was halfway to my face. I lowered it again and let my temple throb instead. "What else could I do?"

"Tell them that when they signed up, they bound themselves to compete until the end. They're welcome to lose the next round, but until then, they'll suck it up. I'd assign a set of trustworthy guards to them though, so they don't go blasting vitriol about you to the crowd."

A brittle chuckle left my throat that felt as sharp and broken as glass. I felt no real humor, only a dull sadness that accompanied my thought. I should have left well enough alone. I should have gone back with Bloss instead of stubbornly insisting that I claim my birthright. *Idiot, Avia. Total idiot.*

“Don’t,” Felipe said, swimming closer and raising his free hand. He stopped his gesture in mid-motion, somewhere between the signal to halt and a reach to touch my shoulder. Tiny rivulets of water traveled from his body to mine and I felt them caress my skin.

I found myself longing for his touch. He’d hugged me mere hours ago. But that was in a moment of dark chaos; now I watched his eyes as he fought to keep the wall of propriety firmly in place because he wanted to say more but knew his place. Part of me wanted him to vault over that wall, but another part knew he couldn’t. He lowered his hand slowly, let it drop to his side.

“Don’t what?” I asked.

His gaze was steady as he responded, “We aren’t better off without you. We’ve never had a queen actually interested in listening before. Nor one who thought about others’ wishes.”

“Definitely not one so completely ignorant.”

"Definitely not one who'd dig through the rubble to save others," he countered. "I can put these bastards off for tonight, let you wait to deal with them."

The offer was kind but while my bones were heavy and my head ached—begging me to sleep, I still had more to do. These four competitors were nothing compared to the man I planned to confront after them. I shook my head. "Thank you but no. Am I covered enough? Or can you still see the results of the spell?"

"You're hidden," Felipe replied, "so long as they stay back. And your face is nearly normal. But … sometimes a bit of a scare can be a good thing." His scarred eyebrow rose, giving me pause. Then, he quickly flipped around and swam for the door, opening it and gesturing with a gracious sweep of his arm so that I could exit my room.

"Okay then. I think I'm ready to face some men who hate me."

"Idiots. You mean idiots," he corrected.

A small smile lit my lips, and I gently tugged my cloak close. "Idiots." I took a step toward the multicolored coral hallway before pausing and looking back at him. "Felipe, can you send over one of the castle mages who worked on the contracts? I'm sure both the contestants and I would appreciate an explanation of the consequences of their withdrawal. Hopefully one is still awake."

He nodded but gestured to Ugo, who swam off to complete the errand, leaving Felipe to guard me.

"Thank you."

"Of course. Anything you need."

I stared at him recklessly for a moment, wishing there was an undertone to that statement, my chest buzzing almost as if I could feel one. Hope was an evil witch that way. She cast her spell and left you with daydreams of things that could never be.

3

I BRACED myself for confrontation as I walked into a small meeting room containing table made from a slab of travertine precariously balanced on some wooden posts. Three mismatched wooden chairs scavenged from shipwrecks surrounded it.

It was brighter than most of the rooms in the mayor's house with at least three lanterns bobbing near the ceiling.

I was grateful they weren't along the walls, or my face would have been instantly lit. In their current position though, they helped my hood cast a lovely shadow, hiding whatever remained of the x-ray fish spell.

I stopped short just inside the door because I'd expected to see men I'd hardly talked to, men I didn't really know. And that's exactly what I seemed to find:

four men crowded behind the table, all standing uncomfortably as they waited, none confident enough to sit. Two tall, golden-skinned sirens stood at the front. I thought I detected a squi-shifter's elongated forehead as the third man. The final man was tucked too far behind the others for me to see more than an arm.

When I stepped through the doorway, they bowed as protocol dictated. But that's when I saw a tuft of red hair from the man at the back of the bunch.

There was only one man in the tournament who had blood-red hair.

Radford.

He wants to leave?

The sight of him cut a jagged hole into my stomach. I stared at the hermit-crab shifter, and I couldn't breathe for a second as the pained shock hit me. The parts of my skin that weren't still translucent burned scarlet in embarrassment.

His eyes met mine steadily, though I saw a sheepish pink creep up his own throat.

Yes. He should be embarrassed.

I was hurt. I'd thought he and I had shared at least a friendly connection. Perhaps not a love match, but something pleasant.

And I'd gifted him with a protective necklace that would stop most magics from hurting him. Of all the men in that entire damned stadium today, he'd probably been safest.

Lashing out at him for leaving wasn't an option, however, because while I'd known he was safe, he certainly hadn't. I'd given him the necklace to counter a spell that had been dumped on him at the opening ball of the tournament, one that made him speak to me in insults. As far as Radford knew, that was the extent of the necklace's power. I hadn't revealed I'd let him wear my rare and valuable elven chain. I didn't know him well enough for that.

Obviously, I didn't know him well at all.

I'd seen a jovial whale-tamer with a drawl, a man who stood out from the many city-born sirens who were as memorable as … well … smooth river rocks. But as he stood there in front of me, rubbing his freckled neck with a calloused hand, I realized that he wasn't quite as tough as I'd imagined him to be. I'd thought his career might make him okay with the unpredictable. I'd thought that coming from the sands of Nowhere, he might bring a different perspective to my court and be a valuable addition to my group of husbands.

Apparently not.

The rejection stung even though we hadn't been a love match, and I'd cried so recently that tears were my natural response.

Unacceptable.

I could feel Felipe's haughty fury wafting through the water as he stood behind me. I envisioned it infusing me, filling me up, because that sort of emotion was preferable to the impostor syndrome niggling at me. If I could misjudge Radford, how faulty was my judgment in other areas?

I felt a fool.

I stared at Radford, trying to embrace my anger and coax it to grow, and eventually, he felt pressured enough that he opened his mouth to speak.

"Your Majesty, we've been honored to—"

One of the sirens next to Radford snorted derisively, a man with short black hair shaped into four spikes framing his forehead.

"—honored to compete. But sometimes, you realize that something isn't a fit. I don't belong in that castle. All those sirens and servants and etiquette rules. Only a few whales to speak of ..." he shook his head. "I thought this would be a new adventure. And we get along well enough. But it feels like trying to put your pants on backward. It's just not right. And it's not fair for me to waste your time."

Sard him. Why did he have to sound so reasonable?

Why couldn't he just be an ass about it so I could hate him and feel justified in binding him to stay?

Dammit all.

I felt like glaring at him for derailing my budding fury and making me feel as though I was sliding across a sheet of ice. It was a struggle to smooth my face so that it was as placid as a pond. My insides didn't match my expression, however. They were a complete mess. I took a deep breath before calmly stating, "I understand." I gave a half nod in his direction before turning to the snorter.

He was one of the sirens who'd made almost no impression on me. His bulging eyes were the only thing that set him apart. His name was Illia or some such thing, and all I could remember about him was that he'd swum down from Sky Stones in the north, a city that had sunk beneath the waves several centuries ago when Macedon had a massive earthquake. Sirens had taken over the city.

Illia hadn't spoken much, and I'd assumed he was a bit shy like Stavros. Perhaps shell-shocked by the palace. Now, I wondered about his intentions for joining the tournament in the first place. The sneer on his face made me think he'd never planned to get very far—but I couldn't tell if that was because he'd come in as a skeptic and detractor or if he'd merely wanted bragging rights back home.

"And you?" I let my voice lash out.

"Tired of nearly getting killed," Illia's sea-green eyes dared me to contradict him. "Seems like you can't go two days without someone trying to whack us off. You're pretty hated."

"One of the many downfalls to royal life," I agreed, though in my head I thought, *With a mouth like his, I'm surprised death threats aren't a regular occurrence for him. I would think this would all be old news.*

"Not every royal's life," Illia countered. "People respected Mayi."

"I happen to believe fear and respect are different," I argued.

"Bullshite. That's the thought process of someone who's never had either." The fourth siren, who'd been silent thus far chimed in, his deep voice reverberating in my ears, that ugly truth sinking deep, dragging up every dark doubt I had about myself.

I turned to stare at him. He had the palest blue eyes, which bulged slightly from his face; one of those faces that could either be extraordinarily handsome or extraordinarily disturbing. Right now, I only saw the latter.

For a moment, I was plunged back into the caves with Mayi, back into darkness and cold and doubt. I was surrounded by ashrays, ghosts of lost sailors, who swirled around me like grey mist and whispered terrible things into my ears.

"You'll never see home again."

"All your wishes are for nothing."

"The sea will swallow you up just like she did us."

"You'll die soon. Alone. Drowning in mediocrity."

Their voices compounded in my mind, layering themselves into a steady drumbeat and I was lost to the real world for a moment.

Until Illia snorted again. That sound drew me out of my own head and allowed me to focus my glare back onto him and his ridiculous spiky hair. If only he knew what a pig was and how much he sounded like one. "Kof's right. You're more naive than anything else."

The squi-shifter shuffled his feet uncomfortably, clearly not a fan of being called out. "That's not exactly what I said."

"Is that why you're leaving then?" I asked Kof gently, turning to him instead of dealing with the siren who was likely to make my blood boil. "It's all right. Tournaments can seem exciting from the outside, just as castles can. But they're full of faults, just like anything else."

Illia rolled his eyes, once again trying to dominate the conversation. "Faults? That's an understatement, like comparing a man-of-war jelly to a sea anemone. If your castle was as faulty as your reign thus far it would be a pile of shards right now."

"Thank you for that constructive criticism," I purred, "but you haven't truly seen me rule yet, so I believe that your conclusion is a bit premature."

Simultaneously, Felipe's spear lowered, tip pointed in Illia's direction as my guard growled, "Watch your tone, finless."

"You can't touch me, spearhead. Not as a contestant."

"You're still a competitor?" Felipe put on a falsely shocked face. "I thought you came here to quit so you could go hide in your hole like the gormless sea cucumber you are."

"Radford, I'll need back that token I gave you." I tried to break up the budding argument with a distraction. Clearly, discussion was getting us nowhere and we needed to move on.

The hermit crab shifter nodded and reached up to unclasp the necklace from his neck.

"She gave you a token?" the squi-shifter burst out indignantly as he turned to stare at Radford. "I knew I was the bottom of the heap! Giving out favors—" he muttered under his breath when Felipe swam a few feet forward, ready for a fight on my behalf.

Felipe's protectiveness felt like a shield countering all the hostility directed at me from the other side of the table. In fact, it felt like a bit more than a shield. It felt like affection. I bit down on a smile, smacked away the giddiness that filled me at Felipe's gesture, and then subtly took a moment to study my hands beneath my cloak. They were still frightful, but at this point, I didn't care.

I held my hand out toward Radford, palm up, muscles exposed, waiting calmly for him to return the necklace. My movement instantly killed the argument that was building as all eyes went right to my fingertips.

If only enchanting people was as easy as terrifying them.

Illia's eyes grew round, the pale-eyed siren's eyes bugged out even further, and the squi-shifter's jaw unhinged.

Hesitantly, Radford reached forward and dropped the necklace I'd given him into my palm. The chain was warm in my hand, the seahorse charm on it heavy. I curled my fingers deliberately around it, giving the men one more opportunity to gawk, to wonder exactly what kind of inhuman monster they were facing, before pulling my hand slowly back underneath my cloak.

I could see clearly in the eyes of all the competitors that they thought they'd made the right choice. Their thoughts practically shouted out their horror and relief.

Assholes.

How sad for them that they wouldn't get to leave as soon as they wanted. I had to speak slowly and deliberately to keep any smugness out of my tone as I asked a question that I was quite certain these men would later hate me for. But they deserved it after their brutish claims.

"Well now, you all came here to quit the Okeanos tournament, without actually losing. Is that correct?"

Each one of the four men nodded.

"No. I need verbal confirmation." I coached.

A chorus of low-toned "ayes" reached my ears. Even Illia was subdued in his response, perhaps because he thought he was getting what he wanted.

It might have been my imagination, but it felt as if the whole room suddenly heated a few degrees. Perhaps their nerves increased their body heat and warmed the water, but I had a sneaking suspicion that wasn't the case.`

For a moment, I scraped my teeth over my tongue, wondering if I should have asked that question. It was a bit cruel of me since I knew so much more than them. I'd grown up taking lessons from a castle mage, despite my utter lack of affinity for magic then. I knew how magical contracts worked. They didn't even know they had signed one.

As if I'd timed it purposely, one of my castle mages, a middle-aged balding merman with a bright yellow tail burst into the room at just that moment. His tail flapped rapidly back and forth like a kite torn between two winds, wrenched one way and then the next. It didn't stop when he entered the room. In fact, he grabbed the door frame so that he wouldn't shoot like a projectile straight through the room. Then he struggled to reach into a pouch at his waist with one hand. He dug out a tiny white seashell, whispered a word or two, and touched the shell to his fin to calm it down. Every eye watched as his tail fin slowed gradually and then drooped like a wilting flower.

"Majesty." My mage dropped his hands from the door frame and gave a courtly bow, tucking one arm to his bare stomach and the other behind him. Then he popped upright, and his yellow eyebrows lowered as his gaze turned to the four men positioned on the opposite side of the table. "Weaklings." He gave them a grin. "Ugo told me you fools think you can just leave the tournament."

I cleared my throat, hoping to keep this matter a bit more civil, at least until we could ensure these men would keep the matter quiet. "Felipe, you can stay if you like, but will you shut the door again?"

Once we had privacy, I turned to the mage, whose name I thought might be Adrastos. "Please let these gentlemen know about the magical contract they signed when they entered this tournament."

A groan went up from the bug-eyed siren standing to the left of Radford. "Magical contract?"

Adrastos snorted. "Of course. Do you really think we'd let a bunch of random commoners have access to the palace without fail-safes?"

My mage was quite the smooth-talker. I attempted to take over before this matter exploded into another round of insults and anger. I turned to Adrastos. "You mean that the castle mages knew that protective measures would be a necessary precaution, right? To ensure safety?"

"To ensure blubbering blubbers like these didn't sard it up, yeah," my mage replied, stepping right into a pile of verbal stink.

Note to self, Adrastos would make a great mage for prisoners of war. Not a great mage for court.

I took a deep breath and pasted on a smile that was hidden by my hood. "What, exactly, happens if a man tries to abandon the tournament without being eliminated?"

Adastros gave me a grin. "Oh, we don't need to tell them, do we? That would ruin the fun. Just let them leave."

I sighed. "Unfortunately, I've been advised not to let them do so without getting disqualified. Hurts the morale of the crowds watching. They'll all have to compete until they're eliminated naturally."

Illia started to make a noise of defiance but Felipe's spear near his face made him close his lips.

My castle mage gazed out at the defiant faces of the four men who no longer wanted to put up with this sham of a tournament. He tilted his head sideways and studied them thoughtfully. "Did they already declare their intention to withdraw to you?"

I hid my grin by clamping my teeth firmly together and responding with a solemn nod. "They did." *I made sure of it.*

"Well then, the damage is already done."

"What the sard? You can't do something to us simply because we thought your sun-dried cunt wasn't worth—"

Felipe's spear tapped Illia's throat and stopped the remainder of the siren's sentence.

Behind him, Radford shook his head, his expression chastising, as though he was disappointed in me.

My lips thinned into a hard line.

"Adrastos, do you know how to put a geas on someone?"

"Spells for preventing speech? Of course." The merman scoffed, giving a dismissive wave of his hand. "Child's play."

"I'd like a geas placed on these four, please. They are neither to speak a word about their desire to leave this tournament, nor a word about the magical contract. Let's add to that—they also aren't allowed to say a negative word about me. Yes?"

"That's sarding wrong!" The bug-eyed siren burst out.

I turned to glare at him. "This is a precaution. You four cannot and will not say anything to contribute to the unrest already rankling Okeanos. I have a country to unite and rule." I bit down on all the further insults I wanted to spew about their cowardly choices. It wouldn't do to make things worse.

Radford sighed and just nodded his agreement.

The squi-shifter remained silent.

"Just do it." I gestured for Adrastos to begin.

"Yes, Your Majesty. Absolutely. Would you like me to do it before or after I tell them that violating the contract turned their dicks into shrimp?"

4

After the disastrously hilarious meeting with the cowards, who'd shrieked and glowered as they yanked open their pants, peered down, and gave terrified sobs of horror … it was quite difficult to get into the proper head space for my next confrontation. I kept giggling as I walked through the hallway.

"You knew," Felipe said, not accusingly, but with a glint of grudging admiration.

"I knew something would happen if they officially broke the contract. But damn. Those castle mages deserve a raise for their ingenuity. What else could make a man stay so invested in the tournament?"

He chuckled and I whipped my head to the side so I could glimpse one of his rare smiles. "True. I am disappointed to learn, though, that if they participate in the next competition, their dicks will return to normal. I rather like the idea of them having to live with a little critter down there forever…"

"I keep imagining them trying to explain it to a woman."

We both collapsed into such a fit of humor that we had to stop swimming. I doubled over, shaking with laughter until I gasped, pain shooting from my stomach because my diaphragm was literally heaving. I couldn't catch my breath. Reflexively, I reached for Felipe's shoulder for support since my wings were hidden. The feel of his skin instantly transformed my mood and my laughter died on my lips as I glanced up. Then I couldn't breathe for a different reason.

His smile dimmed but the fire in his gaze doubled. The water around us seemed to tremble with the intensity of the moment and I was caught up in it, this blissful second of connection.

But Ugo's figure appeared around a corner, and I yanked my hand away as if I'd touched hot coals.

Not in the tournament, I reminded myself.

"I need to speak with Watkins," I said, trying to gain my bearings and put my head back on straight.

Felipe nodded. "I'll take you to his chamber."

As he swam off ahead and Ugo guarded my back, I berated myself. I had to stop this foolish mooning.

I just didn't know how.

The trip to Watkins's room was far too short for my liking. I'd have preferred to get a handle on myself and prepare what I was going to say to my worst enemy, try to rummage up a few quick verbal jabs. But apparently, the wing of the mayor's mansion containing the men's dormitories were not far from my rooms. Drat.

Gazing around, I noted the coral here was not as vibrant as those in my room. Here it was brown and dull, not for show. Part of me wondered if these might normally be servants' quarters, but I didn't ask because, in the scheme of things, such details were unimportant. They were a distraction from my real purpose: Confronting the man I believed responsible for the attack on the arena.

Dammit all, I wish I had proof. Then I could lock him away. But if I did it without proof, then I'd be no better than Radford and his cronies believed.

Maybe he'd confess.

Maybe he'd gloat.

One can hope.

I took a deep breath, wondering how I could possibly still feel a nervous pounding inside my chest when I no longer had a heart.

Felipe swam just past the door before halting and turning, gesturing with his hand toward it to let me know we'd arrived. Ugo stopped on my other side, and I turned to face the door that hid the suitor who hated me above all others. Probably even more than those with shrimps for dicks.

I stared at the wooden door for far too long, gathering my thoughts, trying to predict what he might say. Every confrontation I'd had thus far with the shark shifter had been explosive. He drove me to madness with just a look.

And that was part of my problem. I couldn't even think about him without rage filling me up and blocking my good sense, making it impossible for me to plan what to say. That was a rarity for me. I liked peace, typically got along with most people. Or so I'd believed back in Evaness. The room full of men I'd just left, combined with Watkins, made me wonder about how I defined myself. What if I was wrong?

What if I was unlikeable? Cruel? Selfish? I agreed with their naive comment. But how far did their truths extend?

I couldn't allow myself to believe them, or self-doubt would invade.

Ultimately, I shoved aside philosophy, planning, all of it. I decided that I just needed to get this over with. Thinking wasn't helping anything.

I raised my fist to knock, noting my skin was coming back in rough, splotchy patches. But before my knuckles rapped on the wood, the door flew open, and there stood Watkins, his black brow raised as his dorsal fin erupted from his back upon seeing me and my guards. The rebellious shark shifter was shirtless as always, his pec muscles corded tightly as he dropped the door and his hands clenched into fists. Tight black breeches covered his legs, which backed away from me on the soft sea sand that made up the floor of a room that was hardly more than a cell, fitting only a sea sponge bedroll and a small writing table.

"What's this ambush for? Let me guess ..."

"Don't." I cut him off. "You know why I'm here. Let me in."

My eyes locked onto Watkins's face. The shock of white hair that broke up his black mane fell across his forehead, and he brushed it away as his black eyes went from narrow to mockingly wide. "Of course, Majesty. I'd be so delighted if you came in." Sarcasm was an understatement. Watkins's words were brutal cuts.

The water between us grew charged with animosity and energy as wildly bright and uncontrollable as lightning.

He took a step back into his room, grandly gesturing for me to follow him in.

I did, though there wasn't far to go since the room was little more than a cell. The tension built until it felt like the water was thickening between us. Perhaps our hostility was slowly freezing it. I turned and closed the door behind me, my gaze avoiding both Felipe and Ugo's steady expressions as I shut them out.

They were guards who fought other men.

They weren't equipped to fight monsters like Watkins.

I would have to do that.

When I turned away from the door, I started to find Watkins was so close to me. One step and I could have reached out and touched him, that was how small the room was. But when I took that step, glaring, he took another back.

He must have sensed a predator in the water, one stronger than even him.

Well, he was right.

I was livid about this attack, and I was about to devour him whole.

My power zinged underneath my skin, as dark and mysterious as a stingray. The temptation to use it was nearly overwhelming. I just had to reach out my hand. That's all it would take.

I had no idea how to control the water, but instinct told me I could do it easily. I could peel the waves back from Watkins's stupidly handsome face and watch him struggle to breathe in a little bubble made only of air that followed his head, so that no matter how he bent or struggled, he wouldn't be able to reach the water right in front of him.

My fingers tingled in anticipation, but I curled them shut.

No, I scolded myself, slightly shocked that I'd come up with such a morbidly twisted idea. It had arisen out of nowhere, leeching into my thoughts like poison, dark and sinister.

I took a deep breath and pulled my hands behind my back, linking them. My skin prickled with unease as the black thoughts slowly receded and reason returned.

I hadn't even used my powers yet, but clearly, the loss of my heart itself had some sort of effect.

Yes, I hated this man viscerally, took pleasure in tormenting him, but I'd never fantasized about killing *anyone* before now.

I needed to watch myself carefully, or I'd become exactly the beast that Watkins accused me of being, the heartless queen that Mayi had been.

"What do you want?" the shark shifter asked bluntly, crossing his arms over his chest.

I'd dragged Watkins into this tournament unwillingly, thinking that if he spent time with me, I would showcase just how reasonable and humane I was … as opposed to the previous queen of Okeanos who'd ruled with an iron fist and an empty heart.

Watkins hadn't thanked me for my trouble. He'd defiled my palace and defied me at every turn, no matter how I tried to approach him. But there had been an energy between us that sparked and sizzled, something that felt far more like attraction, than hatred. Or maybe it was like a dessert, a sour citric hatred sprinkled with the sugar of lust, the kind that made me want to bite into his skin. It was attraction-laced hatred. That was it.

Even as he stared at me now with eyes darker than any shadow, I could feel that spark of lust start, low in my belly. Fate was morbidly cruel that way, making me hate and lust after him in the same moment.

My quest to turn him from darkness to light had failed. Utterly. I hadn't shown him I was logical and kind. Instead, he'd driven me to lusty madness at every turn.

I'd punished him by making others think he was my favored, by leaving lipstick marks along his chest. Even now I wanted to do so again.

Watkins glowered down at me. "Come to accuse me of this attack too? Let me guess. Beheading. No trial. Just a farce."

"Yes, well, what more would you deserve? What a naive fool I've been, thinking you could listen to reason." He'd probably faked all of that heated tension, distracting me with his dark stare, getting me to believe the fact that he'd had nothing to do with the attack on our journey from the palace. And like a dunce, like the poor innocent girl I was—with only one suitor to ever speak of—I'd believed him. Because I'd wanted to.

I'd been so caught up in the mysterious tug of his dangerous persona that I hadn't seen the reality others had—he was on the wrong side of things.

Felipe had told me to question Watkins after the attack on the road and I'd squandered the opportunity. Now, the attack on the tournament was my own fault.

Anger at myself cut a blindingly hot gash through my stomach. I gnashed my teeth together and took a deep breath, trying to regain some semblance of poise as he recoiled from me, stepping quickly backward yet again until his gray fin brushed up against the wall.

"I knew it," he spat out as he shook his head. "Sarding bitch—"

"You bastard," I couldn't help the words that burst from my mouth even though I'd managed to hold back all but a small jet of water. The jet blasted unbidden from my curled fingertips and shoved my hood back from my face.

Watkins growled and his teeth grew in his mouth, going sharp and jagged before my eyes. "Always jump right to me, don't you?"

"Because it was you!" I was as taut as a sail in the wind, every single muscle tense. I forced my gaze from his and focused on the wall for a second to ensure that I didn't explode. I counted like a sarding child trying to regain control.

I'd always tried and failed to remain in control with him, but just then, I'd had more than I could bear, and being in the same room with him, breathing the same water, was more difficult than I'd ever believed it could be.

I wanted to scream.

"I'm just your easy target. You're too lazy to look for the real—"

"You dare deny it?" Watkins had conspired to attack *innocents* at my tournament. Innocents. Not me and my guard.

Not my entourage, who willingly signed up to work in my employ and understood the dangers therein. Those rebels had collapsed a stadium with families in it. Children whose unwitting parents had brought them to watch.

And he was the reason this competition, just like the stadium, was falling apart. If I hadn't just given him my very heart, I'd wring his neck.

This line of thought was dangerous for me because my hands unconsciously unfurled and reached out, the impulse to grab him one that I couldn't squash. For a moment, Avia was gone. The peacemaker I'd always defined myself as was erased by a rage that tinted my vision beyond red, it went purple.

"You might not have spoken the spell, but you gave that sea witch every bit of information she needed. Didn't you?"

"No!"

"Liar!" I swept forward with a powerful flick of my wings. My hand reached out, and I shoved against Watkins's chest, pressing his fin uncomfortably against the abrasive coral wall. He grew pale and I couldn't tell if Watkins was more scared of my wild appearance—the translucent patches still apparent on my bared arms—or the look in my eyes. If he was smart, he'd have recognized the look was far more dangerous than my freakish appearance.

Words came to me, but they were slow and stilted as I fought a battle to retain my sense of self. "Thanks to your *friends*, several innocent people were injured, two killed, Keelan's now mangled. The entire sarding city is panicking. And you what? *Lay here in bed—*"

Behind me I heard Ugo mutter, "Some bastards are—"

"Leave us!" I snarled at my guard, not having realized he'd opened the door and entered the room. If I did lose my temper, I didn't want Ugo or Felipe anywhere nearby. I refused, unlike the rebels, to allow anyone in proximity to be injured just because.

Watkins and I both froze until the door closed with a thump.

"What happened to you?" Watkins asked, his eyes finally meeting mine, head tilting curiously.

I paused, thrown by this change in direction. Why wasn't he still yelling? He hadn't said a word about the rebels who hated me, who'd hurt anyone in their quest to dethrone me. He wasn't gloating. But then … he hadn't gloated before. I studied his eyes.

Was that concern in his gaze? Surely not. It had to be just confused disgust. It was simply an expression that I hadn't seen from him before. That was all. Doubt wriggled uncomfortably in my stomach as I answered him with a careless gesture at my face.

"Nothing. My mage had to check me for internal damage." The lie rolled easily off my tongue since I'd told it already. I backed away from him and turned to gather up the cloak I'd tossed down. Doing so calmed me enough to speak. "With an attack like that, additional magic and poison are always concerns for a monarch. The throne isn't the comfortable seat you imagine it to be. Death is *always* lurking in wait for me." That last bit was true enough. Queen Gela, the woman who'd raised me in Evaness, had dealt with assassination attempts regularly.

"And that's fine. I accept it. It comes with the responsibility and duty of the crown I took up. What's *not* fine, is when death comes for my innocent citizens." I glared at him, and annoyingly, my eyes filled with a sudden rush of tears.

Sard it.

I turned away, not wanting him to see any emotion but anger from me. After a few deep breaths, I managed to find my snark. "Of course, my first priority after the attack was getting checked out myself. I'm only pretending to rage about the fact that children could have died today. You know, for the sake of public opinion." My tone was as hard and brittle as ice when I found my control and managed to face him again.

I watched Watkins swallow hard and his gaze drifted to the floor. For the first time since I'd met him, his shoulders slumped. "The movement isn't meant to hurt civilians. I don't know who attacked the stadium, but it wasn't anyone I associate with."

"Try again," I barked out, taking a step closer until my chest nearly bumped into his ribs, flaring my wings so that they made the water swirl around us in the tiny room. One of them brushed against the floating orange lantern and sent the enchanted little glass ball bobbing toward the wall and bouncing off with a *plink*. I glared up at him, hating the fact that he was so much taller than me. I used my wings to lift me gently so that I floated up until we were eye-to-eye.

My comment got a rise out of him. Watkins's nostrils flared as he retorted, "You're so sarding determined to make me your clownfish, aren't you? Paint me with whatever stripes you want. Where the hell was I when this shite happened, huh? Where was I after? When would I have had time to help with this?"

"Doesn't take but a second—"

"Always got an explanation. Always have a reason to blame someone you've labeled. Humiliating me and making me look like a sarding fool and a sellout to shark shifters everywhere isn't enough."

"Me? Acting like you're innocent! *You* desecrated my castle—"

"Doesn't put me in league with murderers!" Watkins shouted, leaning right into my face. "Vandalism and murder are worlds apart."

Behind me, the door opened but we were both brimming with fury, too locked in our deadly stares to bother turning to see who it might be. "Get out," I ordered, thinking my guards might again be trying to play nanny.

"Majesty," Felipe's deep voice was soothing. "Your voices are raised and—"

"Call Lizza to cast a sound shield then," I snapped. "Now leave!" I'd never spoken to him that way, the guard I secretly harbored feelings for. But feelings were the absolute least of my worries right now. Feelings had gotten me into this mess. Feelings had deceived me. Naïve hope had convinced me to invite this utterly despicable man in front of me into this tournament—believing time and interaction would melt his hatred.

The door shut with a *thunk* and for a moment, only tense silence filled the space.

Then Watkins sighed, and the sound was soft. Defeated. "Do you know why I'm against the monarchy?"

"Because my mother was evil," I answered immediately. "Because her reign was full of pitch-black terror and puppetry."

He nodded. "That. But also because I want more for us. I want self-determination. I want more than guilds and trades passed from generation to generation. I want shark shifters to have a chance to integrate more fully with the other races. Do you know how shark shifters have been treated? Most of them have to make their living as beasts of burden, shifted for the sake of hauling shit, or soldiers. My father was told he had to join the army ranks, told he had to fight, not as a man, but always as a shark."

This was news to me because while I'd tried to study the histories of Okeanos, they'd mostly been written by sirens concerned with trade. "You think that I want the same?"

"I think it will all be more of the same so long as there's a queen. I think … no matter your intentions … you'll be just as seduced by power as the last monarch. And all your pretty promises will pop like bubbles."

"So, you're saying that no one's minds will change? These attacks will continue? That I'm at war?"

His eyes grew hard as flint. "I already told you, don't associate me with those madmen attacking people. I'm not one of them."

"Sure." *Liar.*

"See that? Right there? You've already made up your mind about me."

"Well, you made yours up about me before you even met me! At least I gave you an opportunity to be different."

"You ambushed me and set me in your tournament as a plaything!"

"I gave you the opportunity to speak your piece—"

"For all of five seconds!"

"If you hadn't been gloating—"

"If you hadn't flown into a rage—"

I shoved up against him, my entire body vibrating in anger. I had no thoughts, only this hot pulse of hatred.

Without warning, Watkins kissed me.

Immediately, it was like a coiled spring let loose. The anger that had compressed us with each interaction found an outlet, a physical one.

Watkins's teeth were still serrated, but the edge of danger only excited me, heightening when he plunged his tongue into my mouth.

My teeth found his lower lip and bit down while my wings fluttered drawing my legs up against his waist. One of his huge, meaty hands grabbed my ass and yanked me closer. His fingers dug into my skin roughly, kneading and squeezing so hard I thought I might bruise. I relished his rough touch, reaching up to yank at his black hair, surprised to discover his white streak had an entirely different texture, coarser and thicker than the rest. I pulled, hard, holding nothing back, letting my fingernails scrape against his scalp as I sucked on his tongue.

He kissed me back just as fiercely, his free hand coming to my head and roughly gripping the back of my neck and squeezing lightly with just enough hint of a threat that a thrill shot down my spine.

For a moment, the clash of mouths and the press of his chest, the spicy scent of him, surrounded me and I couldn't feel or see anything beyond that. Watkins was everything.

Until he pulled his head back and his hands both dropped me suddenly.

If it weren't for my betta fish fins fluttering reflexively, I would have tumbled to my knees. Instead, they pulled me back from him gently as my chest heaved and I tried to catch my breath.

I could feel the start of a bruise forming on my ass and on my lips as I blinked slowly, recovering my senses.

When I glanced back up at him, Watkins dropped his own eyes.

"That didn't happen," he mumbled, as if trying to convince himself as he ran a hand through his rumpled hair.

"Of course it didn't. Because if you say it didn't happen, I *absolutely believe you*," I cut back before I whirled and grabbed the door.

It slammed shut behind me as I left the man who had my heart in his chest to steep in his own lies.

5

My sleep was fitful when I tumbled into bed an hour before dawn, because even though I spoke with Mayor Deacon, expressed regrets to the families of those killed, and worked with one of Deacon's local heralds to compose the announcements full of both regret and reassurance to be delivered in the town squares the following morning, I couldn't help but circle back to that kiss with Watkins.

Time and again.

Our anger had reached a boiling point, a peak.

I'd foolishly given into it. And in my dreams, I wanted to again. Over and over. In my dreams, we went further; he ripped out the neck of my conservative dress and dragged his lips over my collar bones, squeezing my breasts and pinching my nipples through the fabric. The dream version of Watkins shoved back my skirt and ground his hardness against me, his pants rubbing against me in just the right way, making me wet, drawing out my moans. In my dreams, he drove me to delirium.

But dreams and reality couldn't have been farther apart. I woke angry at myself, furious that my unconscious mind could betray me so. I ground my teeth as I sat up in bed, shucking off my sheets and kicking my feet out. I cracked my neck and was flexing my wings when my maid, Gita, arrived. She was a sweet-faced woman with an amazing talent for hair and I was glad to see her when she came through a servant's door and was at my side with a quick swish of her golden tail. It gave me a bit of a return to normalcy, to a world in which Watkins and I did not get along.

She appraised me thoroughly, clucking her tongue. "Didn't sleep well, Your Majesty?"

I shook my head. "That would be an understatement."

"Don't worry. I have just the thing. A quick seaweed pack for your face will have you looking as good as new." She bustled around the room, digging underneath my bed and lugging out a trunk that I hadn't even noticed. As Gita hummed a sea shanty and prepared some kind of slime-and-seaweed concoction to remove the bags under my eyes, Sahar entered.

My siren advisor strode in slowly and stiffly, as if yesterday had aged her. I could only imagine the years of torment she'd felt compacted into a single moment. I, myself, felt older today, more cynical. There was a shadow looming inside my chest. And I was certain she felt it too. When she gave me a haggard smile, I knew I was right.

"Gita," I canted my head toward my maid, though I kept eye contact with my advisor. "Can you please prepare a second seaweed pack for Sahar?"

"Majesty—" Sahar held up a hand to protest. She was already dressed for the day; her hair was done, her cheeks rouged. But she needed it. She was always solid and formal.

"I insist. Get her a glass of bubble too, Gita." I pointed a finger at Sahar to crumble her protests before she could construct them. "First of all, you need a break. You need not to be my advisor for a little bit. You need to let go. Besides, later on, you're going to be running interference for me with all these outraged Reef City residents. The least I can do is make sure you look fabulous as you face them."

Sahar chuckled and held up her hands in surrender before settling down on a nearby seat. Gita brought over a glass of bubble as my advisor said, "You know, Majesty, you're quite wise for your age."

"I'm trying desperately to catch up to you," I replied with a small shrug.

We spent the next hour sitting on a purple settee in front of my bed with seaweed wraps covering all but our eyes, eating tuna-and-seaweed wraps as Gita fussed with our hair and massaged our hands, claiming that a good hand massage could rid nearly all tension in the body.

"Course, there is one spot that's better, but you'll have to get a handsome sea man to touch that for you!" she joked.

I giggled, though Sahar rolled her eyes. But, with the bubble and a bit of encouragement, even my stoic advisor joined us in gossip, devolving into female chatter about the men in the tournament—sans Keelan, of course. Gita was on the Humberto fan-wagon after his huge stunt saving us on the road.

"Like some hero in a fairy story," she sighed, holding her hairbrush to her heart. "Honestly, Majesty, he's got to be in your top two."

I smiled grandly and gave a nod just to be agreeable, knowing he was a crowd favorite. The cardinal fish shifter and I though ... we didn't share any spark that I could find. It didn't mean that I wouldn't ultimately ask him to be in my harem. I was hoping we'd build a connection before then, however, because that would make it easier.

Originally, I'd hoped to be utterly strategic with my husband selection. But now that I'd given my heart away to Watkins, binding myself to one asshole for eternity seemed like it might be enough. Finding other husbands that I actually enjoyed was a newfound priority this morning.

"I don't know," Sahar said softly. "I think our Queen might have a soft spot for underdogs." She reached for a cup from the tray of breakfast that had been delivered and gave me a knowing smirk that made a strip of seaweed drip from her cheek. Sahar smoothed it back down before bringing the freshly-brewed bubble to her lips.

My stomach tightened. Was Sahar referring to Mateo? I didn't want anyone to notice him, much less scrutinize him. Posing as Felipe's cousin, Mateo was actually the ambassador's son from Macedon. I'd met him and fallen for him while he was still human. He had searched for me high and low after my kidnapping, and my brother-in-law, Declan, had helped Mateo find me. Now, thanks to my guard, Mateo was posing as a merman—and doing a clumsy job of it. Felipe had put out the rumor that poor silver-haired Mateo had been attacked by a hammerhead when he was younger, which had addled his wits.

But their scheme could fall apart if anyone looked too closely. Was Sahar already looking? Should I have confided in her?

Mateo's very entrance into the tournament was forbidden. I was glad for the seaweed wrap; it hid my dismay.

Gita, however, latched onto this little detail like a clam to a rock. "Ooooh! Who? Tell me."

"I like quite a few of them," I hedged. "Julian is so smart that he's fascinating to talk to, even if some of his ideas are a bit radical. Valdez ... he has a delicious devil-may-care way—"

"Oh, is he the pirate?" Gita immediately latched onto that tidbit and ran with it. "Yes, the servants' quarters are full of gossip about him."

"Really? What kind?" I asked conversationally, relieved to have steered the conversation successfully in a new direction.

Gita grinned saucily as she started to remove the seaweed strips from my face. "Well, I suppose it's similar to a lot of the gossip that follows pink dolphin shifters. They're so rare, you know. But I'd be careful with him. That attraction magic they exude is so strong. Plus, I'd heard he only joined this tournament to win a bet..."

"What kind of bet?" I asked.

Gita bit her lip and shook her head as she leaned in conspiratorially. "Well, no one knows. Pirates don't talk outside their own circles."

"Then how do we know the rumor about a bet is true?" Sahar interjected.

Gita gave a shrug. "I don't."

Sahar glanced over at me and deftly moved the conversation in yet another direction. But as Gita cleaned my face, applied my makeup, and did my hair, I couldn't help but wonder if the rumor had a grain of truth to it. True ... it was an extravagant rumor, as glossy and enticing to share as a pearl. But pearls started with a grain of sand and I wondered if this rumor had a grain of truth to it.

Question was ... how could I find out?

PREPARATIONS FOR THE MORNING DURING BREAKFAST were pleasant and lifted my mood despite leaving me with questions to ponder and a pirate to second-guess.

But I did notice that Sahar's gaze often strayed to the door even after our breakfast tray was collected. Her mouth often drooped while Gita prattled on; at first, I thought memories of yesterday were troubling her. But after a while, I began to suspect there was something more.

After Gita wandered off to my dressing chamber to find my outfit for the three remaining rounds of the joust, I turned toward my advisor. I stared at her hair streaked with gray, at the crow's feet around the corners of her eyes, at the perfect poise with which she held herself. But I saw past all of that. I saw beyond the gold patterned skirt she'd worn to show her solidarity with the "golden queen" who'd bring trading riches to Okeanos--a ploy she and my clever seamstress had come up with to help me. I saw the nerves that rattled her.

"Are you afraid of more attacks?" I asked softly, so that Gita wouldn't overhear.

Sahar pressed her lips together and definitively shook her head no. "There will always be those. Even during your mother's reign. No." She chewed her lip thoughtfully for a moment before she turned and angled herself in her seat so that she faced me directly. "I'm worried about Keelan."

My chest pinched and I leaned closer, reaching for her hand. "Is he still unwell? I thought that—"

"Physically, he's recovered. Except for his arm." Her lips twisted and tears came to her eyes. I couldn't imagine it was easy for any mother to watch her child suffer as

Sahar had. She squeezed my fingers hard before grasping my hand and clutching it inside both of hers. "I know that I didn't want him to compete in this tournament." She shook her head, her expression apologetic. "It wasn't personal. I just ... I know how hard this life is. I didn't want that for him. He's always been such an upbeat and fun boy ... right from the moment he was born. His fathers say he came out of the womb with a thumb on his chin and a grin, flipping off the world and already laughing about it." Sahar gave a sigh and her eyes dropped down to trace our fingers. "The royal court has always been treacherous. Not because of you."

"I didn't think you meant that," I said softly, encouraging the older woman, waiting patiently for her to find her pace and continue.

Eventually, she said, "I thought that joining was a joke to him; I didn't think he realized the consequences, and now ... he's torn."

Something caught in my chest. It couldn't have been my heart because that was gone. But it felt like it. I didn't like hearing that Keelan was torn. Did it mean he didn't want to compete? That our connection had been casual to him? An urgent need to know rose up inside my chest, demanding I lean forward and ask, "He doesn't want to leave?"

A sad frown crossed Sahar's face and a hopeless expression marred her features. "How can he joust with a ruined arm?"

"Surely the judges will make an exception."

"It's unprecedented. You have your one pass ..." she trailed off as I froze and gulped, startled by her suggestion as it derailed everything.

I needed that one pass to get Mateo through. He'd jousted but he'd taken a blow to his arm and scored low. He was in the bottom three and the only way he'd get to continue on was if I used my exception. But Keelan ... Shite. I hadn't even realized my conundrum. Sahar's comment earlier suddenly came into context and made complete sense.

Sahar pulled back from my hands and gave a sigh even as she shook her head in understanding. "I know, you need to use it for that merman, Mateo. The one with the bad tail."

Desperation clawed at my insides as I tried to figure out some sort of solution. I didn't want to lose Keelan. But I also, absolutely and irrevocably, needed to keep Mateo in the tournament. He was the only guarantee I'd ever have of true love. He *was* true love.

Sarding shite.

"I see how your eyes light up for him." Sahar gave a soft smile. "It's actually quite endearing. I know… I've known you would use your exception to get him through this round. And I understand." She took a deep breath, fortifying herself to say what came next. "I just don't know how to break the news to Keelan."

I chewed on my lip. "Do you have the scrolls that lay out the rules of the tournament with you? Did you bring them?"

Sahar nodded ruefully. "I looked at them twice this morning before I came to see you."

"And there's nothing? We can't use magic? Lash the lance to his side with leather straps…"

Her eyes flickered down to her fingernails as she toyed with her cuticles, a habit I'd never seen from her before. She was well-and-truly worried, her political persona all but erased as she sat in front of me as simply a mother worried for her son. "There was nothing my son would accept."

"What does that mean?"

Sahar gave a broken little laugh. "There's one precedent —eight hundred or so years ago, mind you—where a competitor had a stand-in compete on his behalf. Okeanos was at war and the competitor was a soldier. He couldn't leave the front lines. But his brother competed in his place. And won."

I stood, excitement rushing through my veins. "That's perfect!"

Sahar reached out a hand to calm me. "No. It's not. The two brothers ended up in a feud over who should marry Queen Karisa because the brother who'd competed fell in love with her."

I blew a raspberry. "As if I would be so lucky."

Still, she protested. "Keelan might not seem like it, but he has a lot of pride. He'd never allow someone—"

I waved my hand impatiently. "Forget he'd never. I'll convince him to do it. But who can compete?"

Sahar threw up her hands as she leaned back against the seat cushions with an exasperated chuckle. I wasn't certain who was frustrating her more—her son, or me and the fact that I assumed I could overcome his pride. "Well, there's another roadblock. Most of our extended family lives in Sky Stones. That's a four-day swim at least. And the joust resumes in just a few hours." She shook her head.

"You don't have any relatives, any friends here ..." I coached.

"I have an eighty-year-old uncle," she returned with hollow sarcasm. "I'm quite certain my son would rather have the lance lashed to his useless arm than allow Waldemar to compete on his behalf."

I sighed, the surge of hope disappearing like a sinking ship. I sat back on the couch next to Sahar and stewed in silence. I desperately wanted Keelan to stay in the tournament. But I had even fewer friends and allies than Sahar. I had no family down here.

Who could I possibly get to compete in a dangerous competition on Keelan's behalf?

At that very moment, Felipe opened the door, bowing his head slightly as he glanced in and realized I was still in my robe. "Your Majesty," his voice was deep and resonant. "It's nearly time to go."

I immediately turned back and stared at Sahar, my brows shooting up, my expression saying *yes*.

Her expression screamed, *no!*

But I ignored her. I turned to my guard and gave a sugary smile, trying to pretend I wasn't close to trembling in thrilled terror as I asked, "Felipe, could you step in here a moment?"

6

To my shocked delight, Felipe had simply nodded when I made my request and said, "Wait here while I find a replacement to guard you."

The nerves I'd built up as I'd hesitantly asked him had all but fizzled by the time he returned with another guard to shadow me around the mayor's palace so that he could go prepare.

"Your Majesty, Paavo will assist you while I'm gone." He gestured toward a massive mer who was at least twice my height, with a black tail and hair. Paavo also had a scar as big as my fist along his torso.

I nodded in greeting to Paavo, who was stoic and silent, as I swam quickly to Felipe's side. Uncertainty ate at me along with a tiny nick of guilt. "I just want to ensure you're actually okay with this," I said in a low voice. "You don't *have to*—"

"It's just a joust."

"Yes, but you could get hurt," I whispered.

Felipe gave me a nonplussed look, the look of a man who's just been insulted. "Please. This is child's play."

I held up my hands in retreat. "Alright."

He gave me a steady look full of swagger that set off a flock of birds nesting in my stomach. They all took flight at once, their feathered wings brushing my insides as they rose. I swallowed hard and gave him a soft, "Good luck, then."

He snorted before he disappeared down the hall with a swish of his navy-blue tail, and I stared longingly after him.

Behind me, Sahar said drily, "I see history repeating itself."

A hot blush rose on my cheeks as I turned to face her. *Dammit.* "Oh, hush. He's just doing me a favor." I tried to take careful breaths to stay calm, but I couldn't control the pink creeping up my neck.

"Mmhmm." Her look said she clearly didn't believe me. "Well, you still have to convince my son of this favor."

I inhaled, bracing myself for what I was sure would be an argument. "Can you have Keelan meet me in the courtyard?"

Sahar gave me a smile. "I'd love to watch this—"

"No."

"Oh, I know you won't let me. I'd just love to see Keelan's reactions." Her gaze sparkled with amusement.

I rolled my eyes. "Just go while I make myself decent enough to meet with him. We don't have much time before the tournament."

Gita did my hair up in a soft circlet that had curls escaping from it. She put on minimal gold eyeshadow and a deep ruby rouge. But she absolutely refused to let me wear the dress she'd selected for the day.

"It will ruin the effect. Here, wear this instead." She handed me a short, lacy white dress with a neckline that dipped to my navel. "But be back before we have to leave. It will take me about ten minutes to get you dressed."

"Yes, Commander," I teased.

She rolled her eyes and shooed me away.

I swam off with my two shadows trailing me, making my way to Mayor Deacon's private courtyard, a square in the middle of his mansion that was free of coral, and let the light from the surface filter down in gorgeous, dancing ribbons.

Unlike the rest of Reef City, which burst with bright colors like an underwater garden, this courtyard was made of stacks of grey stone rising in columns like smoke turned solid. A sunken statue here and there broke up the geometry of the space, but overall, the feeling was simplistic and peaceful as compared to the chaos of the city. I took a moment to breathe deeply and appreciate the cleansing nature of the courtyard before going in search of the siren I needed to speak to.

Keelan sat near the back of the square on a boulder that had been carved into a chair, his eyes downcast, watching the sand beneath his feet shuffle lazily in the sway of the water.

His hair was back to its usual white-blond shade, green lightning bolt zagging through the side. He was shirtless, though his left arm was bandaged and strapped to his torso while black pants encased everything except for his golden feet. Utterly beautiful, like all sirens, he was typically also utterly silly—but not today. His expression was solemn, unlike the teasing, playful man I'd come to know. He was the closest suitor of my age, and his baby cheeks showed it, particularly now, when he frowned.

Behind him, rolling in gentle somersaults, his pet sea turtle, Mr. Whelk, played. The golden-brown and green little creature dangled a strip of seaweed from his mouth like a dog might drag a bit of rope back home in Evaness, always ready for a game of tug-of-war. Mr. Whelk saw me, pausing his flips for a moment to blink his bulbous eyes in my direction before deciding that I didn't have treats and therefore wasn't worth his time.

I cleared my throat gently to get Keelan's attention; he'd been so engrossed in thought that he hadn't heard me approach at all.

"Morning," I greeted him while waving Paavo and Ugo back. They took up posts around opposite sides of the courtyard, facing sideways rather than staring at us directly, the best privacy that guards could give in a space like this.

Keelan's amber eyes rose to mine and the torment in his gaze was clear. His look was as heavy as a bucket full of well-water and though he didn't cry, sorrow splashed down his features.

Alarm bells went off inside my head and I was instantly swept into an internal debate. Soft hand or hard? How did one best snap a man such as Keelan out of his depressive funk? I swam closer with a soft smile. I'd been confident when I'd spoken with Sahar but now I was unsettled by Keelan's demeanor.

“Keelan…”

“I hate the idea of quitting but—”

“Then don’t.”

“I can’t compete.”

“You don’t have to.” I joined him on the rock, my legs brushing up against his as I sat. I could have scooted away but I didn’t. Instead, I stared at him and tried to gather the words to express what I needed without scaring him off. He was jovial and happy and flirted up a storm but that was just who he was. He spread joy around like it was butter. That didn’t mean that he had the same soft feelings for me that I had for him. I searched for words but didn’t find them.

He plucked at his bandaged arm, avoiding eye contact, trying to decipher what I meant but failing and turning toward me, confusion etched onto his face. “I don’t have to compete?”

"I've found a stand-in for you."

He shook his head quickly. "Absolutely not--"

"It would only be for this one event. There are exceptional circumstances."

Keelan's face grew even more somber, which I hadn't thought was possible. "First of all, that's not fair to any of the others. Secondly, I could never ask someone."

"I already asked someone. And he said yes."

"Who?" Keelan's tone was both incredulous and annoyed.

"My guard, Felipe."

"That's not fair to ask him; he can't say no!"

"I gave him the option of saying no. Even second-guessed him. He was quite offended that I could doubt his capabilities. He said, and I quote, 'It's child's play.'" I pulled my palms up and gave a shrug trying to lighten the mood.

Keelan's mouth gave a twist that might have been amusement before it soured into a grimace. "I can't let him do that. He could get hurt. Or worse, he could score better than I would have!"

I let out a laugh, relieved that Keelan still had enough spark to be facetious. "How could that possibly be worse?"

"What will everyone else think? How would the rest of the guys look at me?"

"You barely survived yesterday--they'll think you're lucky to be here at all!"

"Or they'll resent all the strings you're pulling for me."

"Well if they do then they're out," I said dismissively. "They're obviously asses and I have no need of those. My own ass is big enough."

That did earn a chuckle from him. "I refuse to argue about your ass. There is zero possibility of that discussion going well for me."

"I don't know. You could compliment it," I suggested as Mr. Whelk paddled closer, wiggling his neck and dangling his bit of seaweed, trying to entice us into a game. I grabbed onto one end of the weed, taking pity on the poor creature. We wrestled for a minute in silence while Keelan thought over my proposal to substitute in Felipe.

Eventually, he sighed. "Everything's different now. One second and just ... boom."

I dropped the end of the seaweed strand, ignored Mr. Whelk's disappointed whine, and turned to study Keelan's downturned face.

"I just feel like it will be better for everyone if I quit."

He was so infuriatingly stubborn! Couldn't he see how badly I wanted him here? "The only thing you're going to quit doing is wearing that hangdog expression," I chastised. I fluttered my betta fish fins and rose up from our shared seat, turning sideways so that my knees brushed his as I loomed over him, forcing him to look upward.

My words were charged with emotion that I couldn't hold back. "You think I don't know what it's like for life to change from one breath to the next? *Think again.* Of all the men in this tournament, you are the only one who now shares that experience. You're also the only one even close to my age. And you happen to be funny and adorable. With six-pack abs. So, if you think I'm just going to let the perfect man swim away … think again. You're *taking the substitute*."

He stared silently up at me for longer than I would have thought possible, as my confession repeated inside my skull, bouncing around inside, sounding more desperate and pathetic with each internal echo.

Shite. That was too much. Too intense. I've gone and scared him.

The press of his lips into a tight line worried me and I quickly sat back down next to him, dragging his uninjured hand onto my lap as I feared that he'd just swim off.

My chest tightened in anticipation; I couldn't hold his eyes, my gaze dipping down to study his hand for a moment, eyeing the scabbed skin of his knuckles before I reverted to the type of communication he was used to. "Excuse that little outburst. It was a lie. A cover-up. I've grown quite attached to Mr. Whelk, you see. And I couldn't possibly bear to lose him." I bit my lip, and while I kept my words playful, I couldn't stop my truth from leaking into my eyes.

He looked up and studied me silently for a second and something brewed between us—something tender and soft.

"We don't even know if I'll be able to do the next competition." His words were hardly more than a whisper as he squeezed my fingers with his good hand.

"First off, the only test of strength is the first. The other competitions—while I didn't design them—are supposed to test things like your wit. I can see why that might intimidate you," I raised my brows and gave him a hugely haughty look, trying to imitate Lady Agatha from back in Evaness. "I mean, your own mother calls you an idiot."

Keelan chuckled softly. "Right. So, you acknowledge that I'm at a clear disadvantage."

"Are you? Still, though. Even if your skull's a bit thick and you fumble the next competition, you just have to be middling to avoid elimination."

"I don't know if my ego could handle scraping by."

I squeezed his hand. "Then perhaps you'll have to work harder. If Sahar's right, it will be the first time in your life—"

"Stop talking about my mother."

"Why?"

"Because I don't want her in my head while I think about kissing you."

A soft pink glow lit me up inside. "Oh, you definitely don't want to kiss me."

"I don't?"

I gave him a wide-eyed pitying look. "I've been told my kisses are so addictive that once you have one … you'll never want to stop." I had no idea who this absolute flirt was or where my rational mind had gone, but I was floating high and giddy.

Keelan's ardent look only sent me even higher.

"Is that so? Quite a claim."

"Yes, well, if you were to kiss me, you'd never want to quit. Ever. That word wouldn't even enter your tiny, plankton-sized brain. So …" I trailed off and my eyes flickered toward his lips.

"Queenie?"

"Yes?"

"You really want me to stay?"

I gulped and nodded, feeling quite vulnerable. This time it was my turn to gaze down at the rock, overwhelmed as my cheeks flamed and the flirtatious woman who'd briefly inhabited my body fled and left me in her place to deal with the fallout of her brazenness.

Keelan's fingers slid down my own until his fingertips lightly traced over my palm, sending tickles dancing through my skin and grabbing hold of my vulnerability, spinning it in circles until it was dizzy.

"Keelan," I whispered breathily.

He leaned closer and I could see his pulse thrumming in his neck, just as fast and wild as mine.

I swallowed hard before I leaned forward and pressed my lips to his—initiating our kiss.

It was a wondrous tangle of emotions, a soft brushing sensation that sent shivers of delight racing through me and bright sparks fluttering inside my mind. It was beautiful as a cresting wave, as lacy as the water tumbling in an arc.

Mr. Whelk interrupted the moment with a loud, high-pitched whine, and a forceful nudge of his head against my arm.

We broke apart only to see the sea turtle dangling his ragged bit of green seaweed right in my face.

"He doesn't like sharing attention." I smiled over at Keelan, feeling glorious and radiant and gleeful.

"Well. You did say you wanted *him*." Keelan shrugged.

I grabbed the seaweed with a chuckle and gave a few tugs to appease the turtle before turning back to Keelan. "It's true. You're just a bonus."

"Speaking of bonuses … I'll consider your offer of a substitute."

I raised an indignant brow, but only in jest. "My kiss alone didn't convince you?"

He shrugged. "It was nice. But a kiss is temporary. A *statue* … that is forever." An absolutely intoxicating, naughty grin spread across his face.

My own lips stretched wide to match his as an idea formed, one that I was certain would appeal to my troublemaker. "That's true. But you know what they say … two is one, and one is none. So, how about two statues … and what if I sweeten the deal? Let's get them made in secret. And then I'll have them delivered to your mother's rooms while she's out."

Keelan burst into laughter, his good arm clutching his stomach. He guffawed until there were tears in his eyes and he swiped them away as he said, "Queenie, you've got yourself a deal."

7

I WORE a gown with a ruff as tall as my head made of very thin gold that had been pulled and woven to look like lace, though it was as brittle and heavy as armor. The lace had a seahorse pattern, of course, to represent the seal of Okeanos.

The gown itself was light in contrast to that metal yoke which made me feel like an ox. The dress was made of damask, swirling filigree symbols of red on a golden background that puffed out grandly due to a rigid underskirt. The scalloped bottom edge of the skirt wavered in the waves, in and out like a pulsing jellyfish swallowing my legs.

When I'd asked Gita why she was outfitting me in a dress that would be more appropriate on land, my maid had looked me right in the eye. "Because *sard* them."

Her vicious response had steadied my nerves for my first official public appearance since the attack yesterday.

Hopefully, others felt the same.

I swam out of the city accompanied by Ugo and at least five other guards. Emerging from the coral made my eyes blink rapidly as they struggled to adjust from the visual clutter and constant, busy patterns of the reef to the vast space of the open ocean. I took a moment to breathe deeply and appreciate the clean, calm, slightly salty scent of the water.

It was easy to spot the tournament space, though it was also a bit startling to see. It appeared as if all the spectators were floating in midair. Today, there were no banners, no stands, no walls to define the tournament. Only the bodies of those who'd come to watch.

I gazed up at them as my entourage swam forward with me. The onlookers were still in the warm zone, not too far beneath the sparkling surface since reef dwellers preferred warmer waters. But the sight of everyone swimming together, shifters and mer and sirens with all of their different bodies backlit by the sun as they formed a black ring with a white sunburst shining through the midst of them ... that was quite the spectacle.

And there were far more of them than I'd ever expected to see.

At least a thousand Reef City residents floated in a wavering circle roughly thirty feet below the surface. Their chatter rose and fell like a current, growing loud then soft in rhythmic patterns.

I smiled as I drew closer, and watched as word of my arrival spread through the crowd. I could see the news visibly pass from person to person as they bowed, causing the next person in line to do so and the next until the bows made the circle undulate like a wave.

I waited a moment, pausing to acknowledge them with a soft nod, just as Queen Gela would have done. Then I continued over to the near edge of the circle, where I spied Mayor Deacon and his advisors floating.

The crowd seemed friendly enough when they rose and looked at me, which was an improvement from yesterday. Unlike yesterday, however, I didn't see any children amongst the attendees. I didn't see women either, though they were far rarer in our world with the birth ratio of men five times that of women; I suspected quite a few husbands and fathers might not have wanted to risk them coming. I did see men of all stripes and sizes: shark shifters, squi-shifters, jelly-shifters, mermen, and sirens. And nearly all of them were armed. Spears, bows and arrows, sea stars dipped in metal, their edges sharpened to a point. I also spotted potion bottles glowing purples and yellows, hung around quite a few necks with string. Those who'd come today had come prepared for battle.

All of them seemed to take Gita's perspective regarding the rebels: *"Sard them."*

It gave me hope.

My eyes drifted to Mayor Deacon as I reached him. I'd float with the mayor and all the competitors not participating today on one side of the circle, opposite the tournament judges.

The mayor gave me a wide smile, his face a light blue in the open waters, his features much clearer than any other time I'd seen him. I realized with a start that he had a rather large mole just above his lip that I'd never noticed. The painted frogfish shifter's skin naturally changed to match his surroundings. While he was in Reef City, he was multi-hued and his expressions were hard to read; I relied heavily on his friendly tone of voice. I envied him, as those were excellent traits for a statesman, and he clearly made the best of them.

Today, however, I could tell his smile was genuine when he spotted me and waved me over to join him. And I didn't sense worry drifting off of either him or my competitors. But then again, hiding emotion was a valuable skill and I couldn't always trust what I saw.

"Good morning," I said demurely, allowing Deacon to kiss my hand as he bowed. When he rose and I turned to face the arena, he swam closer, clearly wanting to speak.

I tilted my head toward him so that we wouldn't be overheard. "Weapons?" I asked, using a single word to try to avoid any emotion in my intonation, but also to make it harder for the eavesdroppers to follow our conversation.

"Per my request. I made a little announcement about yesterday's attack."

"Oh?" I turned with raised brows to look at the older gentleman whom I'd come to consider a friend. I hadn't been informed of any announcement.

"That attack wasn't just on you. They didn't target you directly when they could have. You had your own raised dais. If they'd been aiming for you, that would have been a hard target to miss."

"True."

"Those idiots want to undermine our sense of security. Make us hide in our bits of reef while they go around and terrorize our families. Well, I won't stand for it."

Despite the horridly heavy ruff I wore, Deacon's words lifted an immense weight from my shoulders. I relaxed them back, then immediately regretted the gesture, as it pinched a nerve.

Curse that seamstress.

I fought the urge to flinch and tried to subtly find a more comfortable position as more spectators joined the crowd. Once I'd shifted enough to ease the sting running down my arm, I turned to the mayor. "You know, your logic has you fast becoming a favorite of mine. Is there anything I can do to help Reef City?"

Deacon tilted his head from side to side a moment as he thought over my question, clearly sifting through the options, trying to select the best one.

I waited patiently, eyes scanning the crowd, noting that no protest signs appeared today. Hopefully, the rebels would keep a low profile after yesterday, though I wasn't counting on it. I saw Lizza and Posey's rotted faces bobbing in the crowd; both the undead women rode large sea turtles in order to stay afloat. Spotting them and some of my guards spaced out along the ring calmed my jangling nerves.

Everyone's armed, Avia. Guards are on alert. Today will go smoothly. Don't be a fusspot. Bloss always used to call me that.

Deacon clicked his tongue when he finally decided what need was most pressing and I turned back to face him as he said, "You know, the edges of the city nearest the coast suffer from sedimentation each year."

"Sedimentation?"

"Apparently, those farmers up in Sedara dredge the land to plant their crops. And they dig out their harbors to keep them deep enough for their ships. All that dirt has to go somewhere."

"And it's been making its way to you." I could only imagine the dust, wondering if it filled the water like a thin fog or if it churned like a muddy flood toward the reef.

Deacon pursed his lips as he nodded. "It's gotten worse the past few years. Pieces of the reef have died. I've had to try to relocate entire neighborhoods …"

I thought for a moment trying to dissect the problem and potential solutions. Sedara would never agree to stop its farming of course. That was off the table. My own powers might be able to help redirect the current … if I knew how to use them. I didn't yet. I made a mental note to have Lizza help me practice at the first opportunity, while I tried to drag out the conversation and find another solution. "So, you'd like to move the soil?"

"Move it, get rid of it … even just reduce it. It's gotten to be too much."

That sparked my mind. Declan's power! No … not Declan's. Bloss's husbands had swapped powers. Well, one of them could reduce the soil anyway. A smile crossed my face and I tried to coax it from a smile of relief to one of confidence. "Excellent. I happen to know one of the kings of Evaness does such things. I shall request he visit."

Deacon's eyes studied me shrewdly and I didn't like the uncomfortable prickle that ran along the back of my neck as he did. I expanded on my answer, hoping that it would satisfy him enough not to question why I didn't just flick my wrist and shove away the mud right now. "You know, I've been looking for ways to build goodwill between Okeanos and the surface kingdoms. And I think that this will be an excellent start."

"Always wise, Majesty. But won't the Queen of Evaness want something in return for the help?"

I sighed. "I'm sure she will. My stubborn sister being what she is."

"Do you have any ideas as to what the price of such help might be?" he fished, trying to understand this negotiation that he'd suddenly been tossed into.

I put a hand on his blue arm. "Don't worry. I'm the one who'll have to pay it. I'm ninety percent certain that Queen Bloss wants to be invited back to my castle so she can lecture my ear off. It's what older sisters do best."

Deacon laughed. "I have one of those. And yes, you speak the truth. Well, so long as you think it would be good for both sides ..." he trailed off uncertainly.

"I do. There's been tension for too long. The sea people have lost many children to the shoreline. I think it's time we start to reconnect."

Deacon bowed his head as a herald swam up above the circle of the crowd and held his mouth to a golden conch shell. "I'm certain the people will be happy to see their extended families once more."

It would be a small thing, the easiest step, to have my sister's country begin to build relations down under the waves.

But I hoped it would help the people of Okeanos see that I was leading them in a new direction, a good one.

A band started up, signaling the start of the morning's joust and the music lifted the crowd's spirits, making my own soar in hope.

After my conversation with Mayor Deacon ended, I only had a few moments of reprieve before several competitors who had jousted yesterday sidled up to me, eager for conversation. As I saw several swim closer, my eyes traveled over the cluster of folk who stayed back, taking note of those who either didn't want to approach or were too shy.

The four men who'd requested to leave the tournament stayed near the fringes, sulks evident on their faces, particularly Radford's. He floated with his arms crossed, red hair plastered low on his forehead today, making zero effort at all with his appearance. His formal black shell shield was gone and instead, he wore a giant white and gray speckled shell on his back that was twice as tall as he was and rose from his shoulders in a spiral that ended in several barbed points. That must have been his traveling shell, the one that the guards wouldn't allow into the palace. Hermit crab shifters were nomadic and slept in their shells as they roamed through Okeanos, though most stuck to the dunes of the Umbra desert, creating semi-permanent residences in the rock caves of Nowhere.

The message Radford sent couldn't have been more blatant. He was done with the tournament and me. I ground my teeth at the way he was being so openly disrespectful, but to make a big deal of it would only draw more attention to the ass. My eyes narrowed in his direction. He could leave if he wanted and keep his tiny little shrimp cocktail forever. I hoped it pinched him. My irritation flared and suddenly my mind began to picture Radford curled up inside his shell, hands tucked under his cheek as he snored. The shell contracted around him quickly, growing smaller and tighter, bumping his head. He jerked awake but the shell contracted again, forcing his knees up toward his chest. And again, making him cry out. And again. I imagined the crunch of bone—I glanced away, trying to shake off that strange vision.

What's wrong with me? I must be in a hell of a mood or something. I'd never had such a horridly and randomly violent thought. Not without good cause anyway. *Well, shake it off, Avia. You have men to cheer on.*

I found someone else to focus on. Keelan also floated off to the side, his feet rapidly vibrating underneath him to keep him from sinking into colder water. He chewed his lip nervously even though he wasn't going to compete and his eyes scanned the crowd, looking for competitors or judges or maybe even his mother.

I suspected he was debating whether or not he should have agreed to our deal, but we'd sealed the agreement with another kiss, which had been just as toe-tingling as the first one. Plus I'd told him that my kisses were just as binding as a magical contract. To me, they were.

Today, Keelan wore a deep blue lightning bolt in his hair instead of the normal bright green. He'd magically altered his hair in honor of Felipe's choice to help him, which I found utterly adorable. Along with nearly everything else about him. Watching him eased the funky mood Radford had incited, and I felt much more myself.

Mr. Whelk paddled in circles around him, the little brown and green sea turtle snapping at his nose and distracting him. The sweet little creature carefully avoided Keelan's injured arm, which was bandaged and tucked tightly against his side. Keelan started to poke at the silly turtle with his pointer finger and the two began a duel. Point. Snap. Point. Snap.

As usual, they gathered a small group of onlookers, including Mateo, who clumsily floated nearby, slightly canted to one side. My breath caught at the sight of him, just like it always did, sending a rush of tender feelings through me. He'd become a mer just to be with me, and now he'd have to remain one forever, since only citizens of Okeanos were allowed to join the tournament. He'd have to marry me and grow old with me as a mer. The fact that he was willing to do that… I had to look away.

Keelan spotted Mateo only moments after I did and produced a little white shell from his pouch, which Mr. Whelk apparently needed desperately based on the turtle's wide-eyed squeal of delight.

It must have been either a treat or a toy.

Keelan tossed the little shell to Mateo who caught it clumsily. But his silver tail betrayed him, sliding sideways with a flick to the right and mussing his silver curls—which used to be brown, back when we were both merely human and desperately in love.

I pressed my lips together and fought the urge to swim over and help "Felipe's cousin" recover. I couldn't send the only guard who knew Mateo was actually human either, since I had roped Felipe into another favor today. I just had to watch from the sidelines and try not to draw attention to the fact that I was so heavily invested in one of the competitors already when we'd hardly met.

The residents of Okeanos would think I'd betrayed them by marrying a "sky breather." They were having a hard enough time accepting me. And while I'd protested Felipe's stupid scheme to pretend Mateo was his feeble-minded cousin, the damage was done and Mateo was part of the tournament now, which meant that he and I had to be careful, very careful, not to give up the ruse.

I could only imagine what the rebels would do if they found out. Immediately, the stuffed effigies that Watkins had made and hung in my castle, marked with black Xs for eyes, came to mind, turning my stomach into a cesspool. That helped motivate me to turn away, even though part of me didn't want to. But I did catch Keelan swimming over and putting an arm on Mateo's elbow out of the corner of my eye, which was comforting. Mateo wouldn't be utterly alone today. Perhaps he'd even befriend the siren that I was pretty certain would end up another one of my husbands. I hoped so.

I glanced around at the crowd again, trying to focus on anyone else, and my eyes caught on my advisor. *Dammit.* Of course, Sahar was watching me. She was far too observant for her own good.

Luckily, I didn't have time to do more than watch her smirk in my direction before other men from the tournament reached me.

Julian was first. The scientifically-minded siren had a darker complexion than most others, his skin a metallic bronze instead of the gold typical of sirens. His pale-green hair had grown a tiny bit scruffy in the week since I'd met him, the tips floating around his ears as his light-brown eyes studied me perceptively while his feet flickered back and forth beneath him so quickly that they were nothing but a blur.

Sirens' swimming techniques were nothing short of magical. Though they looked like breathtakingly beautiful humans, and were quite dangerous, with enchantingly alluring voices to those on land, under the sea, their only magic seemed to be their ability to rapidly flutter their feet as fast as hummingbird wings.

We exchanged greetings before Julian cleared his throat and stated, "I'd heard that tonight there was to be a feast to celebrate the completion of this round of the tournament since obviously it was canceled yesterday."

I nodded and confirmed the rumor. “That’s true.” Mayor Deacon had been quite insistent upon moving the dinner but keeping it, and I understood why. It was important to rub elbows with the locals once more, to discuss opportunities, to end this visit to Reef City with a positive impression rather than the memory of disaster.

Queen Gela always said, "People remember the last thing you say to them, so make it count." It was something I'd taken to heart over the years. *Technically, I can’t take anything to heart any longer.* I swallowed a grin at my own grim joke and focused on the handsome siren in front of me. Though his coloring was unusual, the contrast between his hair and skin was quite beautiful.

Julian’s face broke into a rare smile at my response. He typically looked serious and studious and rarely relaxed, so the sight made me grin a little. He clapped his hands together once in delight. “Wonderful. I’d love to introduce you to a local scientist whose work on a device known as a paint press, which uses paint to stamp out multiple notices in a single day’s time, will revolutionize the way heralds deliver messages. No more memorization. No more shorthand. Notices can even be posted around the town for the literate.” His tone grew progressively more excited as he talked about the advancements.

"That sounds wonderful," I smiled. It actually did sound quite useful, and not for the first time, I wondered if Julian's quest to promote science amongst a world of magically dependent realms wasn't a good enough reason for us to unite. He'd provide a different perspective when I called my husbands together for council. His logic might help me the way Declan's steady thoughts helped steer Bloss toward logical conclusions.

Oblivious to the mental evaluation I was giving him, Julian responded, "Oh, it *is* wonderful! You know the misinformation that gets around these days? Atrocious. Just this morning I swam out to the market, just to see what was being said. Some people called yesterday an omen! A portent!" He rolled his eyes and shook his head. "Ridiculous."

Another man from the tournament joined us, this time a shy siren named Stavros. He had typical siren coloring: blond hair and blue eyes with golden skin. But unlike most sirens who had an aura of confidence, he didn't. He was very reserved. Of course, as soon as I had that thought about him, he undermined it, saying, "Yes, well, if I had a coin for every time my grandmother called something I did an omen …"

"You'd have a million sand dollars?" Julian finished the well-known joke.

"Or more," Stavros agreed. My eyes met the shy siren's liquid blue gaze, which was lit with amusement.

Though handsome, he wasn't as memorable as other sirens in group settings. He was quiet, but witty in a smaller group, and I didn't quite feel like I had the best grasp on his personality. Hopefully, this little exchange would help me learn more.

"My grandmother used to predict I'd have the entire world under my thumb."

"Ha! Bet you loved that growing up!" Julian said.

"Promised her I would," Stavros retorted.

"How's that going for you?"

"I'm not sure. How's my attempt at world domination faring, Your Majesty? Will I make it to the next round?" He gave me a solemn look as he laced his fingers together and tilted his head inquiringly.

"You're doing just fine. Though I'll warn you, I've no plans for world domination."

"Yet," he winked at me and Julian laughed, setting us all off.

"Don't forget, his grandmother said it will happen."

"In that case, we better have your grandmother down to the castle for tea, so that I can learn exactly what she saw." I smiled at the shy siren, suddenly eager to hear more about his family.

Stavros's expression dropped and I froze, unease spreading through me. *Oh no. I put my foot in it, didn't I?*

He confirmed it when he sighed and gave a little shrug with one shoulder, his eyes staring down at the fluttering feet which kept him aloft in the water. The silence grew nearly unbearable before he said softly, "Unfortunately, she's passed on. Most of my family is gone. The ones I acknowledge anyway."

"I'm sorry," I said, trying not to pry, but wondering what kind of rift had occurred in his family line.

"Perhaps your grandmother knew you'd someday meet me, and that we'd revolutionize this abyss and shed some light on things," I contributed.

He glanced up with an odd sort of smile, twisted, as if he were smiling through pain.

Dammit Avia.

"You could be right. Lately, magic has been irritating me."

"I think magic needs to be used in moderation," I contributed. Perhaps these men would spread my view around and buy me some time while I trained with my own magic. Though, neither seemed like the talkative, gossipy type. Oh well.

"My whole family denounced me the first time I tried to use an electric eel to power a lantern," Julian contributed. "Of course, it did scorch mother's hair off, turned it all black, and made it float right off ... but still, you'd think after five years, she'd be willing to forgive and forget."

I struggled not to laugh because while I felt bad, based on the resentment in his tone, his mother was otherwise unharmed, and picturing the incident itself tickled me.

I could just imagine a younger Julian, gangly and buzzing around his shipwreck home in excitement, little bits of experiments scattered along the floor. I could see him calling in the entire family to watch his grand scheme come to life. And then I could imagine the arc of electricity zagging through the water and then lighting his mother up like a fire catching in a fireplace. Apparently, Stavros felt the same way.

"Her entire head?" His hand reached up to cover his mouth but a guffaw escaped.

"I mean, there was a little patch of bangs left at the front. I tried to tell her she could start a new trend—"

Stavros collapsed in laughter and I struggled to contain my own glee, which surged, picturing Julian's mother with only bangs and a look of fury in her eyes as she screamed and pointed, "Out!"

"I'm sorry," I said, reaching out and patting his arm, trying not to undermine Julian's wistful sigh. "I'm sure she'll come to her senses someday."

"I don't know. Sirens are pretty particular about their hair."

At that moment, Humberto came up to join the conversation. "What are we laughing about then?" he asked Stavros as he swam up. The cardinal fish shifter's black zebra stripes stretched as his puffy cheeks bit into a skewer of cooked scallops before realizing it was me he was next to. He bowed with his mouth full before rising, swallowing, and saying, "Well, they didn't skimp on the food out here in the open water at least."

I grinned, relieved to be able to switch topics. "How's our resident hero this morning? I'm surprised you don't have twenty women swooning after you right now."

He pursed his lips into an exaggerated grimace, just as something, indigestion or heartburn, soared up through my throat. I had to fight the strange and unexpected urge to gag as I listened to his response.

"I'm just glad I'm not suiting up again." He patted his belly, which was definitely round in comparison to the other competitors as Humberto was fond of a good meal. But he was brave and decent, which lasted a lot longer than muscles. He took another bite from his skewer, releasing the pungent scent of oily scallops, and chewing as he watched the crowd. My eyes followed his.

"They're much more subdued than yesterday," I noted. "They're on alert," Humberto replied. "One good thing about living around the reef is that people watch out for one another." He gave a yawn. "Wish the match wasn't this early though. It's nearly my bedtime."

"Bed?"

"Been up all night visiting family," Humberto said. "They swam over to check-in. We went down to this little grotto. It's got the most amazing honey bubble. Of course, it costs a fair bit. Honey is hard to get after all."

"Sounds delicious," Julian agreed with a nod that sent his pale green hair wavering. "I've only ever had honey once, after a big storm washed up a ship. Very good stuff."

I made a mental note about setting up a trade for honey. "Anything else from land you all adore?"

"Boots," Humberto said immediately. "There's nothing quite like a well-roasted boot."

I managed not to cringe as I asked, "What about meat?" I immediately thought of Macedon. Perhaps, through Mateo, I could instigate a trade for goat meat and milk. "Have you ever had goat?"

Humberto looked intrigued, but Stavros wrinkled his nose. "Beef is better."

I nodded. I could set up a line of trade with Evaness for cows but perhaps negotiate with Macedon first, to establish relations with that country.

Before I could ask for additional suggestions, the herald blew on his shell, announcing the start of the tournament.

We all turned, shoulder to shoulder, to watch with bated breath.

Two swordfish ridden by competitors swam through the vast space of the open ocean. Each man wore armor as he straddled his beast, gripping the reins tightly. Metallic coverings over the swordfish noses gleamed sharp and dangerous as the beasts swam forward slowly, each swish of their tale ominous.

The circle of spectators separated on opposite sides, letting the jousters enter. Anticipation hissed and crackled inside my stomach as the competitors lined up on either side of the tournament circle as the crowd closed up the gaps behind them.

My stomach clenched and suddenly a new vision ripped through my mind. I imagined the two racing toward one another at top speed, the noses of their beasts tilting up as they yanked on the reins, and a delicious spray of blood as one beast sliced through his target, half beheading the other man so that his neck broke and his skull became nothing more than a floppy appendage as the water turned purple.

Sarding hell. What is wrong with me?

I clutched at my stomach, sickened. Where were these thoughts coming from? First Radford, now this? Something was happening to me. I wasn't certain exactly what. But I had a sinking suspicion that it had everything to do with my forsaken heart. Dread curled its fingers around my neck. Everyone had said that a sea sprite only lost her humanity if she used her powers.

Could they be wrong? Could giving up my heart alone turn me into a monster?

I needed to speak with Lizza as soon as possible.

8

I WASN'T able to speak with Lizza at all yesterday. The tournament had flown by, Felipe confirming Keelan's worst fears and showing everyone else up in the joust. His swordfish had rammed right into the middle of his opponent's armor, making the siren backflip through the water, my chest tumbling right along as I'd stared at Felipe and tried fiercely not to acknowledge how turned on I was.

All of my guards had cheered loudly and been puffed up with pride the rest of the day over the scores and the fact that one of their own won the entire joust.

"Didn't even have to try," Ugo would tell anyone who'd listen. My orange-haired mer guard also often added, "I taught him everything he knows. Man can't piss without asking me which way the current's blowing."

Paavo, poor man, had been more than ready to escape Ugo's incessant second-hand bragging by the time Felipe returned to his post. I couldn't help but notice my favorite guard had a little bit of a glint in his eye and a swagger to his tail.

I'd wanted to compliment him and thank him profusely, but all I could manage was a quick nod and a "nicely done," because Mayor Deacon's arm was around my shoulders as he carted me off to see yet another important merchant.

Sahar and Mayor Deacon had insisted I visit several of the finest establishments in Reef City the second that the tournament had ended and they kept me swimming, tiring out my fins, until moonrise.

There was a money lender with a giant painted sand dollar outside his establishment. He'd been a shark shifter who smelled of roasted eel and smiled far too cunningly for my liking. But he'd been just a part of the whirlwind of people I'd met. The head of the mining commission had been a jelly shifter with tentacles for hair. He'd greeted me with a grin that showcased two missing front teeth and then tried to lead me into the caves to display all their work searching for gemstones.

It had nearly triggered a panic attack for me, being back in the dark amongst nothing but rocks, drudging up memories of my kidnapping. Luckily, Sahar had made some excuse about *her* claustrophobia and gotten us out of that mess; now we sat on couches in his office and spoke over warm cups of seagrass tea.

After that, I'd visited the reef's scavenger association to see all of the treasures collected from trash washed into the ocean. I'd been forced to admire several bedpans that had been repurposed as soup pots, handles welded on by local blacksmiths. Worst of all, when we escaped from that meeting, there was no one to share my horror or amusement with because not one of them knew what a bedpan was, and I longed for Mateo.

But I couldn't visit him.

No, there had been shops to visit, merchants wanting to discuss taxes and trade. Even the weaver's guild had asked us to stop by so they could show me the latest in seaweed tapestries.

Finally it was over. My wings ached fiercely because there had been very little opportunity to walk in Reef City. The rainbow-colored reef buildings were entered and exited by a variety of holes and gaps in the reef that could be anywhere, including in the ceiling. That made for far more swimming than I was used to.

When we returned to Mayor Deacon's mansion to prepare for the evening's farewell dinner, I wanted a shoulder rub and a nap.

But Gita trapped me in a chair for an hour so that she could paint my face with bright orange stripes up the bridge of my nose. She carefully swirled her brush and created fins that fanned out dramatically around my violet eyes, applying the most elaborate face makeup I'd ever seen.

She was careful with every detail, edging the orange in red, then using gold to fill in the spiny fins, along with tiny little diamonds that she magically adhered to my forehead. She added dramatic yellow and orange blush, painted my lips a bright red and edged my eyes in pitch black khol when she was finished with everything else.

I was enthralled by my reflection; I looked like I was attending a masquerade.

My dress was a gorgeous burnt-orange tulle that faded to gold at the ends. It hinted at translucency in the most alluring of ways and I felt absolutely radiant in it, particularly when Gita had gathered up my golden hair into a netting of gold and sparkling tangerine jewels.

For a moment, I perked up, certain that the night would be full of fantastical dancing and romance with my competitors.

It wasn't.

While the scene itself was magical—Deacon's ballroom was full of enchanted floating candelabras from the scavenger association and the candles danced with flames as the waves caused by dancers made them swirl and dip; a foot of water at the base of the room was dyed a deep purple by Deacon's mage for ambiance; giant seahorse ice sculptures framed all of the entryways—I was stuck politicking until the wee hours and my gorgeous dress had been completely wasted.

I ended the night with cheeks that were as sore from smiling as my shoulders were from all the swimming earlier.

Such was the glamorous life of a queen.

I woke determined not to let the same be true today.

We were traveling to Navagio for the next competition and I was going to ensure that I got to speak with several competitors, damn it all. Now that I wasn't dying, I was incredibly invested in who I'd end up spending the rest of my life with. I couldn't afford a mistake.

Mateo was a given—I'd use my single exception for him each round if necessary. Keelan was a shoo-in since his stand-in had won the joust and he currently led the pack. Watkins was ... unfortunately inevitable, though I spent a good long minute daydreaming about locking him up in a tower, like some damsel, from one of the fairy stories before the kingdoms of Sedara were cursed with a low birthrate for women.

I could just picture him brooding and pacing in his tower, chipping away at it and trying to throw bits of glass at passersby. But I'd magically control the current around him so that anything he threw out of his tower window came zooming back in to smack him in the face.

I wondered briefly if I could do that, control the waves in that specific a manner, before deciding I didn't even care if I could. It made for a deliciously satisfying fantasy. Watkins hadn't done anything but glower in my direction last night, as if I'd initiated that kiss instead of him.

Idiot.

I shook my head to clear it of the angry haze that always came on whenever I thought about that shark shifter.

I tried to think about the others in the tournament... but I just wasn't certain. I had no clue who I could choose. I needed to get to know them more. Valdez and I had a vital, very lusty connection...but would a pirate ever be able to become a courtier?

I mulled over each of the remaining candidates as I sat at my dressing table, eating a breakfast of shrimp and sea snails while Gita plaited my hair for travel into this ridiculously elaborate weave, humming a love song while she worked.

When I finished my breakfast, I watched her in the mirror. She created three small braids on either side of my head and then wove them with other parted but unbraided strands of my hair until the back of my head looked like a soft blanket, the ends dangling free. She paused and gestured for me to grab a hand mirror off the dressing table so that I could see the process halfway through.

"You're a hedge witch with hair," I declared, before realizing it was a sky breather compliment and might not make much sense to her.

But my maid only smiled and said, "Yes, I know. But now, tell me what's bothering you. You've had the most serious look on your face all morning."

"I don't know who should win the tournament yet, and that bothers me."

"You're only one competition in. There are still three to go."

"Yes, but there are only twenty men left now." I didn't bother adding that four of the twenty didn't even want to be there, leaving only sixteen true competitors. Out of those, I'd need at least four good men. Maybe five. And I had three picked … but narrowing down the others felt impossible.

Gita tilted her head in thought, staring at me for a moment in my dressing table mirror. "What about that squi-shifter? Basil, I think his name is? I've heard he's really good at spearfishing, which is hard to do. He'd mingle well with all the men at court who like hunting."

I shrugged and didn't mention that my insides instantly recoiled. My only experience with the squi-shifter thus far had been an argument he'd gotten into with Julian about science while I'd been trapped with the two of them in my carriage. It wasn't the best impression. "If I pick Julian, then I certainly couldn't pick him. Those two are like oil and water," I mumbled, thinking. Would it be better to have someone who could mingle with courtiers or a man who had rather odd, albeit possibly useful, beliefs? "How do the servants feel about science?" I asked.

"Which man is that again?"

I pressed my lips together to smother a laugh. "Not a man. A concept Julian's fond of. Life without magic."

"Oh, well. Um, I don't think many would like that, you know. Life's hard enough with it, can't imagine how much harder it would be without it."

I nodded and let the subject drop. "True."

Gita fiddled with my hair a moment, finishing off one of the braids and tying a tiny ribbon around it. When she did speak again, she said, "Hmm… Well, Humberto is quite…dashing." Her cheeks grew pink. "I mean, all of the maids talk about him." She quickly looked back at her work, plaiting my hair with a slightly rougher touch than before.

Suspicion started forming inside my head, but it was completely unaccompanied by jealousy. Strategically, I knew the cardinal fish shifter who'd saved us on the road was the popular choice. He just wasn't my first choice. But it seemed like my maid might be interested … I decided to test the waters.

"Yes, he's very brave."

"Oh, he is. I nearly fainted on the road when those criminals came after us. But then, quick as a flash, he was there."

"It's like a fairy story out of childhood," I agreed.

She nodded and a wistful sigh escaped her lips. "Isn't it? He's like one of those squi-shifter knights from the *Moonlight Tidal Tales*."

She was smitten. *I was right!*

I mulled over the revelation a bit as she continued to plait my hair. While I knew that Humberto would be a strategic match, I'd always wanted a love match for myself. I'd grown up dreaming about one as a second-born princess. Did Humberto really deserve anything less? Gita was fun and sweet. If she and Humberto were a match, he'd still be around. Maybe I could hire him.

I hemmed and hawed a bit before I cleared my throat to get Gita's attention and make my proposal. "You know, Humberto is very fond of boots. Perhaps you could slip down to the kitchen after you finish my hair and get him a few for the road today."

Her eyes widened as she glanced up at me and I worried I might be pushing a bit too much.

"Humberto is sweet," I confessed, "but I can't marry them all. And a hero as grand as he deserves a woman who swoons over him."

Her eyes dipped and she shook her head. "A shifter like that would never look twice—"

"Gita! Don't you dare insult one of my favorite people."

She bit down on a grin. "Your Majesty."

"I could order you to bring him some boots you know," I threatened.

She narrowed her eyes. "If you do that, I swear your next dress will be a corset that compacts your ribs and completely exposes your breasts—"

"Fine," I conceded. "I won't force the matter." But as I settled into my chair and let her finish up the braids, I decided I would scheme a bit on Gita's behalf.

After she left, I called Felipe into my room because I needed to ask Lizza to visit me anyway. I needed her to gather whatever spells and ingredients she needed to test my magic. So sending Felipe on an extra little errand wouldn't be much trouble.

After I'd asked him to fetch Lizza, I added my request that he ensure that Gita and Humberto rode next to one another on the trip to Navagio. I was hardly able to keep a straight face as I asked, giggling in naughty anticipation and ready to face whatever consequences my maid would have for me later, though I fully expected her to be in a giddy daze afterward, not thinking at all about me.

"But he's one of your competitors."

"Yes, but Gita likes him."

His blue eyebrows rose but he didn't make further comment on the matter. He only clarified, "We aren't taking the whale this time so there aren't seats like before."

"Oh?"

"Shorter trip. Not quite a day's journey. We're taking dolphins and sharks and they can fit two each."

"Shark shifters?"

He nodded and immediately, I shook my head. "Nope. No shifters. Animals only." Watkins's rant about shifter treatment popped into my head and I couldn't erase it. I wasn't going to treat people that way.

"There's no way we can rearrange transportation—"

Sard it. "Fine. Then go announce this. Any shifters working today will be paid triple their normal wage. After today, if they want to move into other positions in my castle and work in their human forms, I'll accept letters of recommendation."

Felipe's deep blue eyes gazed fiercely at me for a moment and caught me like a net, dragging my stomach upward into the sunlight zone of the ocean, where everything sparkled and shone. "Of course, my queen. Anything else?"

I wanted to ask him for a dozen other things, including a kiss. But the door was cracked open behind him, he wasn't actually in the tournament, and he worked for me … a million reasons that I couldn't swarmed through my mind, making me sink from sunlight back to the twilight zone, to cooler, more level-headed waters. "No," I whispered.

"Are you sure?"

I glanced up uncertainly.

He swam closer, his spear brushing against my hand as he spoke. "You can ask me for anything, you know."

Oh, what those words did to me. I drank them in like they were the finest wine—they made me just as dizzy.

Combined with his earnest look and the heated intensity of his eyes, I never wanted this moment to end.

I wanted this devotion to morph slowly, like the water around us, swiveling and turning in new directions around our bodies.

Devotion wasn't far off from affection and only a stone's throw from attraction, wasn't it? *Felipe wouldn't do all he'd done for me solely based on his position, would he?* I asked myself.

But I didn't ask him.

Even though he'd blatantly told me that I could, that was one thing I couldn't ask him.

Because if he even hinted at yes, I'd be in a world of trouble.

"I think I pretty much have." I finally admitted, redirecting my eyes from his face to the wagon wheel tattoo just above his heart. I longed to trace it.

But apparently, my answer wasn't what he'd wanted me to say. His shoulders slumped slightly for just a moment, making me feel wretched. I wanted to reach out and touch him and ask why. What had he wanted me to ask? What more could I possibly ask of him? What was it he wanted to give?

But instead of broaching that dangerous topic, I changed the subject. “You know, I do owe you a favor for jousting on Keelan’s behalf.”

He started to shake his head, but I held up a hand to stop him. “I had to bribe Keelan with two statues of himself for him to allow you to show him up.”

Felipe’s expression morphed from downtrodden to amused. “Really?”

“Yes. So think of something extravagant that you want for your part. After all, you did more work than him. He just had to sit there.”

Felipe’s Adam’s apple bobbed up and down as he swallowed and nodded. “Alright. So, shifter announcement—”

“And make sure Gita and Humberto ride together.”

“Got it. I believe my cousin’s scheduled to ride with you in your carriage, if that’s okay?”

I’d intended to do my best to meet more men, but Felipe’s words erased any thoughts of that. I clasped my hands together demurely but a huge smile lit my face. “Yes, I suppose that would be acceptable.”

I was dying to spend time alone with Mateo. And like always, Felipe seemed to know just what I wanted.

If only I knew what it was he wanted in return.

9

"ARE you sure you just don't want to admit that you're a bit of an asshole?" Lizza's question cut like a sword. Her face was skeptical after I'd told her all of my strange and violent visions yesterday.

I ground my teeth and fiddled with the edge of my silk dressing gown because there wasn't much I could say to argue with that. Nothing she'd believe anyway. "It just wasn't normal, that's what I mean. I feel fury, yes. But I don't have the urge to slaughter people regularly."

"Really? Because I'd say I get the urge at least once a week."

"I had it multiple times over a few hours."

"It's not—"

"If you dare ask if it's my monthly courses, I'll have Felipe come in here and … and …" I had no idea what might scare off the old undead bat.

"And what? String up my innards? Isn't that what you say is your problem?" Lizza chuckled as she scratched at her rotting cheek and a bit of skin flaked off and floated away, revealing a tendon or something underneath.

I quickly averted my eyes as I pleaded, "Please. I need your help to try those spells you mentioned to keep my humanity intact while I access my power."

She grunted. "Alright. Have you tried at all yet?"

I swallowed. "Um. No. I thought I should wait since it's dangerous."

With a wave of her hand, the undead witch dismissed my concerns. "Meh, creating a little wave won't do much. Give it a quick try, just so I can see what I'm working with."

I froze, startled, not expecting that response at all. My stomach clenched and my thumbs dug into the cuticles of my pinky fingers nervously. She wanted me to try now? This very moment? It was easy for her to risk, she wasn't the one worried about becoming a violent beast. Though, I supposed, she'd be on the receiving end of things if I did try. I glanced quickly at the door of my bedchamber. It was firmly closed, though I knew

Ugo and Felipe guarded it. Sounds drifted from the hallway as servants packed up and got us ready to leave Mayor Deacon's home.

I turned back to Lizza and swallowed the lump in my throat. I plucked up my frail strands of courage and gathered them into a bouquet. *You can do this, Avia. It's just a simple test.* "Okay. How?"

She laughed dismissively, the sound a loud frog-croak. "It's your magic, girl. Reach inside."

Reach inside!? That was it? Gah! This seemed like an exercise in futility. *Wouldn't I have felt my magic after the spell?*

I hadn't felt anything—just fear and a bit of sadness. Maybe a bit of rage. But magic? I hadn't felt anything out of the ordinary.

I closed my eyes and tried not to let the million thoughts going through my mind distract me, especially not the one that grumbled curses in Lizza's direction. Slowly, they drifted away, like flotsam on a wave.

Magic. I'd never had it before.

What would it feel like? A tickle inside my stomach? Or more of a buzz? Would it have an actual sensation at all or would it be more of a visual thing … an undulating orb of blue light, for instance?

When I found it, my magic was none of those things.

It was a song.

A female voice sang softly inside my head. She used no words, only sounds, but the haunting quality of her voice raised goosebumps on my arms. As soon as I noticed the music, the song grew louder, as if it had always been there, just waiting for an audience.

I listened for a moment to the pattern, the rise and fall of the voice. The notes went up, up, up, crested in a trill of the tongue, then crashed down like a wave, falling quickly. The pattern repeated multiple times in a soothing melody. I found myself relaxing as I listened to the voice, my muscles loosening, hands falling limp. I began to breathe with the voice, between notes, and suddenly I didn't just hear the voice, I felt the reverberations of magic inside my chest as if I were the one singing. My mouth opened and while the song didn't erupt from my lips, they moved silently in concert with it.

What was this song? Was this the voice of the sea herself?

Or was it me—the manifestation of my power?

Whatever it was, this song was the most enchanting thing I'd ever heard. The music was as breathtaking as a sunset painting the ocean waves.

My eyes still closed, I raised my right hand, and I felt the music speed up in response to my movement. I pushed forward and the notes surged higher and faster, staccato.

"Whoa," Lizza breathed.

I opened my eyes to see a sphere made out of steam churning in front of my hand, the heated gas bubbles struggling out of the sphere, escaping to bound up to the ceiling.

My awe was just as frantic as those little bubbles, my conscious mind pinging with excitement.

I took a deep breath and imagined the voice slowing, the tone growing deeper.

The sphere in front of me slowly stopped hissing and churning, becoming a mass of spinning water, before solidifying into ice.

Madness.

I lowered my hand and the song slowly faded as water dripped like tears down the sides of the rapidly melting ball of ice. My gaze rose to meet Lizza's and a flash of fury struck me strong as lightning. An abrasive feeling like a chipped comb dragging across the scalp ran through my chest. Humberto's face appeared inside my head and I imagined thrusting my hand out and wrapping it around his neck, squeezing until his eyes popped from their sockets.

I gasped, breathing hard, and the image fell away as quickly as it had come.

I reached out and grasped Lizza's cold hands, folding my shaking fingers around her palms as I stared into her rotten face and urged, "Please, it happened again. You have to help me, Lizza."

The mage gave me a slow nod. "Alright. Let's get to Navagio. Then we can practice."

I nodded, releasing her hands and staring at my fingers as the lilting song tried to rise up inside of me again.

I couldn't let it. I wasn't prepared for the consequences.

I swam to the door of my room, throwing it open, letting the noise and bustle of everyone in the hall drown out the sound of my magic.

I wasn't ready to harness it again. The next time I tried, I would be.

FIVE DIFFERENT COMPETITORS CONGREGATED AROUND my gilt carriage where it floated, drawn by six white seahorses, on the outskirts of Reef City, just above the drop off of the continental shelf. Deep blue water ebbed beneath it and the cold tendrils from the deep swirled up onto my skin. The scales lining my outer legs and arms loved it. The chill tickled the scales that lined my cheekbones. But the rest of my skin grew cold with goosebumps. I fluttered my betta fish fins harder, trying to warm myself up, cursing my idiocy in refusing that shawl Gita had offered me.

We were about to head to Navagio, the town made of shipwrecks and scavenged treasures. I was equal parts excited and terrified of what I'd find there, after the bedpan debacle.

According to Julian's descriptions, it was a place of ingenuity.

According to Ugo's grumbles as Gita packed up my things this morning, it was a dump.

Still, I found myself a bit giddy for the next part of our journey. We'd made it through yesterday without an incident from the rebels, which I considered a massive win. Last night had been utterly boring, full of facts and figures and careful negotiation, just as a monarch's life was meant to be.

I took a deep breath and grinned at the fact that my biggest challenge this morning was keeping my hands off Mateo before we were closed into my carriage.

I glanced over to the right, where Gita was supposed to be supervising the last of my things after selecting my crown and dress for the day.

She'd opted for a circlet of dangling pearls and a dress with a pale white-and-gold-striped corset that ended just below my breasts. At first, I wondered if she'd overheard my scheming with Felipe about her traveling assignment, but then she'd offered to toss a gauzy wrap over it. I'd declined since I'd be in the carriage most of the day—and I now regretted it. My breasts were on display for the first time, in the style common under the sea.

Gita had mercifully arranged the bottom of my woven hair, pulling the free ends forward so that it provided some coverage. Not quite as much as I wanted, but it was something. When I looked in the mirror at my reflection, with my betta fish fins fluttering free and my short skirt, I felt a little like the vase paintings of water fairies that lined one of the hallways back in Evaness. It was pretty. And I finally looked like I truly belonged to the sea. After experiencing its magic, I was finally starting to feel like I did too.

Of course, I hadn't protested Gita's clothing choice even once, which had made her cock her eyebrows suspiciously at me.

"Who's riding with you in your carriage then?" she'd tried to be casually curious.

"Not Humberto," I'd replied. She'd glared and hadn't asked further.

Gita did have quite an eye for fashion, though today, I more appreciated the easy access this outfit would provide Mateo. It had been far too long since I'd kissed him.

I paused in my swim toward my carriage, instinct stopping me as I watched my handmaid swish her golden tail while she carried my box of jewels carefully out to be packed up for travel. When she reached the crowd of sharks and dolphins wearing leather harnesses with crates and trunks strapped to their sides, I noticed a man swim over. A tall handsome man wearing all black, even a black shirt. A man with pink hair.

With a massive flex of my fins, I sped in their direction, Ugo muttering a curse as he and Felipe tried to keep up. I cut through the water quickly, eyes focused on the pink dolphin shifter.

I hadn't seen Valdez yesterday. Not at all, come to think of it.

Where had the pirate disappeared to? Why hadn't he been there supporting his fellow competitors? Why hadn't he gone to the dinner last night? If he had, he certainly would have stolen me for a dance. The man had zero sense of propriety and oozed sexuality like it was some sort of catching disease, which in his case was true. He made me go daft in the head most of the time.

I would have noticed him swimming through the room last night, and not just because he'd have been the only man wearing a shirt, the only one with rings through his ears, but because he was impossible to ignore.

He was the dashing sort of rogue that women everywhere dream about but are secretly intimidated by. I was no different.

But now, he was setting off a different kind of internal alarm, not one that warned of impending orgasms. One that shouted that something about this scene was off, wrong.

As I got closer I spotted a dark ring around one of his eyes, a bruise. The gold ring at the corner of his lip seemed to hide a small cut. There were also some discolored trails up his muscular forearms, where his shirt sleeves had been rolled back. *What the hell?* What was going on? Had Valdez gotten hurt too during the arena disaster? Was that why he'd been absent yesterday? How had I not known?

Concern made my stomach tighten.

The alluring pink dolphin shifter smiled down at my maid and held out his hands to take my box of jewels—

My concern curdled into suspicion.

"Gita, wait!" I called out.

She paused, her arm already outstretched, the box of jewels hovering just above Valdez's hand. He reached out and snagged it before I could stop him.

A dozen theories slammed into me at once. He was a pirate. Used to doing what he wanted and taking what he wanted. He'd admitted to such himself. Was he really here to compete? Or had he come for some other, more nefarious purpose? That box alone contained enough jewels to set him up for life ...

Misgivings. Doubt. Skepticism. All of them plagued me.

The Kelp Forest wasn't far. If he had a speed potion like Felipe had taken a few days ago, then he could be off and into the plants in minutes. We'd have little to no chance of finding him unless my guards had their own. Even then ...

My throat grew tight.

Valdez turned on the spot. His hazel-green eyes met mine and devilish amusement lit his face. "Why good morning, Your Majesty." He bowed, pale pink hair flopping down and up with the motion of his neck as he held the box securely in his hand. "I'm so glad to see you."

His actions, the exact opposite of what I'd been expecting, threw me off. I slowed since he wasn't speeding off with my jewels tucked against his chest. Of course, I didn't spy a speed potion in his hands so dozens of servants and at least four guards nearby would hinder his getaway attempts.

When I reached him, I let myself flutter in place at his eye level. "And I, you. I wasn't aware that your skills included playing porter." I tried to add a smirk to hide my suspicion underneath flirtation.

Valdez's smile widened in return. "Oh, they don't. I'm horribly bad at it. Eel fingers, you know." He deliberately fumbled my case, chuckling when my eyes widened and Gita gasped next to me. He was right over a very deep span of water; the dive to retrieve my jewels could be thousands of feet.

"Valdez!" I scolded when he chuckled and pulled the box back to his side.

Felipe immediately swam over and held out a hand for the jewels, which Valdez dutifully handed over, loosening the knot in my stomach.

I released a sigh of relief but didn't let up on my glower at the pirate. My glare didn't deter him in the least. Instead, with all the confidence of a courtier, Valdez swam over and slung his arm over my shoulders. I was reminded yet again of how small I was in comparison to him. He was quite tall, though his lazy mannerisms made him less intimidating than he could have been. "While I might not be the best at hauling boxes, I am the best at spotting those who might haul them off." The hand over my shoulder pointed at a shark whose back was halfway loaded with trunks. "That, right there, is Bartrey Rover, part of the Shark Tooth gang. And he was planning to swim off with your gems."

The shark stiffened, his tail went still. And then suddenly, he was off like a shot, jetting out through the water and darting over and under other dolphins and sharks in a mad dash to get away.

Felipe and Ugo hopped into action, yelling orders for the other guards and closing in on me and Valdez.

The pirate's lazy hand on my shoulder slid down to become a hand on my hip and he pulled me against him, grinning when that displaced my hair and he got a view of one of my nipples.

"Don't worry, Majesty. You're safe with me."

My lips thinned and I carefully rearranged my hair to cover myself, conscious of Valdez watching my every move. I chose my words carefully, or as carefully as I could. "This feels like a setup."

Valdez's fingers tightened, but his smile never left his face as he leered down at me. "I'm wounded, Avia. You don't trust me."

"You're a pirate."

"Was." His fingers dragged along my hip, finding the ridge of bone there and tracing it with his thumb over my skirt. Even though I was covered, his fingers tickled the scales that made a small line down the outsides of my legs, creating a deliciously wanton sensation in my low belly. His touch nearly erased all my thoughts, scattered them like plankton sprinkled along a wave.

"Oh really?" I asked, trying not to let him see just how he affected me.

"Yes."

"And how'd you find that out? Who at the mayor's dinner knows Mr. Rover there?"

"I didn't go to the dinner."

"No?" I asked, though I already knew as much.

His fingers gripped tighter pulling me even closer, causing my right nipple to rub against the silky fabric of his shirt. It betrayed me by beading up and I knew he could feel it against him when his grin grew wider and I caught the floral scent associated with his own attraction.

"Stop distracting me," I hissed at him.

"You're the one distracting me," he retorted.

I tried to push him away but it was impossible, he was too strong. Felipe swam closer, spear angled, but I waved him off because I wanted Valdez to answer me more than I wanted him to release me. In fact, a tiny part of me, the part that had been planning naughty things all morning for my visit with Mateo, didn't want Valdez to release me at all. Especially not after I gulped some more of that potent floral scent of his. It made my eyes grow hooded even as I tried to scowl up at him.

"Stop flooding the water with hormones."

"That's like asking you to stop being gorgeous."

I reached out to squeeze his bicep in frustration but ended up admiring how sculpted he was underneath his shirt. Maybe something less pure. I didn't remove my hand. "Tell me you didn't hire that fool to steal from me in order to make yourself look good."

"I didn't hire that fool," Valdez returned easily.

"I can have a mage use a truth serum on you."

"Good. Do so."

There was a long moment as we faced off and I tried to measure whether or not I believed him. But he held steady, so either he was a magnificent liar (a trait that could still be useful in a palace, so long as it wasn't used against me) or he was telling the truth. I didn't have any proof of my accusation. So as I stared up at his hazel-green eyes and watch his pupils blow out with attraction the longer he held me against him, I decided that I couldn't condemn him yet.

"Okay then. Tell me what you were doing last night instead of attending the dinner function you were supposed to."

"I was out gathering information on who might have attacked," Valdez's face grew dark and wrathful, and suddenly, I could see the fierce and dangerous pirate. While the sight made my mouth dry out, it made my lady parts do quite the opposite.

"Mayor Deacon has city guards for that. And I have my own."

"I can go places that pufferfish like those can't."

"Really?"

"Really." He let his hand encase my hip, his fingers quite close to my inner thigh.

"And?" I prompted breathily, very aware of our audience as I reached down and gently slid his hand backward so that it wasn't completely indecent. Of course, that put his palm on my ass because he was a giant. I tried to shove that hand upward to my waist but he tightened his grip and wouldn't let me move it further. I could have protested, but part of me loved the way Valdez *wasn't* gentle with me because I was a queen.

He made me feel like a tavern wench … no, not some woman of the night … he was more like that handsy wool merchant back in Evaness who hadn't been able to stop touching his wife. Every time I'd gone to their shop, his hand had been at her waist, holding her hand, even dipping and kissing her raunchily in public—his affection so strong he couldn't help but reach out and touch her. And woe to any other man that looked at her, because the merchant was possessive.

Though there was a seductive undertone, a teasing to each one of Valdez's touches, he reminded me of the wool merchant, a man whose need spilled over into action. There was something so appealing about that; a man who couldn't help himself around me and didn't care what other people thought… It was the exact opposite of life in a castle court where restraint was everywhere, second-guessing rampant.

"And what happened last night?" I repeated myself, certain Valdez had lost the thread of the conversation from the heated look he was giving me.

"It must have been a lone fish shifter," he shook his head as if trying to clear it. "That's my best guess. Most people in the reef are packed in, it's hard to keep secrets in a place like this. Someone would have heard something and the rumor mill would have started churning. But all anyone could talk about last night, no matter which tavern I went to, was who had attacked the arena. And all they had were theories."

"Only theories? Then why do you look like you got punched?" I reached up to gently touch his cheek, not close enough to his eye to aggravate the bruise.

Valdez leaned into my hand for a second before he straightened and gave a careless shrug. "Some people didn't like some of the theories I suggested. Anyway, that's where I heard whispers about the Shark Tooth fools. A second-rate gang if there ever was one."

I moved my hand back down and squeezed his bicep unconsciously, picturing him getting into tavern brawls, my feet brushing against his pant legs. "But, why did you even go in the first place?"

"I told you, I take what I want. And that's true. But I also protect what's mine."

His eyes glittered with the words he didn't say.

Valdez already considered me his.

10

I WAS STILL SWOONING when I entered my carriage. Valdez's words had sent me into an emotional tailspin, that final squeeze he gave me sizzled like a brand upon my ass. I felt marked. And I liked it.

Gah! I was so physically drawn to him. Our chemistry was so intense I felt like I could touch it, bite it. And his protective nature nearly undid me. But at my core, I wasn't quite certain he was trustworthy. His heroics seemed too convenient.

Either time would tell, or I'd have to test him.

But still, that look in his eyes...

If he'd have asked me to hand over that case of jewels to him just then, I'd have done so. It wasn't payment enough for a look like that.

As I sat down on the padded bench and waited for Mateo to arrive, I tried to clear my mind of thoughts of the pirate but it was impossible. Instead of my fantasies clearing out entirely, I just kept picturing Valdez and Mateo both kissing down my neck at the same time, two sets of warm lips and tongues dragging over my pulse. My eyelashes flickered closed and my head tilted back against the seat until I realized that would muss Gita's intricate work. Dammit.

Mateo and I would have to be careful not to let it go to shambles or it would be obvious what had happened when I emerged from the carriage later. Careful was the opposite of what I wanted. I wanted wild and fierce reunion sex with the man who'd traveled to the far reaches to find me.

My finger trailed lazily up my inner thigh, as I decided that I should probably prepare for our little encounter. I drew little circles on my soft skin, teasing myself as I dragged my skirt up higher and higher, all while picturing Mateo's smile, his dimples, and that curly brown hair that had turned silver when he'd disguised himself as a merman. Finally, my finger reached the crease of my thigh, then the junction that ached. I started to drag my finger across—

The door to my carriage flew open. I swallowed a shriek as I skittered upright in my seat, frantically shoving down my skirt, embarrassment turning me as red as a dragonfish.

Mateo fumbled his way inside, carrying a small bundle of clothes with him as he gave me a bright, "Good morning!" that made me sigh in relief.

For all that I wanted him to do naughty things to me, I didn't want him to catch me doing them. That just … well, I just *couldn't* touch myself in front of an audience, even one I adored.

"Good morning, you handsome—" I cut off my own welcoming statement when I saw that Mateo wasn't alone. One of the other competitors was behind him. A man even shyer than Stavros, who'd just scraped through the joust. I struggled to recall his name as he proceeded to enter the carriage right behind Mateo.

"—man. Oh, good morning," I added to the newcomer, trying very hard not to let my irritation show, though it flashed in my eyes when I glanced over at Mateo.

What is going on? Why the hell is someone else here?

Mateo was oblivious to my unspoken questions, first trying not to stumble as he bowed, then fumbling as he tried to get his mer tail and his brown parcel wedged onto the seat beside me. He had absolutely zero idea how I'd been about to drag him onto me and refuse to let him go until we'd reached Navagio. He was clueless about the ache pulsing between my thighs and my desperate longing to feel his fingers and then his cock there.

I glanced back over at the newcomer, who rose from his bow gracefully and took the bench on the opposite side of the carriage, and I tried very hard not to instantly hate him for interrupting my perfect risqué plan. It was difficult.

The other man smiled apologetically at me as if he somehow knew his presence was an intrusion. He had the broad, bulky build of a merman but no tail, only thick muscled thighs that were visible behind the leather breechcloth he wore to cover his essential bits. His skin had a slightly blue tinge to it while his pitch-black hair cascaded in waves nearly to his waist. The newcomer's eyes rose to meet mine and I was startled to see the irises change color from hunter green to pure white, only his pupil breaking up the ghastly expanse. I was certain that he hadn't done something like that at the opening ball because then I would have remembered that. While he was handsome and his physique was surely an inspiration for statues, he didn't have the sensual quality of a siren, and in the parade of handsome eligible men competing, it was clear he'd gotten lost in the shuffle, which was a shame. If I'd met him on his own, I'd certainly have drooled.

"I'm so sorry, I thought my guard had arranged for only one competitor to ride with me. Yesterday was quite exhausting," I added that last bit as I stared at Mateo, who'd sat down on my left, tantalizingly near, close enough to touch. But with someone else in the carriage…my fingers flexed in frustration.

Hadn't Felipe said Mateo is riding with me? Dammit. Did I make the assumption that it would be alone? Did he actually say alone? I racked my brain, trying to remember, but it didn't really matter. The damage was already done.

Mateo tilted his head and glanced over at me, eyes dipping to my chest, and then back up. "Oh! If you're tired, we can let you rest and swim for a bit. Taft and I don't mind. Could I leave my new cloak here though? It's whale skin. Just got it."

Ah, Taft. That was the other man's name. One of the non-siren competitors. Dammit. I needed Sahar here with a list again. We had cut nearly ten men and I still didn't recall all of the twenty left.

"No, no," I held out a hand to stop them from leaving, though I absolutely wanted Taft to swim out that door. "I apologize. I must have misunderstood my schedule this morning. Please, sit. I'd be glad to have you ride with me." *Tomorrow or any other day. Just not now,* I added inside my mind.

"Are you sure?" Taft asked softly. "We understand if you want quiet." His voice was so soft that I truly believed he did understand the need for solitude. He seemed like the type that hardly talked.

I let out a soft laugh. "A queen doesn't often get what she wants. How about instead of leaving, you tell me about yourself, Taft? I know a few things about Mateo but none about you."

Taft gave a slow nod as Mateo reached for the carriage door and pulled it shut, sliding a bolt closed to lock it. With a shudder, the sea horses began to move and I resigned myself to the fact that this journey wouldn't be the wanton sexual adventure I'd imagined, but instead a conversation that was as dry and stale as an old biscuit.

"I'm from Sky Stones," Taft said slowly, then stopped.

"And he's a nixe," Mateo contributed, excitement coloring his voice.

"Lovely," I said, as I racked my brain to remember if I'd studied anything about nixes in the royal library.

Mateo interjected. "Oh, it's more than lovely. Show her one, Taft."

Taft brought a hand up to dig shyly through his onyx hair and shook his head. "We haven't even made small talk."

"But it's so awesome. If I could do it, I'd hardly be in human form at all."

Taft rolled his eyes at Mateo's enthusiasm before turning to me and said softly, "Majesty, I'd like to change form, if you don't mind."

My disinterest and unfair annoyance at this newcomer who'd crushed my orgasmic plans transformed into a hesitant fascination. What could he do that impressed Mateo so much?

A second later, Taft's body dissolved into bubbles and a small pale blue sea serpent no larger than a loaf of bread appeared in his place. His barbed tail swirled in the water for a moment and he looked like a winged snake with oversized nostrils and the thin mustache of a snake oil peddler. Another moment, and another slew of bubbles, and a blue sea anemone sat in his seat, tentacles swaying.

My jaw hung open like a child's. "You can turn into anything?"

"Anything," Mateo confirmed, reaching out and patting my shoulder with enthusiastic excitement. "It doesn't have to be animate either. And he's not part human, so he doesn't pay a price for his magic! Ask him to become a hand mirror. Or a hair comb. Or—"

"Can you become a scepter?" I faced the little anemone, wondering if Taft could even hear at all in his current form.

Apparently, that answer was yes because another set of bubbles erupted and then a pale silvery scepter set with sapphires lay upon his seat.

"Brilliant," I whispered, awe coursing through me. I knew I needed husbands to help with trade—Mateo was my first pick there—and negotiation. But I also needed a spymaster. I'd been considering Stavros. But here in front of me sat a man who could literally go undetected as he gathered information. What more could I want in a spy?

I turned to look at Mateo, whose hand still sat on my shoulder, gratitude etched into my features. He'd clearly unearthed Taft amongst all the other competitors and brought him to me. My eyes shone my thanks as a final flurry of bubbles appeared and then Taft sat slouching against the other brocade bench once more.

Mateo smiled back and that click of connection I always felt with him returned. His hand slid down my shoulder, thumb gently tracing my skin and reminding me of everything else I wanted to do with him today. Bringing a competitor this powerful but clearly incredibly shy to my attention deserved a reward. My teeth dug into my lip as I thought about what type of reward Mateo might like and what type I thought fitting to give. Definitely one involving my mouth. My change in expression led to a heated stare on his part and I had to turn away and stare down at my lap, knotting my fingers together in frustration.

Damn. What could we do? We were stuck in this carriage with someone else and it would be hours until we stopped for the midday meal. But I wanted to kiss him so badly, whisper my thanks against his lips, have him gather me into his lap and just hold me for a bit before we made slow sweet love, and then had a fast and dirty session after.

I reigned in my imagination by turning to Taft.

The nixe didn't bother offering additional information about himself, sitting silently and awkwardly across from us, doing nothing more than blinking those large eyes of his which had, thankfully, returned to green.

"What does your family think about you entering the tournament, Taft?" I asked.

But the burly blue man just shrugged one of his huge shoulders. "Don't know."

"How'd you find the joust?"

"Different than I'm used to but not bad."

"How's it feel when you're shifted into an object and someone touches you?"

He shrugged. "Dunno how to describe it. It's not like anything else."

"But you do feel it?"

"Sort of. Depends on the object I guess. The harder the object, the more I think it feels like a shell outside of me, not quite getting in."

Fascinating.

Taft's eyes drifted down to his knees and naturally so did mine. He was so completely muscular that it was almost hard to believe his form wasn't at least a little bit under his control. Even Felipe, who exercised daily, wasn't as sculpted as Taft.

But how did one ask, *Do you use magic to make yourself unbelievably attractive?* It wasn't done, so I didn't do it.

Besides, Taft didn't bother to ask any questions about me in return. He didn't try to start up any conversation. He just let the silence grow.

Hmmm. Strong. Silent. Useful. My tongue traced my top teeth as I tried to determine if that was a good combination or a bad one.

"How about a game of Niddy Noddy?" Mateo asked, reaching for his cloak and untying the cord. "My cousin lent me some cards."

"I don't know it." Taft declared.

"Don't know Niddy Noddy! Oh, it's easy! I've been playing it every night," Mateo responded.

Of course Mateo was making friends, I thought as a warmth lit my chest while I watched him dig through his cloak for a small packet of cards. Ever the diplomat's son.

"Alright, so if you have a pair, on your turn, set down one of the cards. The next person has to set down a higher card of the same suit. The suits are the little pictures in the corners: shells, coral, water, and rock. The person who lays down the highest card of that suit wins. See? Easy."

Mateo passed out the cards and we spent a decent hour playing Niddy Noddy by setting down our cards next to us on our benches since we had no table, a thrill racing down my spine every time my hand brushed his. I also noticed how frequently his eyes strayed to my breasts, which was exactly what I'd wanted when I was dressing this morning, but now utterly frustrating.

I purposely fumbled and dropped my cards more than once during the game, using the excuse to bend over toward Mateo, to brush against his tail with my fingertips and let him get an eyeful of my breasts, which ached for his touch.

While we tried to make small talk, Taft was often silent, so Mateo and I ended up conversing about things like trade with Macedon or the sheer size of the swordfish involved in the joust.

"Their noses were massive."

"I wish all the ladies would say my nose was massive," Mateo grinned at his innuendo as he flopped down a coral card.

"I don't want other ladies talking about your nose, thank you," I returned as I set down my own card in response.

"Taft. What do you think of my nose, then?" Mateo turned and let Taft view his profile but my eyes dropped immediately to the true subject of our discussion. Mateo had a very generous ridge building underneath his scales.

Taft didn't seem to catch on to the joke. Or, he didn't play along. "Oh, um, it looks normal. Yup." He laid down his own card as I smirked in Mateo's direction.

"Yes, just normal. Not overly large or anything."

Mateo glared playfully at me. "I'll get you for that."

But I'd only laughed as we continued our little game, flirting with one another a bit more brazenly since Taft seemed so unaware.

After about an hour, it seemed like Taft had had enough. His eyes drooped and he gave a yawn, passing

Mateo back his hand of cards. "Do you all mind if I nod off? Shapeshifting tires me out."

"Of course," I smiled, secretly thrilled to have a chance to be nearly alone with Mateo.

Mateo gave a concerned nod to the other man, and deftly packed up the cards, but I saw a smile playing across the corner of his lips as he bent to wrap them with a bit of string. He was just as pleased as I was.

The nixe laid himself out the best he could on his bench, propping his arm upon the side of the carriage and his head upon that. Within a few minutes—though they felt like hours as I watched him closely and rubbed my thighs together in anticipation—he was asleep.

I eyed the other man cautiously as his eyelashes fluttered against his cheeks, both elated and also incredibly nervous. I wanted Mateo so badly but I didn't really want a stranger to witness everything.

I didn't want him to question our attachment.

I turned to peer out the window of the carriage, which showed nothing but a dull expanse of blue for as far as the eye could see, racking my mind for a solution before I glanced over at Mateo and just lost all my good sense.

"Have we gone into deeper water? I'm suddenly cold." Mateo said, pulling out his cloak and shaking it out in front of us.

"Oh, I do believe you're right, it is a bit colder. Would you mind sharing?" I asked, in a tone that was as innocent as I could manage.

His tongue dug into the side of his cheek as he tried to hide his grin. "Of course not, Your Majesty." He ceremoniously laid the cloak over both of us, scooting closer so that the fabric draped over us both. Underneath the cloak, his hand sought out mine and he squeezed it.

A tingle of naughty victory surged through me and it was quite a fight to keep my face innocent as I said, "Thank you." I tilted my head in Taft's direction and mouthed, "Thank you for him."

He nodded but leaned close as his lips brushed my ear. "He's so quiet that he falls into the background a lot. But I thought you might like him. Be aware though, he doesn't talk about himself. I don't know if there are skeletons in his closet that will come bursting out one day or if there's just a lot of trauma."

"Hmm," I mumbled, but my mind stopped thinking about Taft when Mateo's lips closed around my earlobe. Instead, my hands reached for his waist underneath the cloak and touched him. I dragged my fingers up and down the defined muscles of his abdomen, over the trail of hair that led down to other things. Though he was mer, and his cock was hidden underneath his scales, the thick ridge of his erection still pushed up against my hand like a man's dick would push out his trousers. I gently stroked his scales, wondering if they were as sensitive to the touch as mine were. By the slight moan he made against my throat, I thought it quite possible.

His lips trailed my neck and I fought to remain silent, not to wake the nixe in the carriage, as my mind raced ahead to all the things Mateo and I might be able to get away with without disturbing this cloak. The wild coupling I'd imagined was out ... but what about sitting on his lap?

My plans dissolved into sensation when Mateo's hand sneaked up to my bared breast and tweaked my nipple, then pulled it, tugging rapidly and sending steady spikes of pleasure down my spine as my head tilted back. My mouth opened and my breath quickened but I didn't make any other sound as he teased me. This, this was what I'd been waiting for.

I fought to keep my wings, which I'd tucked down to sit, from fluttering in reaction when Mateo replaced his lips with his teeth, dragging them with a soft scratch over my pulse. I wanted to shove his head down underneath the cloak so that he could use that mouth on my breasts, but my eyes kept straying to Taft where he slept and I hadn't sunk far enough into lust yet to disregard the danger of the other man waking at any moment.

One of Mateo's hands slid down my stomach and to my waist, waiting there in the most polite fashion until I softly growled, "More." Then, quick as a flash, his hand was underneath my skirt, his fingers skimming over my underthings and shoving the dainty silk aside. His hand was warm against my mound and I huffed out a sigh as I slid down slightly on the bench so that I could widen my legs and give him a better angle. My fins grew pinned beneath my back as I reclined, but that only added to the sensation of being at Mateo's mercy—which I was.

With every gentle stroke of his fingers, Mateo drew me farther into a trance. I parted my lips and licked them when he started to trace my opening and then dip just the tip of his finger inside—it was heavenly. My hand made another move for the swollen ridge of his cock, but he whispered gruffly in my ear, "Let me take care of you first."

Selfless. He was always so good to me. I let my hands drift down to the whale skin cloak and clutch it instead of him, ensuring that our indiscretions remained somewhat discreet, though I could smell my own arousal at that point, and wasn't certain the cloak hid much at all.

Mateo was certainly past the point of hiding the hand that thrust into me, which smacked into the cloak and created a very obvious hill each time he withdrew.

I pressed my lips together and closed my eyes, focusing on the sensations he was dragging slowly from my body.

He built me up until I was panting, nearly there, and then he withdrew, despite the protesting moan that escaped my lips.

Taft shifted in his sleep and I stiffened, alarmed I'd woken him. The fear swirled with pleasure because Mateo didn't remove his hand or stop his touch.

"Shhh," he gave me a soft warning as he dragged his lubricated fingers up and down my slit, coating my pussy with my own excitement. He spread me apart with two fingers as he shoved his way back into my heat, the pads dragging deliciously up and down and tapping at me while his other hand plucked at my nipple aggressively in a pattern that made me nearly delirious.

It was dangerous, letting Mateo go this far with me while another competitor slept only feet away, and it was clear Taft was a light sleeper. We were trodding on thin ice.

But when the mer pulled his soaked fingers out, denying me an orgasm for the second time, I dropped the cloak furiously, exposing his hand on my nipple as my own hand flew down to shackle his wrist.

His mouth whispered gently against my ear. "Don't worry, Avia. It will be better this way."

I released his hand with a warning glance before tugging the cloak back up to hide myself again, eyes flickering once more to Taft, but the nixe seemed out.

Slowly, Mateo reached back down and began to caress my clit. As he worked up a rhythm, all my worries dissolved like salt in the water.

My eyes found his while his hands worked their magic and I could practically taste his excitement as I felt heat slinking through my belly and pooling right where his fingers teased until I burned and ached twice as much as I had before.

He pinched my clit lightly between his thumb and forefinger and I arched into his hand, rising off the bench, hips thrusting in a primal response that I couldn't control—and didn't want to. Nearly there. I was nearly there.

He tugged lightly, the motion on my clit matching the tug upon my nipple.

I shuddered.

Oh. Yes. Bliss.

I knew nothing for a moment as my body bucked and slick release flooded Mateo's hand.

When I came back to myself, I realized with a start, that Taft's eyes were cracked open.

He'd seen us.

11

PANIC SLUICED THROUGH ME, gushing from my head as quick and fast as a flood as I stared at Taft. Dammit.

I had to fight to get my logic to take charge and come up with some excuse.

But Taft shut his eyes before my trembling lips could spout off something stupid. And when he kept them shut for a moment, my fear abated enough for an explanation to pop up inside my mind.

If rumors get around about why I saved Mateo, at least they'll have one explanation for it. They'll think he's sleeping his way to a crown, which isn't true but it's better than the truth. I glanced nervously over at Mateo, but he hadn't noticed our traveling companion was awake, he was too busy peering down at my body behind the cloak, his eyes hungry as he watched my pussy pulse near his fingers.

Taft gave a loud yawn and stretched, and Mateo instantly straightened, yanking his hand away from me without subtlety, gaze going wide with guilt and alarm.

"Well, I've got a crick in my back," the nixe stretched his arm across his chest, carefully avoiding eye contact with us. "I think I'll just hop out and swim for a bit. Stretch it out." He pushed open the door of the carriage and it slammed behind him with a solid thunk.

I turned to Mateo, chewing my lip. "He knows. Do you think he'll—"

Mateo ripped the cloak off of me, his eyes dragging down my front as he yanked me toward him, then rolled me up onto his lap so that I straddled him on the bench, his actions ignoring every bit of the panic surging through me. My betta fins splayed out automatically as he moved me to help me keep my balance as he clasped my waist and dipped his head down to bring his mouth to my nipple, to continue where we'd just left off.

"Mateo! Will he be a problem?" I tried to smack his back but his mouth on my breast was too compelling and I ended up just raking my fingers down his spine. "He could be out there right now, telling everyone that

I'm sleeping with you, making them suspicious as to why—"

The mer let my nipple slide from his lips and punctuated his next statement with kisses as his mouth traveled across my chest and climbed my other breast. "No. He. Wouldn't." He sucked harder when he reached my pink peak this time and I groaned at the sensation, finally able to make noise now that we were alone.

"Why not?" I breathed when he abandoned my breast and slid his hand down between us.

Mateo smirked up at me, those chocolate eyes of his one of the few things that had stayed the same when he'd become mer. "Because Taft wants to win as much as any of us or he wouldn't have entered. And he knows he's socially awkward. He knows I'm his ticket in."

I was still a bit skeptical but then Mateo roughly shoved aside the row of glittering silver scales that hid his cock from view and my focus changed, aligned with Mateo's dick, which was clearly as desperate for me as I was for it. It popped forward instantly, a bulging pale organ. I was surprised how different the shape was from his human cock. The shaft itself was as wide as three of my fingers at the base but narrowed as it rose from his body until it flared out into a very thick mushroom tip twice as wide as the shaft. Another unique feature I spied instantly was the sucker on Mateo's pelvis that sat just above the base of his cock. It looked like one of the suckers from an octopus and instantly, I knew exactly what it was for ... that little appendage would perfectly enclose my clit.

Oh. Yes.

I shoved at Mateo so that I could scramble backward off of his lap. I stood, crouching over him so that my head didn't bump the roof of the carriage, hand braced on his shoulder as I quickly discarded my skirt and undergarments. I wanted to feel that cock inside of me. I wanted to worship Mateo's new body and kiss him until I couldn't breathe.

I didn't bother removing the corset—it had too many strings and my breasts were already free anyway. I climbed carefully back up onto the bench and straddled Mateo again, hovering just above his cock. I wrapped one of my arms around his neck and with my other hand, I positioned him at my entrance, enjoying the brush of that soft helmet and the lubrication that eased from his narrow tip.

I slid it back and forth across my slit a few times, making my eyelashes flutter, and Mateo grit his teeth in anticipation.

It hit me at once that we were here together again, despite fate's every effort to keep us apart. Tenderness filled me at the thought that we'd beaten such odds because the man in front of me refused to give up. It didn't matter if dragons and mountains or an ocean and fins stood in his way—he'd come for me.

As I sank down onto him, I whispered, "I love you."

He groaned at the feel of me, at the way we fit together so perfectly with our new bodies, the head of his cock gently rubbing against my g-spot, which felt so much longer than it had when I was merely human. The sensation was definitely more intense for me than last time. And when he bottomed out and that suction cup attached to me. *Oh. Oh yes.*

My head tilted back and Mateo leaned in, kissing my neck as he said, "I don't just love you, Avia. I worship you."

My mind turned the color of clouds at sunset, a soft rosy pink, and I stared down at the top of his head as soft tears came to my eyes. I needed him, needed this level of acceptance so badly that it was an ache. Only he could ease it.

Our lips met in a kiss that was full of promises and starlight.

I held onto him the way I clung to hope, fiercely. Tongues dancing, our bodies connected, I felt like we were melting into one another. It was exquisite.

Only when we were both panting, out of breath from our frantic kisses, did we pull back and stare into one another's eyes.

The moment grew potent as Mateo's hands fell to my hips and then he lifted me up slowly.

I gasped, worried I'd lose the delicious suction at the base of his cock. But the little appendage stretched, tightening up on my clit as I drew away from him, and continued to suck more gently when I plunged back down. Perfection.

No wonder humans walked into the sea chasing singing mer.

Sarding hell, it's so good.

It only took five thrusts before a rolling orgasm started, making my hips shake and my bones turn liquid as pleasure sparked inside of me and shot out to all of my limbs. It sizzled and simmered but didn't quite fade away, leaving me moaning and utterly useless.

Mateo was forced to grab onto me and use his arms to thrust my body up and down on his, which only drew the trembling sensation out longer as a pleasurable pressure I'd never felt before built deeper inside of me, making the brilliance of the surface orgasm on my clit seem like it was only an appetizer for headier, darker things that I'd never experienced.

"Oh. Yes. Via. Dammit," Mateo swore into my ear as he lifted me and slammed me back down onto his lap repeatedly.

As we continued, either I grew tighter or he grew bigger, I wasn't sure which—whether I was clamping down on that thick cock head or if he was expanding. I just knew that it caused red lines to shoot across my vision and burst like fireworks behind my eyes.

The world became sensation. Moans. Grunts. The friction of our bodies. I ground into him and the scales of his mer tail created this delicious sensation against my inner thighs. His fingers dug into my ass and then he held me still, perched an inch above him before his hips slammed into my pelvis and he swapped our motion, pistoning in and out of me.

All I could do was grab onto his hair and the back of the seat behind him as he dipped his head and bit down on my nipple. My hips swiveled in response and then and there, I reached the peak of sensation, bursting through the clouds to a height I'd never reached before. My mind filled with the most brilliant blank bliss.

When I came back down, Mateo's head rose from my nipple, his pupils dilated with lust. "Climb off of me and grab onto the other bench," he ordered.

Shakily, I did so, though my limbs were tangled threads that didn't want to cooperate. My hands could hardly hold me up as I braced them on the opposite bench; I had to flare out my fins to the side to help, but that made me glance back. "Did I hit you with my wings—"

Mateo's cock plunged into me, erasing my question and my inhibitions. I leaned down as he grabbed hold of my hips and started steadily stroking in and out, using his tail to thrust, finding his rhythm, one that set my breasts bouncing hard against my chest. His motion set the water inside the carriage swirling and it danced deliciously over my nipples.

Once Mateo had a steady pace and I felt less light-headed, I used one hand to prop me up against the seat back of the bench while I rested my cheek on the seat padding. My other hand reached back and touch my swollen clit, which—to my surprise—was still longing for touch even after the massive orgasm I'd just had. I circled my clit as my cheek slid across the bench with every thrust, the abrasions only adding to the utter wicked pleasure of the moment. Mateo's sucker at the base of his cock latched onto a patch of skin on my ass, and it felt like a kiss, then a painful yet satisfying sort of suction. I was certain I'd have a hickey.

The water swirling over my breasts was nice but not quite enough sensation and the naughty vision I'd had earlier of Valdez joining in returned. In my imagination, the pirate sat on the ground, his mouth and fingers plucking at my breasts and awaiting his turn. I imagined his cock, wondering what it might be like … if it would be smooth or knobby, thick or thin. Could it make me feel this good?

The prospect of both of them playing with me at once sent heat rumbling through me and my breath came shorter and quicker as my finger circled my clit faster.

"Via," Mateo breathed, and then suddenly he reached forward underneath my chest and dragged me up so that my back pressed against his chest. My wings flew back and arched around him, fins folding themselves around his back as my arms wrapped around his neck.

The sensation was intense—for both of us, it appeared—my fins started to shudder just as Mateo started to grunt his release. One, two, three times, he pumped into me. Then his forehead fell to my shoulder and he gave a contented sigh. But he didn't release me.

"I want you to clench around my cock after I've come in you," Mateo whispered, his words leaving a warm trail along my back at the base of my wing. "I want that pussy to clench and suck up my sperm, Via."

Oh shit. His dirty talk made me shudder, and when he brought his fingers back to my slit, running them up and down my sensitive lips, I bucked back against him. He didn't release me, he held me still whispering,

"You're mine, Via. You might belong to lots of men eventually. But right now, in this moment, you're mine. And I don't ever want you to forget it."

With that, his fingers slid up to my clit.

I nearly blacked out.

12

Raj

I side-eyed Humberto as the idiotic dolphin I rode skidded happily through the waves, cresting annoyingly every so often so it could breathe.

Stupid sarding animal. Why couldn't I have been assigned to ride a shark?

My ride and Humberto's prodding questions had thoroughly ruined my morning. The cardinal fish shifter had kept poking around asking about my background.

I should have taken notes on what I've told everyone—though I've tried not to speak much—but it had been hard to shake that entitled, paunchy little hero off because he thought he was being "friendly" and I hadn't just been able to peel the skin from his tongue to shut him up like I normally would have.

What an annoying exercise in self-restraint that had been.

I sighed.

"Don't worry, today's a much shorter jaunt," Julian, my saddle mate, said from behind me.

I made a sarcastic face mocking him, but only after I ensured no one was looking.

Humberto was too busy chatting with some golden-tailed mer woman beside us.

Blech.

At least I hadn't been forced to ride with him but all this play-acting was getting tiring. I wished this stupid farce of a tournament was over already so that I could unleash my wrath and reveal myself to the pathetic Avia right before I obliterated her. I imagined her face covered in tear tracks and smiled at the thought.

She would actually be lucky. Her death was only a means to an end, so it would be relatively quick. It was a way to take control of Okeanos and lure Bloss back down here for another battle. But this time, I'd be prepared for her tricks. This time, I'd defeat that upstart bitch.

I inhaled, the scent of impending victory invigorating me.

And maybe it was the thought of progress, or perhaps the sunshine itself, but as we crested the next wave, I felt happier. Giddy and excited even. It had been a long time since I'd faced an opponent like Bloss, one who'd managed to surprise me. I smiled as our mount jumped through several waves, not even upset when the motion pushed Julian closer to me.

In fact, the press of his cock against my ass stirred something in me. A flash of attraction blinded me for a moment and as the dolphin dove back under the waves, I found myself getting turned on.

Of course, my thoughts immediately went to Bloss's stupid curse, but this attraction was just a low simmer, not a kettle boiling over. It wasn't the mindlessness of those orgasms she'd forced on me.

Was I really getting hard over the press of another man's thighs against my hips? The way his cock nestled in the crack of my ass?

I felt the urge to reach down and stroke myself, though I resisted, fascinated by the feelings swirling through my chest.

Even when I'd taken men occasionally over the centuries, I'd always been a top, not a bottom. But there was an undeniable stirring in my loins.

I cleared my throat, wondering if it was possible.

It faded a bit when Humberto's idiot dolphin ended up thwacking his tail against the waves and splattering water into my eyes.

Shitehead.

I touched my ring on my finger, tempted to twist. But I didn't. I breathed slowly until I was calm again.

"So, what do you think the next challenge will be?" Julian asked, his tone pondering, oblivious to my troubles.

"I heard it was wit," I replied shortly, wanting this conversation over.

"I'm glad of that. I'm much more suited to mental battles than physical ones. You're pretty bright too, so I assume you feel the same?"

The compliment sent a little thrill through me that it shouldn't have, and my dick, though only half-hard, twitched slightly. I scolded it for its stupidity. The damned thing was being a fool.

"I suppose."

"I hope we have to build something. I recently built a little device I like to call an astrolabe that can allow sailors to navigate without magic—"

He was speaking without prompting, one of my pet peeves. I hated when people prattled on uselessly. I often pulled their teeth out for it so that they'd be self-conscious every time they opened their mouth from then on. His talk was even more boring than most. Who cared about some unnecessary device that didn't use magic?

His words should have made my dick shrink but it only throbbed in longing. Perhaps I'd been neglecting it too much lately. After the orgasm curse from Bloss, I hadn't been very inclined to repeat the sensation of mindless pleasure, much like one doesn't want to drink for a bit after a night of inebriation that ended with hurling their guts into the gutter.

Now, I wondered if I'd made a mistake.

Perhaps I should have cleaned out the pipes more regularly because my body was clearly malfunctioning. First my heart, now my dick—perhaps siren bodies were inferior.

I tried to shake off the sensation and think of something else, but Julian put his hand on my shoulder to point out a school of fish nearby, as if that was something special. The warmth from his fingertips drifted into my skin like sunlight and my chest grew soft and warm.

Sard it. What the hell is going on? I don't get soft and warm!

He kept talking. And talking. And I battled to make my throbbing dick shrink back to normal because I was never going to mindlessly orgasm again.

But then, Julian mentioned surgery.

"Wait. What is that again?" I asked.

"Well, it's a medical procedure intended to replace magic."

"Yes, but the knife?"

"Well, yes, you use the knives to cut a body open in order to access the area of trauma or illness."

"You cut them open while they're still alive?" I had to clench my hands down on the reins I held as my heart suddenly throbbed in time with my dick.

"Yes, I know, a lot of people find it ghastly, but it can actually be quite effective—"

"I don't. Tell me more," I urged as my mind finally caught up with whatever my dick must have known all along. Julian was brilliant. "How do you make these cuts?"

"Well, ideally, the person is passed out. But if not, I've seen it done by strapping the body down and pouring vinegar or whiskey on the wound—"

Sarding hell. He went on and on. He talked about torture in the most exquisite way. I wanted to turn around and kiss him full on the mouth. I wanted to plunge my hand into his trousers and see if he was as turned on as I was. I slowly stopped fighting the heat gathered in my loins.

He discussed surgery for hours and my opinion of him blossomed like a flower. He was so smart and charming and sweet as he spoke about blood and entrails in a detached way, as only a true killer could.

I began to treasure his words, crave the sensation of his breath trailing down my neck as he used these amazingly seductive words: dissection, laceration, trephining the skull with a hole.

His brilliant evil was as majestic as the sun across the desert sand dunes which held nothing more than glittering golden death. Julian was that magnificent.

I saw a dozen fish swim nearby and suddenly, I was reaching back, grabbing his thigh as I pointed the creatures out for him, ecstatic when he leaned forward over my shoulder, pressed close against me to get a better look.

A silly little smile lit my lips even as my cock strained against my pants, brutally tapping against the hem repeatedly.

I said his name inside my head as I touched him, whispered it gently. *Julian.*

A fleeting thought came to me as he squeezed my bicep and exclaimed over some rare fish. I hoped we rode an actual dolphin and not a dolphin shifter, who'd recognize my arousal and wonder about it later. But that thought fled when we reached a slightly more turbulent patch of water and Julian's arms came around my waist, clutching me, sending my mind into a flurry of naughty images where he held me tight and slid his swollen dick in and out of my ass, rubbing against my perineum, making me moan loudly while he stroked me off.

I erupted in my pants.

I came so hard that dark spots filled my vision and I nearly blacked out.

13

Avia

Navagio gleamed like a pirate's treasure box in the distance. The golden rooftops glittered and glowing colored glass towers peeked like enchanted gemstones out from behind the town's defensive wall, which was constructed out of the hulls of sunken ships. At first, I found the sight magical, but when I thought about it, I realized how macabre it was that all of the beautiful treasures of the city came from the death of people from my former world.

Mateo swam out of my carriage a few hours before we arrived at the city walls, partially to avoid speculation from the crowd, who'd see him inside with me and wonder who he was, and partially because Sahar swam up with a list of Navagio's "notables" for me to learn.

"It smells like you had an enjoyable *ride* over," Sahara smirked at me as she unfurled a long scroll on her lap.

My cheeks burned in embarrassment, but I knew better than to deny her charges. It would only draw out the teasing. "Are you going to tell me who is who and what's what or are you going to mock me?"

"Perhaps a bit of both your highness," Sahar flicked her golden hair behind her shoulder with a grin. I narrowed my eyes at my adviser but that didn't seem to deter her in the slightest. Secretly, I was quite glad for the deal that I made with her son. I was going to quite enjoy her reaction when she stumbled over two life-size statues of Keelan. *Perhaps I should commission four,* I thought. *Or maybe I should just fill her entire bed-chamber.* That was a gratifying vision: dozens of winking Keelan statues surrounding her bed so that she'd have to swim up and over them in order to sleep. Maybe they should watch over her as she slept, granite eyes staring down at her.

It was difficult to set aside my silly thoughts of revenge, but Sahar settled into work by pointing at the first name on her list, and so I had no choice but to take a deep breath and calm myself to listen.

"I need to warn you that the mayor here is not like the mayor back in Reef City. He's not a big fan of the monarchy. Believes in 'local government.'"

“In other words, he wants all the power for himself,” I commented dryly.

Sahar pointed her finger at me and gave a tongue click. “Exactly.”

I chuckled, then asked, "So I shouldn’t expect much of a greeting then?“ I slunk back in my seat, tracing my fingers along the brocade pattern of the seat cushion, trying not to cringe as I reached a rather sticky spot—evidence of my earlier pastime. *Ew.*

I placed my hands onto my lap instead as my hopes for this next visit spiraled downward. It had been so nice and so wonderful to have an ally in Mayor Deacon. I hadn’t even considered the fact that this new mayor might utterly resent the intrusion of the Okeanos Tournament into his domain.

"The opposite actually." Sahar startled me with her response and I glanced over as she gave me a superior look followed by an eye roll as she said, "This mayor is as competitive as they come. Gorgono can’t stand Deacon, and always tries to beat him at everything. So prepare yourself. You're going to get both the grandest and yet the coldest welcome imaginable.”

I gave a careless toss of my hand, feigning an arrogance I’d often seen used by courtiers. “Well, as long as it’s grand …” I finished it off with a posh laugh, which made Sahar chuckle.

"Don't underestimate him," she warned, her serious face quickly returning. "He and his wife, Marea, are monogamous." She scrunched her nose up at the term.

"What?"

"He wouldn't let her choose a husband group. Said it was him or nothing. Actually, back in the day rumors circulated about him. It seems like he threatened a lot of people off when she was younger. She's a mandarin fish shifter, pretty rare, utterly gorgeous. Her coloring is electric blue and lava orange in patterns of stripes and circles and she keeps those colors even when she's shifted to human. All the fish shifters go insane for that."

"Hmm." I was learning new things about this underwater world daily. Sometimes, I wondered if the learning would ever stop or if I'd always feel like a foreigner. "And what's her attitude regarding government?"

Sahar shrugs. "It's hard to tell. She doesn't talk much. Lost a brother to a fishing net once though, when she was younger, so my guess is she's not the biggest fan of sailors."

I nodded. The odds were stacked against me then.

"Alright. Well, there's the first set of people to know. But I've got more," Sahar stated with sarcastic enthusiasm as she pointed at her list.

She really was quite fun when we were alone together. And quite socially perfect when we weren't. Damn her for being the perfect adviser, because my plans to make her room a statuary faded.

She dug into the list, rattling off names, stations, and holdings for the next two hours until we arrived.

I was ready for my ice-cold greeting by the time she'd filled my head with a hundred facts and figures, mostly because I would at least get a cup of fermented bubble to go along with said greeting. But as I peered out the window of my carriage, past all the competitors on their dolphins and sharks, I realized that Sahar's description of Gorgono as "competitive" had been an understatement.

The city gates were gaudily decorated in mirrors set onto gears that rotated so that the glass was constantly spinning. Someone had designed the contraption, which rose on a wooden arch above the gates, so several mirrors caught the sunlight and pitched it over to the next. The mirrors played a game of catch with light, sending beams crisscrossing over the open gate until it looked like a pattern created on a loom.

"That's incredible," I breathed, nose up against the glass as I tried to work out which mirrors were first in the sequence.

"That's Gorgono." Sahar sighed. "He's going to try to prove to himself he's more clever than you, so watch out for that," she warned with a wave of her golden finger.

I nodded. "Got it. Yes. Be stupid to make him feel superior."

She smacked my shoulder. "No! Don't *let* him feel superior. Men need a pecking order. He needs to know he's not in charge. Just be on guard."

She glanced over at the gate, which we were rapidly approaching. "Come on. Let's get out and ride with the driver. The people will want to see you and wave."

We got ourselves settled onto the narrow bench on the front of the carriage. Bortie, the driver, a siren with a spine as twisted as a piece of seaweed and wrinkles deep enough to poke your finger into, welcomed us aboard with a grin and a wink.

All the men of the tournament brought their animals to a halt over to our right, next to the entrance gate, and clambered off their mounts. Watkins was the first off and instantly, his mount shifted and they began chatting in low tones. My eyes narrowed suspiciously at the shark shifter because he was always planning something. Part of me wondered if I should force him to stay at my side so he'd never have the opportunity. But then I'd be torturing myself with h There was no way to win.

I scratched at a plankton that had brushed past my cheek, annoying as a gnat, while I watched the others.

Per the direction of a few guards, the servants stayed with the animals and all the crates full of traveling necessities. Meanwhile, the competitors fell into single file lines on either side of the carriage, as if they themselves were my guards.

I heard Felipe and Ugo grumbling about this, but they were perched on the back of my carriage, holding onto the luggage rail with one hand and their spears with the other. They were close, but not close enough for my nosy tendencies because I couldn't make out a single word they said.

I glanced over at Sahar, who was straightening her spine and looking proper, just like I should. But mischief struck me and I gave her a grin as I shot my hand forward, announcing to the driver, "Onward, to heartache and hatred! Let's go make people who hate me pay for my dinner."

The driver snorted, while Sahar just shook her head as if I exhausted her. "I take back anything I said earlier about my son. You're no longer allowed to be around him. He's obviously a horrid influence."

"Keelan," I called out loudly, searching the lines of swimming competitors for him. Instead of Keelan, I saw Mateo struggling near the back, but burly blue Taft was helping him, letting Mateo lean on his arm.

I saw Humberto in line, his eyes straying over to the sharks and dolphins loaded with trunks, giving me a bit of hope on Gita's behalf. I'd have to follow up with her later.

Valdez gave me a slow nod as he swam in formation, the competitor behind him giving him a large berth. Stavros was swimming next to Julian, instead of behind him, their conversation animated as if they were becoming fast friends. Good. I hoped more competitors formed friendships.

Keelan appeared seconds later at my right side, Mr. Whelk perched lazily atop his head. He gave me a grin, those amber eyes of his dancing merrily.

My giddiness increased once my co-conspirator arrived.

"Yes, Queenie?"

"Your mother just had the most wonderful suggestion. She thought that you all could do flips as we swim through the city to entertain the crowd. And the man with the most can sit next to me at dinner."

Keelan pumped his good fist, displacing Mr. Whelk, who scolded him with a soft whine before swimming over to me.

The turtle settled snugly onto my lap and I patted his leathery head while Keelan asked, "Who's judging?"

Ha. I knew it! I knew he wouldn't second-guess this plan at all.

The mayor might hate me, but the children would love me and my competitors.

"Well, since it was your mother's idea, why doesn't she judge?" I asked brightly.

Sahar narrowed her eyes at me.

Keelan's expression grew skeptical. "I'm not sure she can count that high."

Sahar's scroll went flying and bonked her son in the head. He chuckled and caught it as she berated him.

"You ungrateful little slime. You cruddy little barnacle! Just you wait—" she shook a threatening fist in his direction.

He merely stuck his tongue out at her before handing me the scroll. Then he swam off to go announce the miniature competition to all the men.

As we made our way through the net of light into Navagio's crowded main street, where people lined the road and also hung out of windows and floated above rooftops—every single competitor in the tournament began to perform acrobatic feats. Not just flips, but backflips and cartwheels through the water.

Stavros and Julian decided to balance on one another's shoulders like court jesters, though where they got the idea, I didn't know. Julian just swam right up and perched on Stavros's shoulders. The other man's hands held steadily onto Julian's calves and marched down the road as Julian waved, trying not to tumble backward as the water pushed at him. They had several accidents—they were completely bad at it, but they made the crowd laugh. Even serious scientist Julian laughed and Stavros smiled, so everyone was enjoying themselves.

I heard the crowd gasp in enthusiastic surprise when Valdez spun three times in a row like a court dancer, one foot kicked out into the water, which had to be incredibly hard due to the drag of the waves. The squealing delight of children danced in my ears as I blinked and my eyes adjusted after the onslaught of the light array, looking for the next amazing performance.

That's when I had to hold in my own gasp of surprise.

Navagio was a fascinating amalgamation of buildings. My carriage floated just above a sandy road that stretched straight through town toward the mayor's home. On either side, there were pure white brick constructions that resembled the most stately houses on land. But there were also bulging buildings that were made out of wine casks that had been sawed in half and stacked, then mortared together with bubbly colored glass so that they were odd, bumpy little constructions.

There was a mill that rose taller than most of the structures in town. But instead of having a windmill turned by air, the giant rotor was sideways so that the current made it spin until it was a blur.

We passed a small square, traversing around a giant sculpture made of anchors collected from sunken ships. They were arranged into a tall spiraling pinnacle and pink and orange starfish had been strategically placed to provide pops of color against the rusting metal.

Down a side street, I did see a fence barring a mountain of what could only be called junk—a pile of items scavenged from shipwrecks. The crowd grew even more dense down the side streets, mer people with purple tails and wide eyes drawing my smiles, distracting me from gaping at the town like a newborn who'd just seen his mother.

We reached the final three blocks of the main corridor leading to the mayor's home. That's when the decorations began. The people of Navagio had spared no expense in hosting the next challenge for my suitors.

The promenade was draped with the brightly colored sails of sunken ships and painted with the banners of the competitor's various houses. All around bobbed lanterns made out of sailors' pants, which had been re-purposed. The leg holes and waist had been tied shut with bits of rope and then the cloth had been inflated with air until it bulged. I wasn't certain where the interior light sources came from, but they were all different colors, soft reds, light greens, orange. Some of the lanterns were tied to windows. Others were carried by children with strings, the pants bobbing like kites above their heads.

I wasn't certain if the balloons were a normal celebratory activity or a dig at sky breathers, so I just smiled and waved.

Scattered about the final blocks were vendor shops and stands. I heard mermen and sirens hawking various trinkets and other items from sunken ships. Some of their re-purposed wares were quite beautiful - coins with holes bored into them strung into necklaces and broken glass from bottles crafted into earrings. Others, like the forks and spoons I saw twisted in people's hair —tines and heads diving into teased and curled strands as if someone invisible was about to devour hair rather than noodles—were quite hilarious.

But then we arrived and the crowd stopped, leaving me to press my lips together to tamp down on my awe. We entered a large sandy square right in front of the mayor's palace. The palace itself was a work of art. The roof was made out of golden bars collected from treasure ships. They had been stacked like tiles. The rest of the edifice was made of pure white bricks with columns in the front made out of carved whale bones.

Floating just before the massive front doors were Gorgono and his wife. Marea was indeed beautiful, the patterns on her skin were enchanting lines of blue and dots of orange, but most fascinating of all for me was the fact that she didn't have any hair. Instead her head was crowned by a very delicate, scalloped, pale orange fin that wavered in the current.

Next to her, Gorgono was absolutely plain. He was a large mer with a bit of a belly and a green tail and matching hair. He had a sharp face and it would have been hard to guess his age if thick bands of gray in his green hair hadn't betrayed him.

"Welcome! Welcome, Your Majesty!" He gave the world's smallest bow before straightening. "Please join my wife and I up here to watch the festivities."

"Festivities?" I asked as I swam up and turned so that I floated next to him, my betta fins fluttering lightly.

"Yes, just a little welcome celebration. Please, everyone, gather around!"

The twenty competitors left swam closer to us, lining up alongside me, Valdez instantly darting forward and claiming the spot at my left side.

I raised a brow in the pirate's direction but he simply smirked, making his lip ring gleam. "I won your company for the night."

I hadn't realized that Sahar had picked a winner, but then I'd been distracted by our surroundings and not paying much attention.

"Wonderful," I responded, with a bit more enthusiasm than I might if Gorgono weren't overhearing our conversation. I was still highly suspicious of Valdez. But that was a matter for another moment.

I was shocked, however, when Valdez leaned around me and clapped the mayor on the back. "Good to see you again, old man."

Gorgono's brows lowered. "Old man, huh? That's what you call your best patron?"

"Perhaps you just need some hair dye from a merchant ship to cover up that awful grey. I hear that Lored has been testing some magnificent new dye on their silks. Arsenic. It's supposed to make the most luminescent green..."

Gorgono pursed his thin lips as he considered the offer.

Meanwhile, I used my "courtier" face to remain pleasantly unaffected while I reeled inside. The mayor here associated with a pirate?

All of the amazing recycled shipwreck items suddenly became suspect. Pirates captured ships, took what they wanted...did they sink them too?

My unease only doubled as the crowd filled in around the square and then the show began. Gorgono's festivities seemed to confirm my worst fears.

A group of mer children swam up from one of the nearby glass topped buildings, and then swooped down toward the open space in the middle of the square. Their silver tails gleamed and they giggled as they swam—adorable and energetic, bouncing and happy. The little ones tried to swim in synchronization. They put their hands together, tails out, to make a spinning flower. But a few of the little ones were slower than the others, so the flower always had gaps as if it were missing a few petals. Then they tried to dance together, and did a half decent job until one accidentally elbowed another, leading to a bit of squabbling that set off titters in the crowd.

"They're adorable, aren't they?" Valdez whispered.

"Quite. I want to squeeze one in a hug."

"I volunteer as a substitute."

I merely rolled my eyes, enjoying the kids' attempts to swim in three darting lines, zig-zagging simultaneously. Their performance was sweet and endearing in its heartfelt simplicity, and at first it caught me off guard because it wasn't the pretentious sort of thing that Sahar had told me to expect from Gorgono. But I was naive to think that the children were the entirety of the show. They were just part one.

A shadow appeared above the square and I craned my neck up to see a ship sailing beneath the water. Only... it was upside down. The ship was drawn by two dozen burly mermen, with harnesses strapped to their chests. They pulled the wooden boat down through the water in one of the greatest demonstrations of brute strength I'd ever seen. The shadow grew.

Valdez leaned over and whispered in my ear. "You might want to close your jaw. Not to dull your adoration, but I've heard that mer have the tiniest cocks."

"Really? I swear I thought that's what people said about dolphin shifters," I replied without turning my head to see him, too fascinated by the upside down ship as it grew closer.

The white sails were unfurled and billowed in the current while on deck, ten absolutely gorgeous siren men danced upside down.

They were dressed as sailors in pure white as they stomped their feet on the deck in unison. Stomp, stomp, clap. Stomp, stomp, clap-clap.

They repeated the pattern, somehow speeding it up and keeping it uniform even as some of them did flips across the deck. I tilted my head to the side as I watched them, wondering if all the blood was flowing to their brains, if they were dizzy. The crowd that had spilled into the square didn't seem to have my inhibitions. They started to stomp and clap along.

That's when the men on the deck began to sing.

What more could we crave

Got the life of a knave

Dancing on a pretty wave

With a dilly dilly ho

No mistress nagging

Just friends all a'ragging

Each one lying and bragging

With a dilly dilly ho

One scrambled down a mast until his head was nearest to the crowd. He put his hand up dramatically to shade his eyes as if he was peering out into the distance.

I watched as the children who'd been dancing for us just moments before, swam upward, directly in the path of the ship, zooming past and above it so that they floated around near its base.

The scout on the mast gave a whoop, which made all the singing and dancing men on deck spin and flip their way over to a compartment. They dragged out a huge net and made a dramatic show of unfurling it before they flung it over the side of the ship, where it was caught by the children, who immediately pretended they were trapped and crying.

"Bastards!" Someone in the crowd shouted.

"Stupid sky breathers!" Another anonymous voice broke through the din.

Horror rushed through my veins and if Valdez hadn't slyly caught my hand in that moment, I might have turned and slapped the mayor across the face.

But it got worse. As the sailors on the ship started to haul aboard the net with the mer children a cry went out.

"Queen Avia! Save us!" The little children caught in the fake net began to scream, their plaintive little voices growing louder.

The crowd grew hushed and every eye turned expectantly toward me.

My blood boiled while my stomach writhed—I was both infuriated and utterly terrified.

Gorgono had not only put on a show that deliberately sabotaged my purpose of uniting the sea kingdom with those on land, but the bastard had put me on the spot to display my magic.

Sarding hell.

14

GORGONO GESTURED WIDELY, a fake smile on his slimy lips—the bastard. "Well, your Majesty? I believe you've been summoned." His emerald green eyes glittered cruelly as his hand invited me to go help the children who pretended to be caught in the net.

He has to know that I don't use my magic. Word must have spread after the attack on the way to Reef City.

I fought to keep my limbs from stiffening under Gorgono's look and decided that it was better just not to look at the fucker. Instead, I diverted my eyes and glanced over at his wife to find her head bowed in shame. So at least I knew that she didn't agree with her husband's actions. But she didn't say a word, so she was a complacent bystander and hadn't sent word ahead as forewarning. Wonderful. This relationship with Navagio was going to hell quickly.

When my eyes left her, I felt that flash that I feared. My anger grew like an enchanted dragon, morphed and changed shape like Taft had in the carriage ride over—it turned darker and more twisted than I'd have believed possible just weeks ago.

I imagined that my magic was strength and that I could grab stupid Gorgono and lob him through the water like I was a catapult. His dumb, rock-hard head would smash through the inverted ship and everyone would cheer for me.

I took a deep breath, trying to calm the phantom pounding of my heart.

No.

Thankfully, I couldn't do that.

Sahar was the next person I looked to, trying to regain my center. But the glance didn't really help me—her face was just as shocked and furious as I felt. Her courtier's mask slipped for a moment and I saw raw fury painted across her cheeks.

She'd been right.

Gorgono was a beast and he needed to be shown his place.

I took a deep breath, steeling myself – glad that Lizza and I had practiced at least once so I knew how to pull in my magic. But this was the absolute last way that I'd ever wanted to test it. Around children. Around crowds who might get hurt if I fumbled. And what if I sarded it all up so badly that it became obvious I had no control?

What kind of opening would that give the rebels?

I swallowed and it felt like knives lined my throat.

I glanced out at the crowd for half a second. They were cheering, waving, clapping, excited for the grand show they expected to get.

I saw balding mermen placing bets, sand dollars slipping from palm to palm. I saw children in the crowd clasping hands with one another in rapt attention. The mermaids were all staring expectantly in my direction, most of their gazes full of confidence, certain that I'd impress.

Do something grand, Avia. Don't sard this up, I told myself, before giving a smile full of teeth and fake happiness and launching myself off the stoop with my betta fish fins.

As I swam upward, leaving the the mayor's home and the crowd beneath me, it felt like the water pressure around me was building not lessening—as if I swam into a dark trench where the water was so dense that many creatures were crushed to death instead of rising up into the turquoise shallows. There was no dark trench here, only the looming shadow of an upside down ship that hovered above the square. With all the poles and ropes and rigging, it looked very much like an elaborate gallows to me—one on which I could end up hanging.

I could feel it in my bones: this would be a defining moment for my reign.

I wondered if rulers often knew that in the moment, or generally only realized their mistakes after the fact.

Gela had often told me about her stumbles. But she'd never mentioned when she realized she'd made a mistake.

Was I about to make one?

Sard Gorgono!

Another flash of anger slid through me, along with a sliver of strange delight that tumbled and twisted with it until I couldn't quite tell which was which.

Was I excited to prove myself? Test myself? Where did that random emotion come from? Was there some secret part of me that was aching for destruction? It felt like there was. And I didn't know what to think about that. It didn't correspond to my definition of self.

But that definition had been solidified when I was a human.

Now, I was anything but that.

I glanced at the ship, no longer seeing it as an entertainment but an obstacle.

What could I do to affect the ship and not the people?

Was there a way that I could freeze and crack the planks without hurting the sirens performing?

Could I somehow sever the net with ice? Mayi had used ice spears and daggers against me, and I knew that it was one of her favorite weapons. But what if I hurt someone? All I'd ever done was practice making a sarding ball of ice!

Indecision swam through my ribs like a swarming school of fish and made my torso feel too crowded, ready to burst.

I couldn't find a safe solution with logic, I just kept imagining disasters play out. The ship exploding into fragments and a sharp wooden shard piercing a child. Creating a whirlpool that then ravaged half the town. What if my power burst out too strong and fierce?

Could I just swim over and rescue each child in my arms? But that was me thinking as a human.

These people didn't want a human queen.

They wanted a sea sprite.

Should I embrace my darker instincts?

I took a deep breath and closed my eyes, searching for the song inside me, deciding I should find my magic first and see if the song itself led me in any particular direction.

Last time, I'd gotten caught up in the tune, perhaps I should do so again and just see if instinct could guide me. Just a little. A bit. I wouldn't let it drag me too far in the wrong direction.

I listened.

I didn't hear the sea's song.

I searched again.

Silence.

I panicked when I couldn't find my magic—the crowd was too loud, the need of the moment was too much to find that tiny strand of music that I'd only ever acknowledged once.

But then a strong hand threaded fingers through my own and my eyes shot open.

I turned and was startled to see Watkins, of all people, floating beside me. The shark shifter gave me one long look before he turned down to the crowd below. His white shock of hair fell across his eyes as he stared down before he bellowed, "What's wrong with you people! Those are your children under attack! You can't wait for a queen or a mayor or an army! Otherwise, you yourselves are no better than these children, calling out for someone else to save them!"

His words caused a tense moment of frozen silence as the crowd exchanged looks, wondering what they should do—follow the plan of their mayor, a known entity, or a stranger, a shark shifter whose name they probably didn't even know, who held hands with a queen they'd never met.

That moment of silence was what I needed to find the song inside. It surged up into me—a precious vocal run that started deep and rose through an entire octave as if it was surfacing through the waves, utterly gorgeous.

It brought me relief because I knew I could do something with my magic. But what exactly was best?

As I searched for the answer to that question, trying to let the song tell me what to do, I glanced over at the shark shifter holding my hand. His handsome features were inscrutable as his eyes turned from the crowd beneath our floating feet back to me.

Is Watkins actually helping me or undermining me?

Should I move forward and destroy the ship with my clumsy magic or should I wait to see what the crowd would do?

The shark shifter squeezed my hand in solidarity and for some reason, the song inside of me surged forth.

My free hand unfurled to the right instinctively as the voice inside rushed up through my chest and made my ribs start to vibrate with her song.

A low note echoed inside of my head as my fingertips shot a hundred balls of ice out into the water, where they floated in a straight line, the size of dinner plates.

I swallowed hard, in shock as the frozen spheres slowly began to rise in place.

I didn't even mean to do that.

But Watkins capitalized on the moment, seizing the opportunity. In a loud, fierce voice he yelled and pointed at my glittering creations. "Citizens, grab your weapons! Attack!"

An enthusiastic howl went up through the crowd and I stared down in awe.

They were thrilled to be invited to participate.

To them, this was fun.

It was silly.

It was a game.

Sea men of all shapes and sizes zoomed upward through the current in a flurry of bubbles, plucking the ice from the water. They hurled their frosted globes at the inverted ship, pummeling the side boards. Cracks and holes formed in the ship. The sirens kept playing their part, some panicking and running about on deck ridiculously, grabbing at their hair and screeching.

One yelled, "We need to lose weight or we'll sink!" And then he chucked a fellow siren off the side of the ship, where the man proceeded to flip and spin in the water as he died in a very agonizingly theatrical way.

The mermen tugging the ship got into the game, tilting it from side to side.

Meanwhile, some of the other sirens on board tried to haul the net of mer children in faster. "Get 'em in! Then we'll plug that hole."

Watkins tugged at my hand, and chuckled. Then he swam up a few yards, dragging me with him as I tried to process what was happening.

"More ice, Majesty," Watkins shouted, with all the fierceness of an army commander.

I lifted my hand, letting the song inside of me shake my bones, and another row of ice balls shot out, spinning through the water in a neat even row. The citizens of Navagio were into the game now, hurling insults as they hurled the balls of ice.

"You filthy sand-walking fools!"

"You stupid scallywags!"

"Your mom wouldn't know a barnacle from her butthole!"

While some mermen from the crowd pummeled the ship with the ice, another group formed a "rescue" team, swimming at the ship from behind, grabbing one mer child at a time and passing them down the row of rescuers to safety.

One of the children ruined the illusion of the battle when she yelled, "Daddy!" and planted a big kiss on her father's cheek.

But that just caused a chuckle to ripple through the crowd as her father rumpled her hair and then handed her off, continuing on with his role. He yelled, "We've almost got them all! Those sky breathers won't know what hit them!"

It wasn't long before all the children had been freed.

Then mermen swarmed the ship, all of them singing.

One of the siren men on board clasped his hands and batted his eyelashes before saying, "Oh, I surrender. With a voice like that you can do whatever you want to me!"

The audience chuckled as the rest followed suit, each siren trying to top the other's surrender with something more outlandish until they were all on their knees.

Watkins again took up his role as a faux general and shouted, "Victory is ours! Navagio you did it!!!!!"

The roar from the crowd was deafening as a storm.

My chest crackled with victory and excitement surged through me as Watkins released my hand, picked me up by the waist, and whirled me in a circle. My hands fell onto his firm shoulders and I stared down in awe at my greatest enemy. His eyes were black as ever, pupils dilated as he stared up at me, the single white shock running through his black hair sweeping across his forehead. But unlike the scowls I was used to from the shark shifter, he wore a fierce smile, one that was as dangerous and sharp as any of his shark teeth.

In a moment of need, he'd suddenly become my greatest ally. *But why?*

The question must have been etched across my face and he pulled me down against him, then whispered in my ear. "Your declaration about the shark shifters. Thank you."

I nodded slowly as comprehension dawned that he liked the changes that I'd made this morning. "Of course."

Watkins gently released me from his grip and looked down, almost shyly. "I misjudged you. And I'm sorry."

I nodded again, like an idiot, completely at a loss for what to say.

"Anyway, Gorgono is an idiot."

I laughed, finally able to release some of the odd tension building up inside of me at this absolutely unbelievable scenario. Never in a million years had I expected Watkins to change his tune. Especially not over something as small as treating shifters with a bit more empathy.

Suspicion hovered at the edges of my mind. Was there an angle to this? There had to be.

Watkins ran his tongue over his lower lip before saying, "I know it might not be possible, but it would be really nice…I'd like it if we could start over."

He swam off before I could reply, leaving my thoughts as mangled as the inverted ship still drifting above us.

15

GORGONO MIGHT HAVE BEEN a horrid person but his ballroom was a masterpiece—and he knew how to throw a party.

I watched the last of a tittering group of noblemen as they escorted their wife into the building through the skylight in the roof.

Then Felipe and Ugo turned and nodded to me, clearing me for the approach to the tall octagonal tower with no windows and no doors.

On land, it might have looked like a prison, a tower from which no captives could escape, but this tower was in the sea, where anyone could swim right up to the roof. Its tower burst out of a long small building and was decorated with a row of rainbow quartz every few feet.

No one could quite keep their eyes off the flashy crystal, and jaws dropped until Gita leaned forward and whispered into my ear, "Julian told Humberto this morning that they've painted gold onto the crystals to give them that iridescent sheen. Wish we could do that with fabrics."

I nodded. She was right. The effect was unearthly. All the tiny facets of the rough crystal sparkled in the diffused sunlight—bright oranges, deep blues, unnatural greens, and pinks as vivid as an azalea bush. It turned the plain tower into a wonder to behold.

We swam forward but stopped when I was ten feet above the skylight, staring down, though I couldn't see in. The opening just looked like the top of a water well from my perspective.

Music floated up from the skylight and out into the water as I waited while Felipe and Ugo, in their most formal stamped seashell armor, swam forward and flanked the entrance on either side so that I could safely descend through it.

Once they were in position, I turned to Gita.

"You knew the entrance was in the roof, didn't you, you minx," I jokingly accused.

She gave a shrug but her expression was smug. My maid had clearly planned for my descent because she'd wrangled me into a hunter green silk dress with golden lace fringe that hardly covered my nipples. The dress had a train twenty feet long. I'd argued with her when she'd initially suggested it, hoping to find something less ostentatious. But she'd persevered and won that battle because Sahar was in the room the entire time backing her up—I couldn't win against them both. Nor could I ask the questions I was dying to ask about Gita's ride over with Humberto.

I fingered the deep green skirt as Gita giggled and she adjusted the precarious train carefully tucked over her arm.

"Now wait here, Your Majesty," she instructed as she swam down below me. With a flourish, she dropped my massive train through the skylight, the fabric as thick as the opening, clearly blotting out the light and creating a scene below as the music stopped.

She glanced back up, a mischievous expression on her face. "Alright, descend slowly."

I gave a nod and let my wings tuck back a bit so that I drifted down through the skylight to find every eye in the room upon me, my train already puddling on the marble floor.

My tall golden crown slid inside my tightly woven braids as I nodded softly to the fully packed ballroom. They bowed in unison, which still gave me a tiny thrill, though I probably should have been used to it by then.

When all eyes rose, I found Gorgono's face instantly, and he did not look happy about my entrance.

Good. I hoped he hated that as much as he hated the crowd's cheering earlier. Involving the crowd had been Watkins's stroke of brilliance. I could still hear chatter drifting through the room about it as the music resumed.

I maintained steady eye contact with the mayor, until he was forced to look away by someone asking him a question. Still, that felt like another tiny victory in this battle of wills.

I felt a bit smug, considering the asshole had tried to publicly humiliate me. I couldn't lie to myself and pretend I didn't care because I did. I'd have to find a way to thank Gita later for the dress. And Watkins...I still didn't quite know what to make of him and his help.

I turned to see some of Gorgono's servants closing the skylight, making the ballroom darker, though it wasn't completely black. Somehow, the remaining walls, those that weren't white, had a luminescent quality, and people who swam near them were lit up, their arms or tails glowing slightly different colors. I swam over to investigate.

No one immediately approached me, so I had a moment to examine Gorgono's ballroom. The crystals were clearly only on the outside of the walls. The octagonal room was made out of perfectly pure white plaster walls. Against one, an orchestra floated and strummed mostly on stringed instruments, accompanied by a low hand drum thumping occasionally. Against another wall were refreshments. A third was obviously set aside for dancing. But then the others walls were fantastic art pieces.

I blinked as I stared at them. They didn't quite look like murals. But what were they? There were absolutely gorgeous tableaus of mermaids perched upon piles of gold and sand dollars, strands of pearls dripping from their necks and wrists. The only odd thing was, they were upside down. Suddenly, one of them moved, slowly lifting her arm and pushing her hair back over her shoulder.

Julian and Stavros approached me together, the scientist stopping right at my side. "Those camera obscura scenes are amazing aren't they?"

"The what?"

"Gorgono has an inventor who came up with this tower. There are pinholes drilled into the walls. That lets in light from the adjoining rooms. Those rooms are set up with a lot of magical lanterns and several mermaids hired to pose for the night."

"He definitely likes to showcase his wealth," Stavros added.

I stared again at the wall. "Fascinating. But why are they—"

"Upside down?" Julian puffed up a bit, eager to explain further, happy to find me interested. "Nobody knows. There's a strange effect. It can be counteracted with mirrors apparently, but this room was set up when the obscura was first invented, before such advancements."

A mermaid on a wall full of golden goblets sneezed in her spot. "It's like a living portrait."

Julian nodded. "All due to the brilliance of science."

"Yes, but don't you think a spell could possibly have done the same?"

"Perhaps, but the ingenuity?" Julian countered, raising his bronze hand to gesture at the wall. "The incredible power of the mind…isn't that a great feat in and of itself?"

Stavros smiled brightly at Julian and I felt admiration swell inside my own chest. I tossed a hand onto Julian's arm. "You're right. That's true."

Julian gave me a shy grin in return but as soon as he did, a flash of anger hit me with the force of a portcullis smashing down on my head.

Shite.

I stepped back from Julian, giving the mint-haired siren an apologetic look. “Excuse me. I need to go get a drink before I mingle endlessly.” He and Stavros gave me polite nods, though Julian did seem slightly startled that I was swimming off mid-conversation.

But the consequences of my magic must have just hit. There must have been a delayed effect. I was glad to have the excuse of my heavy train to dig my hands into my long silk skirt and clench something.

I made my way to the refreshments with Felipe and Ugo trailing me. Of course, Felipe didn’t miss a beat. “Everything alright, Majesty?” he asked in a soft undertone, once we reached the heavily laden tables.

“It’s perfect,” I lied as I grabbed a chilled silver goblet of fermented bubble.

Felipe reached for the cup and pulled it out of my fingers before he deliberately took the first sip to test it. “Liar,” he whispered as he handed it to me with a nod.

I tried hard not to stare as he licked his lips.

“You’re right. But it’s not something we can discuss here.”

“It *is* something we can discuss?” Felipe asked gently.

Tension mounted as I stared at him for a long moment, weighing everything from the steadiness that radiated from his eyes to the fact that he'd done everything I'd ever asked of him and more.

Lizza and Bloss would tell me I shouldn't…but I nodded. I wanted to trust him, needed to desperately. Perhaps there would come a free moment soon where I could whisk him and Mateo away and pour out all my secrets.

I didn't want to repeat Bloss's mistakes. I didn't want to be alone, with years of wary silence and regret to separate me from happiness.

"Yes." I gave a slight nod, my nerves giving way to fluttering sensations in my belly—excited, relieved, and utterly terrified of what he'd think.

"Wait. Am I missing something?" Ugo piped up from where he'd stuffed his cheeks with crab roll since we'd stopped near the table.

"Nope," I told the orange-haired merman as he tried to chew faster in order to swallow and ask more questions. "Not a thing."

But Felipe's gaze sparkled and he had to bite his cheek to hide his grin and maintain his formal demeanor as Sahar approached. I let the siren lead me off to mingle with the locals—a big crowd of inventors—so that I wouldn't have to endure any other questions from Ugo.

After nearly an hour of maintaining perfect posture and the perfect smile, my goblet was empty and I was ready for a break.

Sahar, political genius that she was, noticed my fatigue and deftly ended our conversation with a delusional man who was trying to convince me that wheeled wagons had a future under the sea.

Right. Because whales are so inefficient, slow, and untrustworthy.

"Thank you for the rescue," I whispered as Sahar led me over to a table.

"Part of the job description, Majesty. Guards protect your body. I protect your mind from drivel."

I raised a sardonic brow. "Is that what you were doing tonight? I thought you were exposing me to the drivel."

She gave an impertinent shrug that made her beaded silver dress shudder. "Perhaps my job is a bit of both."

A gentleman swam over and she excused herself to chat.

Meanwhile, I sunk gratefully into my cushioned seat, hardly even caring that Gorgono hadn't set aside a throne space for me apart from everyone else. Valdez, the winner of the ridiculous flipping challenge I'd engineered during the afternoon, swam over and ate with me. There wasn't much conversation between us, because apparently, tall dolphin shifters were starving at the end of the day and attacked lobster as if it was the most glorious thing on the planet.

At least he was neat about it—not leaving splatters everywhere and meticulously cleaning his plate—but he definitely had his priorities.

I might have interrupted his gorging to speak, but courtiers kept stopping by to chat with me. I only got through an appetizer or two, some kind of fried sea cucumber creation, while staring around at the townspeople in the gaps between interruptions.

After the stunt with the ship had gone so well, the vibe inside the ballroom wasn't quite as antagonistic as I'd expected, though I suspected it was different behind closed doors.

However they felt about me, mermen groups and their wives kept swimming on up and introducing themselves, eager for the memory of actually meeting the queen face to face.

In between one of those rolling, repetitively bland introductions, the orchestra began to play a melody that was sad and slow, one perfect for a dance.

I swayed in my spot, fingers tapping on the table, and Valdez stood up next to me. His hazel eyes locked onto mine as he floated close enough to bump my hip. That got my attention and I swung my gaze up to look at him, his head far above me because he was so damned tall.

The pink dolphin shifter backed up the slightest bit, bowed formally with one hand against his firm stomach and the other tucked behind his back. He was shirtless tonight, which was a rarity for him, and a massive distraction for me because it turned out that I found the rings on his pierced nipples quite…eye-catching.

"You could almost be mistaken for a true gentleman," I commented as he rose, the rings in his ears glinting in the projected light from one of the camera obscuras.

"Don't insult me, Majesty. I'll never be one of those."

I grinned as he held out his hand, that intoxicating aura of his immediately snagging me and drawing me in. "May I have this dance?"

"You're asking, not taking?" I teased, but he grabbed my hand before I even finished speaking, drawing me out to the ballroom dance space, a wide cube of water set aside for dancers to swirl and flip at various heights.

Rather than politely dancing at the bottom half of the dancing area like most couples entering the space,

Valdez swam right for the top near the closed skylight. My green train snaked through the water, winding around other dancers blocking their view, and evicting a pair dancing just below us when he finally stopped.

"You did that on purpose," I accused him.

"Of course I did," Valdez responded as he pulled me in tight before gentling the grip of his hand on my waist. His expression was not repentant. "All eyes should always be on you, my beautiful queen."

I shook my head at him. "You know slathering me with compliments won't—"

"Are you sure? Not even if I tell you that your lavender eyes are the most beautiful thing I've ever seen?"

"Stop."

"And the way you handled yourself today, even after that ambush—"

I smacked his shoulder lightly. "You've worked closely with Gorgono."

"A pirate doesn't get to choose his customers, Majesty. Not anymore than a Queen gets to choose her subjects."

"Touché."

He did have a point. Perhaps what I didn't like was the fact that they had seemed a bit friendly. But I could hardly be less than friendly in public to this politician who clearly hated me. Still, I wasn't fully satisfied. Valdez was too full of clever answers for me to really believe him.

"Other than hair dye, what has our wonderful mayor gotten from you?" I asked with wide-eyed innocence, laying it on a bit thick.

Valdez threw back his head and laughed until I reached up and tugged on a lock of his light pink hair. Then his eyes grew hooded as he gazed down at me. "You like hair-pulling, Avia?"

Immediately, I let go of his locks, but my traitorous fingers couldn't help smoothing them down when his floral scent drifted through the water. "No."

"Liar."

"Stop with the distractions and tell me what Gorgono buys from you."

"Can't say. Pirate's code."

"Pirates have a code?"

"Oh yes. Steal. Cheat. Lie. And never ever, under any circumstances succumb to torture. Otherwise we'll be locked into a trunk and tossed into a volcano."

"Torture! I hardly think a question constitutes torture."

“Have you seen the way your eyes grow luminescent and round when you stare up at me? Definitely the worst torture imaginable,” Valdez whispered, bending down low and placing a kiss on my cheek.

With a second kiss, one edging a bit closer to my lips, he murmured. “And these lips. Watching them without being able to kiss them is definitely akin to being stretched on the rack.”

Warm giddiness spiraled up through my belly and heated me up. My fingers curled into Valdez’s hair, playing with the tips at the nape of his neck. His fingers slunk lower, from my waist to my ass, and he pulled me tighter against him.

“How do you know what it’s like to be stretched on a rack?”

“How do you think I got so tall?” he asked.

“You’re full of shite.”

“But you love it.” His lips hovered just over mine, daring me to close that gap between us, daring me to give in to his seduction.

I leaned forward, our breath mingling, our lips about to brush.

“Majesty, may I cut in?” a deep voice asked, destroying the moment as solidly as if someone had dropped an anchor on my toe.

I pulled back from Valdez, who cursed, as we both turned to see Watkins floating next to us, a hand extended.

The shark shifter's fin protruded from his back, making him as intimidating as ever, but tonight I noticed all the things that had drawn me to him upon our first meeting—his air of mysterious confidence, his guts as he came up and interrupted another competitor, that cut of his jaw that was sharp as glass. And the muscles. Lots of muscles.

"She's busy," Valdez responded curtly, clearly annoyed that our kiss had been interrupted.

"Please," Watkins was politely earnest, his normal sneer completely erased for the moment.

I glanced between the two, uncertain what to do. I was making no headway with Valdez, and I did have questions for Watkins—questions like what the sard got into him today? Did he really intend to try to start over? Did he even think that was possible after all the vitriol that had passed between us?

"Hasn't your favorite gotten enough attention?" Valdez growled, latching on tighter to my rear.

Amusement slid through my belly. I grew warm and then quite turned on as I realized that Valdez was jealous.

My nipples tightened at the very thought that he didn't want to give me up. I let my hand play with the bottoms of his pink hair, let my fingernails drag softly over the skin on the back of his neck, as I asked, "I don't know, have you gotten enough attention, my favorite?"

The smirk that erupted on Valdez's face was worth it, crinkles near the edges of his eyes were playful and another jolt of that floral scent of his swept over me, almost as if he was scent-marking me as his.

"Never enough." He leaned in again for a kiss but I was ready this time.

If he was going to deprive me then I was very well going to deprive him. I leaned back away from his tempting lips and the amazing sensations I knew lay in that direction. "Well, now, that's not very fair to the others though, is it?" I pretended to reprimand him, but Valdez's fingers just dug into my ass and pulled me tighter against him, so that I could physically feel just how much he liked this little game.

"I've already told you pirates cheat."

"Yes, well I've already told you I wanted an answer to my question. How about this? When you're ready to answer, you can come cut into our dance." A pout erupted on Valdez's face and the thrill of victory dipped down into my low belly at the downward curve of those lips which was adorable and made me want to kiss him all the more.

It was difficult to wrest myself away, but I did it anyway.

With great strength of will, I untangled myself from the tempting pink dolphin shifter and used my fins to swim over to Watkins, where I immediately grew more clear-headed, no longer surrounded by Valdez's seductive presence.

Damned floral pink dolphin magical bullshite, I grumbled internally, wondering if I could ever counteract Valdez's magic long enough to see if we shared a true connection. But that wasn't going to happen tonight. I focused instead on my target, another competitor who was twice as confusing as the pirate: the rebel.

"I hope you're up for the challenge of an eighty-pound dress," I stated wryly as I wrapped my arms around Watkins's neck and drifted slowly into his torso, glad not to have to bear the weight of the material alone for more than a minute.

While Gita was a genius, she hadn't counted on me dancing in this outfit. To be honest, after the last flubbed ball, neither had I—though I did quite enjoy this change in circumstance.

Dancing with my competitors was preferable to jawing endlessly with inventors below, pretending I understood all the nuances of their technical conversations while trying to ensure I didn't financially commit the crown to anything. What an utter headache.

Julian's place amongst my husbands was almost assured based on all those conversations.

But what about these two men? I pondered as Watkins wrapped his arms around me in a willing fashion for the first time, his fingers leaving a scalding trail as our kiss blazed through my memory.

The shark shifter held me formally, unlike Valdez, who'd tried to wrap me around himself—pressing us close together.

In contrast, the rebel was respectful, one hand on my waist while the other clasped my fingers delicately while managing to still somehow relieve me of the weight of my dress. Watkins was completely in control of himself, restrained in a way I hadn't seen—the polar opposite of how he'd been when he'd kissed me.

He was a contradiction and a puzzle all wrapped into one I thought as I studied him a moment, trying to discern his end game as my arm brushed over the jagged scar on his bicep.

"Good evening, Watkins."

"Majesty," he replied.

"You don't have to call me that when we're alone," I clarified.

"We aren't alone. We're in a room full of people." He pointedly stared around the ballroom and turned us in a slow circle, my train spiraling beneath us.

I rolled my eyes and pinched his shoulder lightly in warning, admiring the strong curve and the solid mass there. "Don't be difficult on purpose, otherwise dancing with you is no better than dancing with Valdez."

He grimaced. "I just...I don't know how to do this."

"Not hate me?" I asked, my tone light but my eyes grim. Based on his tone, he was serious about wanting to start over, which made me both relieved and annoyed because it extinguished that fire in him that I'd come to crave.

"Pretty much," he confessed. "I just...I don't know."

"Well, I don't know either, if it makes you feel any better. And, for all we know, there's a chance you could be right about me. One day I could turn into that monster that my birth mother was."

Watkins's black eyes snapped to mine at that declaration.

"We can't predict the future, and as much as we think we know how we'll react when hatred is flung our way…we don't. I never thought I'd make a snap judgment to invite a rebel to join the tournament and yet here we are." I trailed off as I considered him.

"Perhaps what we need isn't to start over," I said as I leaned closer. "Perhaps we just need to finish what you already started."

His hands tightened slightly on my fingertips and I watched him battle temptation—it was the closest I'd seen to the Watkins that I'd come to know since we'd started dancing. That burning ember inside of him wasn't fully extinguished then. Good.

"If you make it to the end of this tournament and I choose to keep you, Watkins, it's not because I want a nice man," I whispered, watching the current swirl over his ear and rustle his black locks. "It's because I want a man who won't back down just because I'm queen."

He swallowed hard and I felt his fingers dig into my waist, though he didn't drag me to him as Valdez had.

Interesting.

So the pirate wanted to break me and make me lose all sense of propriety. Meanwhile, I craved doing exactly the same thing to the rebel.

Watkins studied me silently for a moment, his looks broody no matter his expression, because his brows were thick and his eyes were deep-set, allowing mysterious shadows to gather and hide his true thoughts.

He chewed on his lip for a moment before asking in a husky voice, "Favorite childhood memory?"

This man was so full of twists and turns that he could have been a tangleball, the ocean's version of a tumbleweed.

"You don't really care."

"I asked, didn't I?"

"My dress is too heavy," I lied and used the excuse to slide both my hands up around his back so that he'd hold my waist and pull me closer.

He grinned and shook his head as if he knew exactly what I was thinking but I didn't give a damn. If Watkins actually wanted to know something about me, he was going to learn it on my terms.

I thought for a moment before I remembered a memory that always brought a smile to my face. "I played hide and seek with my older sister, Bloss, quite a bit when we were younger. She's six years older and grew out of loving the game faster than I did. So she used to volunteer to count and then would claim she could never find me."

"Rather mean."

"Yes. Well, I figured it out. And so the next time we played, I let her count, and then I snuck over to our fathers' rooms. I stole sweets hidden in their drawers, mixed up their clothes—dragged them to the wrong rooms, jumped on the beds, and then…when I got caught, I told them all Bloss threatened to cut off all my hair and made me do it."

Watkins shook his head. "Ruthless. I knew it."

"Must run in the genes, you're right. Swim away now while you can."

"Yes. Well, now I blame you and your evil ways for the fact that Humberto's underthings ended up in my trunk." He gave a playful shudder.

I snorted an unladylike laugh. "What? Really?" I didn't particularly want to imagine Humberto's underthings but an unwilling image of striped braies like my fathers had worn—short pant-like undergarments—popped into my mind and wouldn't leave. Nor would the idea of Watkins growing increasingly angry as he tried on pair after pair only to have them all fall down.

The shark shifter sighed and nodded with mock seriousness. "It was a bit traumatic getting ready for this ball when nothing would stay up. I had to go get help to find my real clothes. A couple of servants helped me look—took thirteen trunks before we found mine."

I closed my eyes, letting my eyelashes gently brush my cheeks as I said, "I love it. I'm currently imagining you wandering the hallway naked."

"Well, be sure to double the size of my dick—I'm sure you're not imagining it large enough."

I smacked him even as I tilted my head back and teased, "Bigger or smaller than a sea slug?"

"Definitely bigger."

"Bigger or smaller than an eel?"

Watkins's laugh stopped his answer, but our entire conversation was cut off by someone who pressed their body up against my spine. My eyes flew open, wondering who would take such liberties.

Valdez would.

And did.

He pressed up against my spine, his lips curling down to my ear. "I don't like you laughing with this crown-hater," he murmured.

"Are you willing to answer my question?" I spat back rather harshly because Valdez's words were a slap to the face. I felt my cheeks heat, but this time in anger, instead of attraction.

“He’s not wrong to be protective,” Watkins’s grip loosened on my hand but I clutched at his wrist, refusing to let it go.

“Valdez doesn’t get to dictate the terms of what I do,” I snapped.

Instantly, I watched something flicker in Watkins’s eyes, a hint of that hot fury that had simmered between us for so long. Only, this time, I didn’t interpret that spark as anger—I realized what it really was—attraction.

The shark shifter watched me steadily with that gaze of his, frozen, waiting to find out what I’d do.

I looked up at Valdez, whose hands clutched my hips, annoyed when he was so damned tall and pressed so close to me that all I could see was his chin. “If you aren’t answering my question, then you can’t cut in.”

“I’m not cutting in,” Valdez replied smoothly, pressing against my betta wings. I shifted forward in an effort to get away from him, but the stubborn pirate just sandwiched me firmly between himself and Watkins. “You should have been more specific, but since I’ve only been banned from cutting in, I’m joining the dance.”

The pirate chuckled and slid his hands down to the front of my hips as I found myself trapped in the middle of two intoxicatingly dangerous men.

16

SAHAR INTERRUPTED my dance with the two devils. She dragged my unwilling body away from the sinful pleasure of the press of Watkins and Valdez, just as the pirate whispered in my ear, "You like dancing with two men at once, don't you Avia? Just wait…one day we'll both dance with you again."

Watkins let out a low moan as a seductive thrill rushed down my spine because I was very, very certain that Valdez didn't mean dancing. I had to swallow hard and turn away from Watkins's glare at Valdez because that glare did unnatural things to me and it would have been disastrous.

Instead of allowing my competitors to corrupt me, Sahar swam me down to my own personal politicking hell. I spent the rest of the night smiling through Gorgono's verbal jabs and watching while Radford and his fellow shrimp dicks lambasted the other competitors to anyone who'd listen.

I wanted to stop them, but Sahar put her hand onto my arm, holding me in place with that gentle but firm way she had. "No. Only you know they're serious. To everyone else, they look like foolish boasters."

Radford tilted back what had to be an eighth cup of fermented bubble, his glazed eyes full of anger. The red-haired hermit crab shifter slurred and swayed as he said, "Bet Keelan's turtle does better than him tomorrow. Unless the competition is about getting crushed by rocks. He's pretty good at that." He was the only one who laughed at his own cruelty.

I couldn't believe I'd ever considered him as a contender. It appeared that whatever magic spell had made him spout off to me might only have multiplied his mean-spirited tendencies, because who could possibly laugh at Keelan's injury? Who could possibly hate the sweet, silly siren?

Luckily, Keelan was on the other side of the room, playing a game of cards with a few of the local merchants, so he didn't hear anything.

Next to Radford, Illia--the bug-eyed siren who'd been so aggressive about leaving—raised his glass to a merchant and said, "Good on you for not entering this —this—" The geas prevented him from finishing his sentence so he simply polished off his drink instead and slammed an empty tankard back onto the table.

People started to drift away from the negative little cluster of men as Radford continued to rail on Keelan's weakness, having someone else compete on his behalf.

As Radford's listeners slowly left, I watched him bury himself using his own tongue as his shovel. His reputation would be dead by morning and I doubted the man would find easy employment for himself in the future after revealing this awful side of himself so publicly.

I felt a tiny bit of guilt nudge my chest because Radford was only stuck in this tournament because of me. Then again, no one had forced him to sign up, to begin with —his family had been against it. And he could be counting down til tomorrow was over, til the time his cock would be restored because he competed but lost, fair and square as any other competitor.

My capacity for pity evaporated when I turned and realized I had to face off against the mayor himself.

Seeing me alone but for my guards, Gorgonio sidled up to me, his tail fin sliding along the underside of my feet and sending chills up my spine. I felt certain he did that deliberately, to throw me off balance as he gave me a toothy grin that looked as friendly as a hungry shark's smile.

"Majesty, I need to inquire, for the safety of my citizens —of course—about what precautions you're taking for tomorrow's event. Wouldn't want a repeat of the last disaster now, would we?" His voice was droll and he gave a dry chuckle before sipping at his own goblet, which I noticed was encrusted with sunshine-colored citrine jewels around the top.

I opened my mouth to respond with some vagary, because who could plan against a random attack? Battles were for battlefields but armies couldn't defend against such sporadic acts of violence—which made the rebels all the more dangerous. But before I could get a word out, Felipe swam forward from where he was shadowing me.

"Permission to speak, Majesty?" Felipe asked, all formality as he gripped his spear.

"Of course," I nodded and gestured for him to answer because I had an idea of what he'd say. Sahar and I had discussed security along with local politics during our last hour in the carriage. We'd come up with a few ideas that she'd pitched to my guards while I'd gotten ready for the ball.

Felipe cleared his throat before saying, "The commanders have gotten together and agreed upon a morning sweep of the city since the challenge doesn't begin until noon. We'll also be taking some confidential precautions, ones we can't discuss for security purposes. But, rest assured, we'll be on top of things."

I watched Gorgono's lips protrude as his tongue traced over the front of his teeth and he took in this information. He didn't look thrilled that we had a decent plan.

"Well, what are you doing about the threats?" the mayor added, clearly trying to throw a wrench in our plans.

"Have you gotten reports of threats throughout the city?" Felipe asked evenly.

"You'd be required to report those."

"Not official reports," Gorgono quickly and smoothly covered his bases, like any good politician. "Just rumors."

Felipe didn't bat an eye, didn't change his expression a whit, but his tone made his threat clear. "Well, be certain to pass along any rumors. The royal guard wouldn't want anything or anyone to slip by us and harm you."

Gorgono had clearly anticipated that sort of response and just grinned maliciously. "Yes, we wouldn't want that. Particularly since I'll be floating right next to your queen."

I decided I needed to defuse the moment. "Well, I suppose if we're going to go, at least our last moments will be together, Gorgono. That, at least, has to be some consolation for you. You'll get a royal funeral out of it. Perhaps we should discuss colors. I always wanted a casket of green glass. But we should color coordinate. What were you planning for your coffin? I'll be certain to let Sahar know so she can make arrangements."

Gorgono stared at me a long moment, unable to determine if I was serious or joking. I quite enjoyed seeing him uncomfortable.

"Excuse me, Majesty. I believe my wife is summoning me. We'll have to continue our funeral coordination later."

"Not if you pass along the news of those rumors," I retorted with a smile as I waved my fingers at him delicately while he swam off in a disgruntled manner, his shoulders bunched and tense. *Oh, how I'd love to replace him,* I thought.

But the inventors loved him here. He accepted them and their crazy creations even as he swindled them, but they —like Julian—were so desperate for acceptance that they didn't care one whit. I couldn't get rid of him. Yet, anyway.

I watched his retreat into the crowd for a moment before I huffed out a sigh of relief before turning to Felipe and Ugo and speaking in a low tone. "Is he right? Have there been threats?"

Ugo shook his head but Felipe remained silent, eyes darting around at those nearby.

When Felipe mouthed, “Later,” in my direction, I knew without a shred of doubt that there *were* rumors of another impending attack.

After the ball, when the moon was nearly ready to set in the sky, I made my way back to my rooms with my guards—one thought pounding through my mind.

What kind of attack are the rebels planning?

Leaving Ugo outside the door to keep watch, Felipe came into my bedroom, dragging the massive mess of my train, which had gathered endless amounts of sea sand in it on our swim back to our room. He dumped the speckled green mass in a coil on the marble floor before he turned to look at me.

“Well?” I asked softly.

“You promised me you'd discuss certain matters that have been bothering you,” he said gently, but not forcefully, because Felipe always treated me gently.

I cleared my throat, his statement not expected at all, not top of mind for me. “Um, actually, it's something I'd kind of hoped to tell you and Mateo at the same time,” I hedged, uncertain if the combination of my inebriation, the late hour, and my anxiety over the rebel rumors were good circumstances for life-altering confessions.

"You look nervous, and I'm not trying to make you uncomfortable. I just…I just want to be able to take care of you…" he trailed off, running a hand through his navy hair, which caused his armor to clink softly in the silence.

I stared at him, the man who saved me constantly. Who gave and gave and had only ever asked this one thing… Had he meant to say "take care of" instead of "protect"? Was that a slip of the tongue?

If so, was it a slip of the tongue that meant he cared or a slip of the tongue because he was tired? My mind spun in circles around me and until my emotions were dizzy with possibilities.

How I longed for him to mean it the way I wanted.

I wished for it like a child placing all their hopes on the brightest star.

He swam a tiny bit closer. "Avia…" he breathed, so softly that I might have just imagined it.

I found myself blinking rapidly, my lips parting, and then the words just spilled out of me in a rush. The secrets poured forth and I watched Felipe's eyes grow wide when I mentioned my heart and why I'd been ill.

He sat down on one of my closed trunks when I spoke about Lizza's spell. But he straightened up to his full height when I confessed to my violent delusions and my fear that I'd one day manifest them.

Saying everything was painful, hearing my own opinion of my weakness in the face of magic made me cringe because I didn't want to be this weak and cowardly woman. I didn't want to be an inadequate queen.

"I have no idea how to be both a powerful protector and a good queen—they seem mutually exclusive," I finished, feeling as though I'd swam from Palati to Reef City—empty and drained—as my confession came to a close.

"That's why you don't use your power." He made it a statement, not a question, as if he could read my mind and thoughts more clearly than I could.

I gave him a small nod, my chin dropping, my eyes dipping to his fin.

"Does Sahar know?"

I shook my head.

"And Mateo doesn't either?"

"Only Lizza. And my sister knows the first bit." I glanced tentatively up at him only to see his jaw clenched, his hands shaking as he curled them into fists by his sides, and his eyes, those deep blue eyes that reminded me of the ocean on its calmest days—they blazed. His breathing was stilted, short, I could see the rise and fall of his armor.

For a moment, the current seemed to stop flowing between us, even the water droplets stilled in expectation.

Something built…and built…until we both trembled in place.

Come on Avia, just swim forward and kiss him, I told myself. But I couldn't do it. Not when I wasn't sure… not when I might be projecting. Not when he might not feel he had the authority to say no to me.

What we had was so precious that I couldn't bear to shatter it.

We had trust.

I had just given him a gift greater than anything I'd given the others.

I'd given him my truth.

I tried to tell myself that honesty meant more than kisses…but my heart didn't believe me.

Felipe's dusky lashes fell to his cheeks and he hid his eyes from me for a long moment and I stared at his graying hairline before he gave a strained, "I'm honored, Majesty." When his eyes reopened the blaze was gone and the wall of propriety was back in place.

My heart recoiled in disappointment because I'd somehow secretly wished that my confession would make him melt, make him rush forward and take me into his arms. Instead, my eyes filled with tears that I had to rapidly blink away so that he didn't notice. I had to turn to the side and bring a hand to my flaming cheek to hide my humiliation. "I need you to keep it a secret…"

"You don't even have to ask. I'm your guard. I'll take it to the grave."

I gave a stiff nod and glanced over at the disastrous mess that was my train—it was better to look at anything other than him. "Right. Well, um. I'd wanted you to tell me what rumors you'd heard about the rebels."

"A few of the less reputable taverns had some chatter. There's a local rebel leader and we'll pay him a visit tomorrow. He's sort of the local equivalent to Watkins."

I nodded. "If you hear anything…"

"I'll let you know."

I nodded again, still staring at my train, unsure if I could even make any other gesture, because I felt broken.

Felipe swam to the door and I heard him lift the latch. There was a long, drawn-out pause and the back of my neck prickled, so I knew he was staring at me.

Did he know? Did he pity me? I could have sworn I'd seen something more. Once. Maybe twice.

But then the current wrapped around me as the door opened. The latch fell.

Felipe was gone.

I cried and stripped out of my dress myself, climbing into bed a naked and fragile wreck.

17

Raj

JULIAN'S HEAD twisted toward me, and I watched his glazed eyes, each stripe of his tan irises lit by the magical lantern I'd pilfered from the ballroom so that we could swim out into the town, out of the town, anywhere we wanted to go. The glowing orange glass ball was warm where it was tucked underneath my arm, even warmer than the rest of me, which had been heated up by wine and Julian's presence all night.

I'd never appreciated before just how beautiful someone could be when they were in their element. I'd always been too busy in the middle of my own element —death and destruction.

But I'd watched Julian discuss the dissection of a deceased octopus shifter with a colleague, fascination imbuing every inch of his body, every gesture while the other man described the way the back of an octopus head contained the stomach and digestive tract of the animal.

Julian had been as thrilled as I had the first time my father allowed me to perform an execution. His smile had been contagious. Even now, hours later, he practically glowed with excitement as we swam through the sea, only broken streaks of moonlight mixing with my lantern to break up the vast expanse of blackness. It almost felt like flying through the sky above the clouds, like we were stars in the universe.

How his star shone.

"Thanks for agreeing to stay out with me. I'm just still too edgy to go in, even though I know we should be sleeping, resting for the big event tomorrow. Today? Ha! I don't even know what time it is. Do you?"

I shook my head.

"That's what happens when you really connect—time just flies!"

When you really connect... Is he talking about me? A soft hope, so different and foreign to me, unfurled inside my stomach, smooth and delicate as a rose petal. I tried to shake off the feeling—this strange effeminate weakness—but it clung to my ribs and wouldn't go away. I wanted him to be talking about me, I realized with a start. I really wanted it.

“Tonight was amazing, don’t you think?” he said. “I know I’ve only been away from town a week but I didn’t realize how much I missed intellectual conversation. You know?” He gave a yawn and stretched his bronze arms, drawing my eyes to their sculpted muscles and the outline of his fingertips.

But instead of the flare of lust that I expected based on my reactions to Julian’s body earlier in the day, I felt fluttering inside my ribcage—as if a moth had wandered in and gotten trapped. I rubbed at the spot, trying to erase that sensation.

Strange. I was feeling strange again.

Perhaps from the heart palpitation. Maybe the spell hadn’t been enough. I’d have to think on it.

In fact, I realized…I’d gone through this entire day without planning how I was going to attack Avia next. I hadn’t thought about what I was going to do in order to set her on edge, disrupt this tournament.

Julian had distracted me from my quest, an offense normally punishable by dismemberment at the least. But I glanced over at the way his lips quirked, slightly higher on the right side…and I couldn’t find my normal stores of annoyance or dismissal. Instead, that softness brushed against me again.

He spoke, and I had to remind myself to listen to the conversation instead of wondering so much about what was going on with my fool body.

"I suppose that I thought more men of intellect would compete for Queen Avia's hand, you know?" Julian sighed dolefully. "Of course, the world is run by brute force and I didn't take that into calculation—the number of brutes competing for her. Did you see Watkins and Valdez earlier? I swear, I thought they'd shift and fight. Savages, I tell you. So glad I found you amongst the competitors."

The way my fingers tingled at that compliment and my face stretched into a grin was absolutely childish. I might have preferred to continue to get rock-hard erections around him, instead of this syrupy sweetness. I tried to hedge against my emotions by turning his conversation down a serious path. "I think a man who can encompass both intellect and brute force is best suited to run the world."

Julian laughed in response.

Shocked, I paused in our swim, my feet slowing their rapid paddle so I could turn and stare at him, my teeth clenching—memories of my courtiers laughing at Bloss's shite orgasm wish filling my mind. I hated being thought a fool.

His pale green hair wavered in the current and when he noticed my expression, he stopped laughing. He put a hand to his lips instead and my eyes naturally followed.

"I'm sorry. It's just that you said a man should run the world."

"Yes. Why not?" I shrugged.

"Well. It's just that the queens have always controlled—"

"If you can envision a world without magic, why not one where men rule the world instead of women?"

He grinned and tossed an arm around my shoulder, clapping my triceps. "True enough. Good point. Good point. I'm sorry about my reaction. I didn't mean any offense. I don't often think about politics, unless it relates to medicine. A bit outside my wheelhouse. But you have a fascinating proposition here. How different would the world be if men ran it? Would there be fewer wars? I mean…the Fire Wars were just horrific. Then you have the recent debacle with our own queen." His face took on a somber quality as he processed my proposal. "I wonder… Stavros, I can't tell you how glad I am that you decided to compete so I'm not alone amongst these over-muscled idiots."

Julian was agreeing with me, complimenting me, but I was more focused on the fact that he was freely and willingly touching me, on the way the pads of his fingers felt against my skin. Perfect.

It was an unsettlingly pleasant sensation that was rapidly followed by the realization that *no one* willingly touched me—they were either ordered to or else I touched them.

When's the last time I'd been touched by someone out of basic affection?

It had to be hundreds of years…so long that I wasn't even sure if my memories were true or false.

His touch revitalized me in ways I didn't even know I'd needed. My nerve endings bloomed like desert flowers who hibernate beneath the sand, his touch life-giving as rain on a parched land. His scent was as refreshing as the smell of rain on heated sand, that delicious scent of wet rock associated with pop up storms.

The warmth of Julian's arm across my back, the comfortable weight of him leaning into me, the spark in his eyes…they caused a change, a reversal of the tides.

Instead of sluffing off the softness that kept invading my system, for a moment, I embraced it.

Then something grew between us, there in the dark water, something that I suspected might be even bigger and more dangerous than the physical attraction I'd experienced when he touched me earlier this morning.

What was it?

"You know, your ideas are a bit out there. But so are mine. And you have something more going for you than I have."

"What's that?" I asked, genuinely curious about someone else's opinion for the first time in decades.

"Your grandmother did say you'd take over the world," Julian gave me a smirk that curled up one side of his mouth in the most delicious way.

I had the sudden urge to lean forward and trace the corner of that mouth with my tongue—but I resisted.

Why?

I had to ask myself that question because I hadn't resisted my impulses in ages. I trusted my instincts, particularly those that set off alarms.

But Julian wasn't alarming, he was the exact opposite. Charming.

I realized with a start that I didn't give into my impulse because the prickles on my fingertips were nervous sensations—I didn't just lean forward because I wasn't certain Julian wanted me to.

Somehow, I cared what he wanted.

Another person's desires were more important than my own.

My heart gave a jagged, uneven set of thumps as I stared at him, wondering why the sarding hell some random stranger under the sea could suddenly rearrange my innards and make me feel all these…things.

He didn't have magic. He'd already confessed to me that he couldn't even change the color of his hair.

So it wasn't that.

He wasn't enchanting me, unless he'd gone to some hedge witch. But the sarding bastard was so utterly against using magic, that I couldn't see him doing that. Especially since he had no idea who I really was.

That meant this feeling was something else.

I stared at him long and hard, until his teasing grin turned into an awkward expression and he slid his arm from my shoulders.

No! I wanted to protest, to scream. But again, my lips stayed shut.

Instead, my insides tangled and writhed in agony as Julian withdrew to a more formal distance and said, "Well. Anyway, if you do take over the world, do a better job than that sultan in Cheryn, alright? He bungled it big time."

My throat closed.

I should have been furious at the insult, raving mad. I should have disintegrated him on the spot, twisted my ring and just ended him with a wish.

Instead, I could only think, *He'd hate me if he knew.*

And all those soft feelings tumbled down to my toes, replaced by the gut-wrenching agony of the knowledge that Julian would want someone good.

Kind.

I was anything and everything but that.

I looked off into the wavering darkness and nodded emptily at his words as Julian retreated from me and the cold water filled in the space he'd occupied while I tried not to notice the utter shambles and emptiness that defined my life.

18

Avia

I DREAMT of milky-eyed witches and a rockfall inside a pitch-black cave where I had to navigate the falling stones based on sound alone—all while the shrill laughter of my birth mother echoed off the walls as she shrieked, "You wanted your birthright! Take it!"

I awoke shaky and feeling like a fool.

Though the tournament didn't start until noon and I could have slept in, I hadn't wanted to spend an extra minute in that bed. I'd dragged myself out of the uncomfortably hard bed I'd slept on in Gorgono's grand house, grumbling, "No wonder I dreamed about rocks, I slept on one." I stuck my tongue out at the square mattress, which looked like a normal bed but was clearly designed as a torture device. Then I went about basically trying to rouse myself and lift my spirits so that I'd be in the right frame of mind for the tournament.

Meditating on the white marble floor didn't work because my fins ended up bent against the ground and quickly protested that position. Pacing didn't work, because this room hadn't come with its own dressing chamber so my trunks were scattered around the walls, creating a miniature maze. In fact, other than the fact that the red sails that looped through chains hung from the ceiling and decorated the windows, the room itself was rather plain. There were no portraits or tapestries. My dressing table didn't have a mirror. I'd been put into the "ugly stepsister" of guest rooms.

I was doing calisthenics in between one of the trunks full of my undergarments and the case of my jewelry that Valdez had supposedly saved—though I still had my doubts about that—when a knock came at my door.

I shoved out from my push up, chest heaving, taking one barefoot step across the marble toward the door as I waited for Felipe to crack it open and announce my visitor. I brushed back my hair from around my eyes as I wondered who it could be. Neither Sahar nor Gita were allowed to be announced, I'd told them I didn't want such formalities from them. But both had already come together—I suspected Gita was avoiding letting me speak to her alone about Humberto—and gone for the morning. Sahar had run through the basic structure of the event while Gita dressed me in a short golden tunic that had slits cut for my betta fins and full deep purple bell-shaped skirt that brushed my ankles.

Hair and makeup would only come the hour before the tournament. So…if it wasn't Gita and it wasn't Sahar, who could possibly want to see me?

Felipe's eyes met mine and he gave a formal nod as he announced, "Keelan would like to speak with you, Majesty."

Keelan! I nodded. "Of course, let him in."

Felipe held open the door and the siren entered, a purple lightning bolt on the side of his white-blond hair this morning. His amber eyes sparkled but he swam slowly, cradling his injured arm as if it pained him. When my guard went to shut the door again, Keelan turned to him. "Can you stay please? Just for a moment?"

With a neutral face that hid his curiosity, Felipe shut the door and stayed just inside, floating by the wall.

Why would Keelan want Felipe to stay? Was something wrong? I watched the way the siren cradled his arm, which was still wrapped in bandages.

I swam slowly over to him, hesitating to reach out and touch him. I didn't know if his ruined arm came with residual pain. Lizza had healed his other injuries, but men returning from war often ached—pain lasted for years and varied with the weather, according to my fathers. "Are you okay?" I asked, not quite certain what else to say. "Has something happened to you or Mr. Whelk?"

He shook his head. "The bastard's just sleeping. Don't worry."

"But you?"

"Queenie, my arm is aching so badly I can hardly think straight." He grimaced, clenching his teeth. "I just… don't know how I'll even be able to think through this pain."

"Oh." My eyes widened and my hand came up to my chest. I felt like an ass for not even considering the possibility that Keelan's injury might affect—

"In fact, I don't know if I'll be able to complete any of the challenges…"

I was rattled and thrown off balance by his statement. We'd already discussed him quitting. We'd already made a deal! And our connection was strong—or so I'd thought. We were a perfect match, his playfulness the perfect relief to offset all the serious tasks I had to take on. I swam forward, placing my hand on his good shoulder, ready to shake sense into him. He couldn't threaten to leave me again. I'd build that entire damn statuary he wanted. "You can't quit!"

"Quit? No. I thought...I could have a substitute. Like before." Keelan's eyes swung to the side where Felipe was silent, standing in position by the door with his spear.

I blinked at my guard and watched his eyebrows shoot up in surprise at this proposal.

"It just hurts so terribly bad. Like fire." Keelan reached over to clutch his injured arm.

I noticed he didn't actually flinch. If pain was shooting up his arm, wouldn't he react, at least a bit, when he touched it?

Suspicion peeked out from behind the rock where she lived and wagged a finger in Keelan's direction.

But I didn't say anything. I simply turned to stare at Felipe to see what he wanted to do. I wouldn't ask him again, wouldn't force him to keep competing because that wasn't fair to him. That put him in a position he might not like.

Sahar's murmured precedent about Queen Karisa and the two brothers who fought over her did drift through my mind.

If Felipe decided to stand in for Keelan…if he completed every round of the tournament…could I have them both?

I didn't consider myself a greedy person but at that moment, I wanted it all. Everything. My funny courtier and my perfect knight. I wanted to wrap my arms around both of them and call them mine and never, ever let go.

But that's selfish, I reminded myself.

Felipe had had a dozen chances to kiss me, to tell me something more. He never had.

Then again, he'd always been my guard and not a competitor.

If he accepted, this would change his status.

It could change everything.

Could hope explode out of a person? Could it become so big that it burst through their skin and just couldn't be contained any longer? I wasn't certain, but I felt like it must be so, because every fiber of my being filled with hope. Even after last night's utter debacle…the tears that still probably bobbed through this room, mixed with the current.

He'd still been a guard last night.

Did he want to be more?

I glanced up to see Felipe's blue eyes bright, an inferno sweeping through his gaze underneath the carefully smooth expression he always wore.

My blue haired guard stared steadily back at me in what somehow became a battle of wills—each of us staring at the other, wanting them to speak first.

Keelan glanced between us before dropping his hand from his arm and saying, "Well, I suppose I could ask Ugo instead—"

"No!" Felipe and I spoke simultaneously, both of us nearly shouting.

Keelan's expression just became smug. "Well then…"

The stare off threatened to resume, but Keelan broke it by saying in a high falsetto, "Felipe, I'd really love if you'd compete for my hand and give me little blue-haired mer babies." He switched to a deep tone, shoving his chin into his neck as he play-acted Felipe's response. "I'd sarding love to give you all the silent little mer babies you want."

I gaped at him as he kept talking, resuming his normal voice. "Well, now that that's all settled, Felipe—you'd better go find someone to replace you. And Avia, I think we better seal this deal the way we did the last one."

Disbelief clouded the room like perfume.

But Felipe didn't argue.

He didn't scoff as I'd feared.

He didn't tell Keelan he'd gone too far or asked too much. He didn't even counter the mockery that Keelan had made of us.

So, feeling like I was walking on the very edge of a cliff, I gave a small nod.

He gave me one in return, his lips tweaking just slightly—so slightly I couldn't tell if he was fighting a frown or a smile until I released my own very small, tentative grin.

Then his lips curved up and took my heart with them.

My dashing guard, who'd stolen my breath from the very first moment I'd met him, gave me a small bow before leaving the room as my phantom heart fell like a raindrop onto desert soil, seeping into all the cracks of uncertainty and filling them with promise instead.

I waited until the door was latched and my sense of awe faded.

But then I whirled on the smirking bastard Keelan in a scolding fury. "What were you *thinking*?"

Keelan didn't even flinch—probably used to irritating his mother. "Did you notice we match?" He gestured at his hair with his good hand. "Did it to match your eyes, but your skirt makes it a bit more obvious."

"Stop that, idiot! You're not even sore!" I poked at his bad arm—not too hard—trying to prove my point and he didn't even flinch. Guilt flooded me and I considered swimming after Felipe to call him back. "You're forcing him—"

"Avia, please. The sexual tension between you two is so thick that even being in the same room is like wading through mud."

"It is not!"

"Ask Gita. Or Ugo. I can call him in here."

"Don't you dare!"

"Look, if you don't like to acknowledge reality, fine. I'm selfishly stacking the deck."

I raised a hand to rub my forehead, suddenly pitying Sahar and all the shite she put up with from her wayward son. "What are you talking about?" I couldn't get past the fact that he'd used his injury to manipulate Felipe.

"I know you're keeping me around because after that kiss," —he dusted his fingernails on his chest—"I'm a shoo-in. But I'd like to have a couple of co-husbands that I can actually stand."

Laughter burst from my lips, bubbled like a fountain and kept spilling over, layer after layer of laughter. "So…this is all about you?"

Keelan swam closer and put his good arm around my waist gently, holding me while my giggles subsided. "No. But we can pretend it is until you're ready to admit that it's all about you."

And then Keelan leaned down and swept me into a kiss that made my wings flutter and my phantom heart pound.

19

MIDDAY CAME SOONER than I expected, though, once Keelan's lips slanted over mine, the morning had passed in a bit of a blur. I was certain, however quickly the time had passed for me, it was gone in a blink for the anxious men waiting to prove themselves.

The twenty competitors remaining, with the exception of Keelan—who floated with Mr. Whelk at my side—lined the edge of Mayor Gorgono's golden brick rooftop, floating slightly above the bricks stamped with the insignia of Rasle and Cheryn, even some crests that looked older—a dragon curled into a ball that I didn't recognize was blazed into several of the older bars. The men studied the gold as I studied them while we all waited, impatiently, for the announcement of their next challenge. Felipe was among them, next to Mateo and Taft—the trio spoke quietly.

Behind them, the sea was a bright cornflower blue with the sun directly overhead. The chatter of spectators drifted lazily through the current as people gathered in the streets, on the rooftops, or just hanging out of windows to watch a bit of the spectacle. The current was soft and lazy, it felt like one of those summer breezes on land that gave up halfway through its journey and dawdled along the path so slowly that it wouldn't even nudge a fly off course much less bring any relief.

I looked around at the buildings, wondering if there were pennants or any visual markers that might tell me what exactly today's competition was—but I saw nothing. Only smiling faces, mermen waving, and shifter families playing catch appeared to populate Navagio. I watched a siren family struggle to create a makeshift rooftop tent so that the sun didn't burn their golden skin. The little boy couldn't stretch his corner far enough and kept making the thing collapse. Finally, his parents dismissed him from helping and did it themselves, while he laid back on the brick rooftop with a satisfied grin. His parents had foresight though, they would be cooler and more comfortable while they waited through the afternoon for the competition's results.

Results of what though?

That was the question. And I wanted an answer.

I glanced over to the three chairs on the far side of the roof, which held three elder men from Navagio: a surgeon, a traditional healer, and a portly man with a mustache that hung to his shoulders—the local barber. They all reclined in their wicker chairs with goblets of chilled fermented bubble and chit-chatted randomly. Beside them sat a table with nothing on it, though it was set with a tablecloth so it clearly served some purpose.

Gah. Not knowing was driving me to madness. I wanted to pace but had to remain still and regal, smiling at the judges, who smiled back serenely.

They were the only ones on the roof who were relaxed. Soldiers were stiff and alert, the contestants spoke in low voices, even Keelan glanced from side to side, cracking the knuckles of his right hand as he asked, "Do you know what the battle of wits will be?"

"Your mother didn't tell you?"

He snorted. "I'm the last person she'd ever tell."

"Probably smart. I'll make sure I keep state secrets from you."

He poked playfully at my side until Mr. Whelk mistook the exposed finger for the start of a game and snapped at it. Keelan retracted his hand quickly.

"Good turtle," I praised, petting the little creature on the head. He leaned into my hand and I could have sworn he purred in delight.

"Traitor," Keelan muttered, but with affection in his amber eyes as he snatched the turtle out of the water and tucked him under his arm.

Gorgono floated over to a seat near where Keelan and I floated. He gave me a perfunctory bow of the head before he settled into it but didn't greet me. I might have been annoyed by the brush off, but if he had said hello, I was quite certain I'd pointedly ask him if he'd made his coffin choice yet. *Perhaps that isn't the best way to start off the competition,* I thought wryly, realizing I had a bit more of Bloss in me than I'd imagined.

Marea, his wife, trailed behind him as usual. At least she did bow and give me a hesitant smile, which I returned. I had hardly spoken with her, but I could only hope that she didn't share her husband's clear loathing for me.

I glanced around at the city one more time, scanning a multitude of colored glass rooftops: lime green, ruby, sapphire blue—wondering where Lizza and Posey had wandered. I knew that my guards and mages were posted around the town, on high alert, but suddenly, I wished they were closer—that this portion of the tournament was more closed off and contained because anything could happen to my competitors out there in the city.

The rebels could hide in alleyways, sneak up behind my men in a tavern, attack them in a shop—and I wouldn't even know.

Protocol dictated that my mages would send up a column of steam if the rebels attacked so that everyone could congregate in the right spot.

But would they be able to see? And if they did, would we be fast enough?

I only had four castle mages plus Lizza. Posey was an undead soldier, but didn't have magic. The rest of my guards…I didn't discount them, but I didn't exactly know how they'd fare. We'd had a hard enough time with the attack on the road.

I didn't know how bad it could get today, but the fact that we were surrounded by thousands of innocent civilians troubled me. I couldn't let the fight go on like it had with the whale…which would mean if something happened, I needed to use magic.

But what if I did? Would this time be the time that I finally slipped into madness?

Lizza had said we'd practice my magic once we reached Navagio, and I thought she'd originally intended for us to get together this morning before the main event. But with the possibility of an attack looming, she'd gone out to sweep the city with all the soldiers and discourage any sort of uprising.

But if there were rumors and whispers, could the soldiers actually stop the rebels who didn't want the crown? Or those who used rebellion as an excuse for looting and pillaging?

Navagio was even more full of human wonders and gold than Reef City. It was definitely the more posh of the two—my quarters notwithstanding. It would make a tempting target.

I tapped my foot in the water nervously before realizing the old habit from humanity didn't quite have the same effect in the water.

Well, if you're nervous, do something about it, ninny. Talk to her!

As always, scolding myself drove me to action. I swam over to where several of the guards huddled, those assigned not just to protect me, but to protect the mayor's home. Though they'd soon spread out, they'd congregated on the back corner of the roof, drinking bubble and eating their lunch before their shifts officially began.

They bowed upon my approach. "Does anyone know the mage, Lizza?" I asked.

"Yes, Majesty," A shifter wearing Navagio city shell and chain mail spoke up. I glanced up at the tall man. He had a black stripe that ran across his eyes and a bright pink forehead. His chin, on the other hand, was a pale green that almost made him look ill. He pointed off to his right. "She's actually stationed nearby in order to keep an eye out for you and the mayor."

That was good to know. Part of me liked that Lizza would be close. But another part of me wanted her to do a spell to duplicate herself—was that even possible? —so that she could be everywhere.

I smiled up at the guard and asked, "Could you fetch her please?"

He gave me a quick salute before swimming off with his trident.

At my side, Paavo grumbled. "I could have done that."

"Not and protect the queen, you couldn't," Ugo retorted, his orange brows dipping down in judgment.

Paavo sighed and added, "No offense, Majesty."

"He's used to wall watch, pacing all the time." Ugo stated, the jolly guard trying to ease whatever annoyance he imagined I had toward Paavo.

Actually, I couldn't have cared less what Paavo thought right then. There were too many other things on my mind. I started to wave them both off when Ugo added,

"Sides, he's probably jealous you just sent off a slippery dick. Paavo hates them."

"Ugo!" I said, a bit scandalized he'd use such language.

"Oh! What? Wait. No. It's a type of fish shifter, Majesty." Ugo couldn't contain his snort. "Sorry. Sorry. It's not funny." His laughter belied his words.

I turned drily to Paavo. "And what don't you like?"

"Cause they slide right in. Get it? Slippery dick! Gah! Sorry. Can't help myself. Their hammer-throwing team always beats Paavo's. Those dicks give them a pounding! Oh. I'm dying. I'm dying." Ugo started chortling and couldn't stop.

Eventually, I just had to roll my eyes at him and turn to Paavo. "I can see why you prefer the ramparts."

Ugo's jaw dropped in offense before I nudged him with an elbow. "But apparently, a requirement to be my guard is you don't only have to like dicks, you have to be one."

I didn't know if Paavo's laughter was real or faked, but I didn't care, because Ugo said, "Well, if you're insulting me, I know I'm not in danger of getting fired. It's when your boss is polite that you've got a problem."

I chuckled at his wisdom. "That's right. You're family now."

He waved his hand in an "awe shucks" manner. But the banter with my guard came to an end when Lizza flew up over the edge of the rooftop on the back of a giant black stingray. The creature flapped its triangular wings and gently lowered itself so that she could climb off, her leather armor nearly as crackled and careworn as her face.

"Majesty." She didn't bother to bow and I didn't bother to remind her because who knew what flap of flesh might come flying off if she tried.

"Can I have a word?" I asked, leading her across the roof to the doorway that led from the roof into a small access room. The entire rooftop was treated like a veranda or porch on land, and there was a small attached room set up behind Gorgono, the contestants, the judges, and myself. It had been filled with drinks and snacks for the comfort of the mayor and his guests during the competition. Thankfully, a group of male servants was leaving as we entered, so we had the space to ourselves.

Lizza swam immediately over to the right wall, where a round table was set with food. I grimaced when she dipped a finger into a large serving bowl of soup and then licked the rotten appendage.

"Well? What's more important than watching for attackers?"

"My *issue*," I said in a low strained voice, very aware that anyone could come up the stairs or walk in from the roof at any moment.

Of course, Lizza immediately caught on to the fact that I was speaking about my magic. "You did just fine when we practiced."

"Once! That was once!"

"What about the parade thing-a-ma-jig? You did fine then too!" Lizza said as she moved over to some little clam dish and peered down at it suspiciously.

I followed closely behind her, a bit perturbed that she wasn't taking this seriously. Then again, it wasn't as though I had physical side effects. Just emotional ones, which were much harder for anyone else to see or recognize…until I went completely mad.

"We haven't talked since then…but later that night, I was hit with a bolt of rage. It was bad as lightning, Lizza. What if it's worse next time? What if 'next time' is today?"

She shook her head dismissively. "I've been all over this city and let me tell you, I haven't seen a thing out of the ordinary."

I didn't point out that Lizza's ability to see was questionable since one of her eyeballs was slowly turning opaque. I felt that would be counterproductive, but I wanted to shake her. "We didn't think anything was out of the ordinary on the road."

Lizza stuffed a jumbo shrimp into her mouth just then and I had to wait while she chewed before she could respond. "Have you considered an alternative reason for these feelings? What if giving away your heart to someone else means they can affect you?"

I glanced around, alarmed, worried that someone might overhear. But the room full of hors d'oeuvres was still empty.

"What do you mean?" I hissed.

"Well, you gave your heart to an asshole. You sure that's not what's causing all this? I mean you did say you wanted it to go to your worst enemy."

Her words gave me pause. "But…Mayi gave her heart to *me*."

"Yes, and who knows how it affected her. Ever think that your sweetness made her feel soft so she overcompensated and ended up heartless?"

"But Posey said a sea sprite had to give up her humanity."

"Well, Posey might be right. She might not." Lizza gave a lazy shrug as she popped something black into her mouth and I heard a gross little crunch. "Just playing devil's advocate here. You said that your fury was delayed. That's odd, isn't it? Most magical prices have to be paid immediately by part humans."

That was true. I chewed my lip, thinking about Watkins. He did have quite the temper. But lately… lately it had settled. He thought it had to do with the way I treated the shark shifters…an explanation I still hesitated to believe because I didn't think one decent act could undo a lifetime of hatred. But, what if he had my heart?

"Would it change the other person as well?" I asked, unconsciously reaching up and rubbing my chest.

"Hmm?" Lizza asked with another crunch.

"If they have my heart, will they change?"

"Possibly." Lizza grabbed a goblet and took a swig, some of the bubble spilling out the rotted corner of her mouth. She finished with a satisfied "ahhh" and wiped the back of her arm across her lips. "These are all just theories."

I nodded, but something about what she said made sense. It relaxed me and calmed me.

Maybe the whole legend of losing your humanity was just the best explanation people could come up with at the time. Just like people used to blame fairies for stealing when really, they'd turned forgetful and misplaced things in their old age.

Perhaps.

Yes.

"Can I get back to my real job now?" Lizza asked, before giving a small belch.

I tried not to make a face as I swam out of the stench. "Of course. Thank you."

Lizza marched off then and I thought I heard her mutter something like, "Queens. Always worrying about something."

It was time.

A bell rang out somewhere in town, singing that noon was upon us.

I was back out on the roof with Keelan and Mr. Whelk, darting looks at the sun to see how high overhead it was, though the water distorted it.

Right after the first chime, Sahar swam out from the little guest room onto the roof, declaring that everything was set. Her entrance caused a stir and everyone straightened a little more where they stood.

Automatically, my eyes traveled over to the competitors and met Mateo's in a silent wish of luck. Then I looked to Felipe to give him the same. To my surprised delight, my former guard grinned openly back at me. It was a look I'd pined to see from him, one I'd imagined a thousand times. Open happiness. A little ribbon of pleasure wove down my spine to see it in real life—directed at me.

Keelan bent to whisper smugly in my ear, "Told ya," but I ignored him.

Instead I continued my well-wishing. I nodded to odd-man Taft. His waist-length hair was pulled back with a series of leather straps today, his loincloth the same as always though. He pressed his pale blue hands together in a prayer position, acknowledging me, before his eyes drifted down to the golden roof and stayed there.

I gave a look for luck to both Stavros and Julian, who hovered together, the pair whispering rapidly to one another, though Julian did acknowledge my glance with a quick wink. Stavros didn't—he was probably a bit worried about the coming event.

I crossed over the "evil four" as I randomly dubbed them at that very moment. The shrimp dicks didn't even have the decency to have proper posture, they slouched and waited as if this was all a great inconvenience to them. I couldn't wait to officially be rid of them.

Humberto was humming to himself and as I caught a couple notes of the tune, I could have sworn it was the same one I'd heard Gita sing as she'd done my hair this morning. A secret little bubble of joy floated up inside of me. Good.

I looked left. To my surprise, I saw Watkins and Valdez standing together—laughing over something. I narrowed my eyes at the two men who drove my hormones wild but the two I thought I could trust least of all. Valdez was a pirate. And Watkins's change of heart was so sudden. Though perhaps Lizza had provided an explanation for that. Maybe he was in earnest.

Sarding magic, making things so difficult to tell. I wished my price was bursting into boils or something. Then at least I'd know for certain it had been paid.

I studied Watkins's strong jaw as I wondered if I might be able to feel the same things that he did.

My eyes flickered back over to Valdez, who leered and tapped Watkins on the shoulder to alert him to my ogling.

Watkins added his pouty smolder to the mix and their combined lust force was too great. I had to look away before I combusted.

When is this damned tournament going to start? I need them out of here before I end up doing something foolish again—like asking them to recreate our dance.

As if she could read my mind, Sahar quietly appeared by my side. Her graying gold hair was swept back into a simple, single braid today and she wore a high-waisted skirt with a white and green seaweed pattern running up and down its length.

"Majesty, I believe we're ready to begin." Behind her trailed a herald with a conch shell. He was a skinny older siren with an underbite—I didn't recognize him, so I assumed he came from Gorgono's servants.

When I nodded, he swam to the edge of the roof and blew a high bugle-like note into the water, causing all sound on the block to cease. To my amazement, his shell was magically, or perhaps scientifically, connected to shells throughout the entire city. I heard the blast reverberate through a street a block away, then fainter, through the block behind that, and on and on. The herald waited until the sounds had faded in the distance, until the entire city had gone still and silent, awaiting his next words.

Even I felt on tenterhooks as he sucked in a breath and announced, "Today, the Okeanos Tournament will host the second competition of four. Those battling for the queen's hand must show us their wit!" A pause for the news to spread had me nervously clasping Keelan's hand. "Today's challenge will be timed. Contestants have three hours to try to retrieve three items and bring them back to the queen." Another pause and I had to remind myself not to fidget, not to break my smile, not to yell at the herald to get on with it. My nerves frothed. "Points will be awarded based on the amount of time contestants take as well as how many items they are able to find." Pause. I was surprised I didn't snap the bones in Keelan's hand, I squeezed so hard. "Citizens, if you have any of our scavenger hunt items, then you may allow contestants to take them if you wish. Or, you may prevent them from doing so. Remember, this is a battle of wits for the contestants. Make them work for it!" A cheer went up from the crowd and I smiled over at Sahar. The clever woman. Part of me wondered if she'd added more citizen involvement based on how well it had been received yesterday. Or maybe she'd always planned the competition this way. She was brilliant, after all. In either case, that pause was the longest as the herald had to wait for the news to travel and the cheers at the far end of the city to die down.

"And now, for the information you've all been waiting for…the items that contestants must find within the city limits and bring back are: a sewing needle, a horseshoe, and the heart of a land animal."

"What the sard is a sewing needle?" Illia's face screwed up in confusion, his eyes bugging out more than usual.

I had to refrain from an eye roll at his utterly male ignorance.

On the far side of the roof, all three judges stood. One pulled a sewing needle out of his trouser pocket and held it aloft for the contestants to see. The next man, the one with the long mustache, bent over his chair and retrieved a box. He opened it to display a small organ. "A bird's heart," he declared.

The final judge also reached under his seat and produced a horseshoe, which had rusted under the water.

"These are all sky walker items," Radford protested.

One of the other sirens not associated with the evil four, looked concerned. "How would we even recognize them?"

Sahar turned to the group as whispers broke out amongst the competitors. "Gentlemen, this is a tournament of wit. I expect you to use it. Now stop talking. It's each man for himself as soon as the shell blasts."

The conch erupted just as her words finished.

"Three hours starts now!" Sahar declared.

And with a swish, the rooftop emptied—all the competitors, even the evil four, were gone.

Keelan turned to me and untangled our hands. "You know, next time I think I'll stand on your other side."

"Why?"

"I've already got one mangled hand. I don't need two," he said wryly as he made a show of stretching and flexing his right hand.

I just glared and reached out for Mr. Whelk, who paddled happily into my arms. "We don't like him, do we, Mr. Whelk? Do we?" I slipped into a baby tone automatically.

Keelan just chuckled and turned to his mother. "So, how can we actually monitor what's going on?"

Sahar just smiled. "We can't."

His good shoulder fell. "Are you joking? We just have to sit here and wait? For three sarding hours!"

"Don't worry, I'm sure the pain in your arm will keep you distracted while your stand-in does all the work," Sahar batted back, ruthless as ever.

"True. I'm an invalid now. I might need my dearest mother to feed me while they're gone."

"So long as you like the poisonous bits of puffer fish."

"My favorite."

I felt like dragging the pair of them into a tight hug, telling them their snarking was adorable and I wanted to turn them both against Bloss whenever she returned to visit. My sister wouldn't know what had hit her.

But I didn't. Instead, I said, "Well, I suppose we can make this time useful at least."

So I sat down next to Gorgono—who pointedly ignored me and opened his mail, reading over a long parchment. But his rudeness sparked an idea. I requested writing materials and a lap desk. Then I wrote a letter to Bloss asking for help on behalf of Reef City. I wrote another to Macedon about trade. And another to Rasle, to see if we could establish some sort of treaty regarding visitors, since so many part mer lived on their shores.

I'd taken a break to shake out my cramping hand when a yellow-tailed merman flew through the water toward us. I glanced around the city, but no jets of steam shot up through the waves.

Were we being attacked? Or was this mer a lone madman? A distraction?

Ugo and my replacement guard, Paavo, closed ranks in front of me, their spears jutting out as their eyes darted around, constantly returning to the yellow haired man approaching us. Ugo reached into his armor and I saw him pull out a vial of speed potion, the kind that Felipe had used to move me from harm before.

I reached out and gently put my hand on his freckled arm. "I won't need that," I whispered.

"All due respect, Majesty, but this is the one area where I'm not allowed to let you make that call." Ugo spoke out of the side of his mouth—eyes still on the stranger, who shouted hoarsely as he approached, as if he'd been shouting for a while.

"Attack in the quarry. Attack!" The merman's words beat him to the edge of the roof.

I shot up out of my seat, the lap desk tumbling to the side, ink trailing around me, my betta fins flapping hard as I gained height. Gorgono did the same.

"Show us," I commanded.

In synchrony, all the guards surrounding our building turned to follow the yellow-tailed mer, who nodded and turned south. We swam swiftly, my pulse crackling. The song of my magic welled up easily inside of me when I called it this time, the wispy voice growing stronger and louder as we rose through the waves. The beat of the music seemed to fill up the space inside of me where my heart had once kept tempo.

Fast, my mind urged. *If we want to help—then we need to get there quickly.*

The yellow-tailed merman shot off to the right, swerving around several tall metal towers. I darted between them instead, taking a more direct route, energy infusing every pore in my body, fear and the need to do something driving me.

Of course, we can't get through one event without an attack. Damned bastards, I thought fiercely.

I vaguely heard members of the public, swimming up as we passed overhead, asking what was going on.

To answer all of their queries at once, Paavo announced loudly, "Rebels are attacking the quarry."

Quite a few mer drifted up from the crowd to join us. "Bastards!" one spit.

"Stay back," Paavo warned them.

"Don't tell me to stay back. This is our home!" a mer with a gap between his teeth retorted. "We've a right to defend it!"

"Let them," I said, because I agreed. I also appreciated any and every citizen who saw these rebels for what they were—a threat to stability. They weren't even making demands! Who just attacked like that? They were little more than common criminals then. If their hatred for me was the only thing uniting them, then they didn't have a cause great enough to warrant respect.

They deserved ferocity.

Our band grew larger as more and more citizens spread the word while we swam through the city, until a mob swarmed behind us, shouting and threatening.

Ugo said nervously, "I don't know if I like them at our backs, Majesty. Untrained men…can be unpredictable. Trained men make mistakes, but regular ones filled with testosterone? I think we're courting disaster."

I couldn't disagree, but also, what was done was done. And we didn't know what kind of threat we were facing.

My eyes around, subconsciously looking for threats or columns of steam shooting up from the gem-colored glass rooftops. An unnerving thought came to me, one that made me suddenly glad for the throng of men behind us.

Shite. What if they attack multiple places at once?

Shut it, Avia. Don't worry about things that haven't happened yet, I scolded myself as I darted through the water with my wings as if I'd been born a champion swimmer, instead of a girl who'd been kept away from the water.

I had plenty to worry about with one attack already, my frazzled nerves and blazing fury didn't need any more fuel as we swam all the way across the city, to the far reaches of the town, so far that I could even see the blue-tinted dunes of Nowhere in the distance.

I poured on speed, worried we weren't fast enough, until sights began to blur around me, and it took a moment for me to realize someone was shouting at me.

I stopped, and turned, realizing the yellow-tailed merman had paused at the edge of a chasm. I glanced around and realized we must have reached the quarry, stone cliffs whose sheer edges had been carved away for bricks and blocks to build out Navagio when scavenging alone wouldn't do.

Chest heaving, I glanced around, down into the man-made canyon, searching for anyone out of place. But the shadows and the rocks made it nearly impossible to tell what was there.

The crowd roared in anger, and my guards closed in around me, several of the city soldiers organizing them into groups—attempting to coordinate whatever moves we might make.

But where the hell were the attackers? Adrenaline made my mind rush like rapids, churning my body up to such a pitch I thought I might vomit. But I swallowed down bile, flexing my fingers, searching for my inner song. I tried to focus that mad rush of energy where I'd need it.

I wouldn't be the damsel in distress rescued by my guard again. I refused to be.

I spotted a small group of shadows farther down in the quarry, near a giant system of pulleys and ropes.

I darted in that direction, Mayor Gorgono and the crowd following like a massive school of fish.

The yellow-tailed mer stopped short when several shadows armed with picks and spikes swam out of a cave-like opening.

This was it.

I lifted my hand, willing the song inside my ears to sing a high-pitched note. I'd sear the bastards with boiling water.

"WAIT!" The yellow-tailed man shouted at the top of his lungs. His solitary word reverberated around the canyon, echoing and repeating, bouncing off the rock until it sounded like someone behind me was shouting it as well.

We halted, and my guards turned, crisply barking out orders to halt to the guards behind us before swimming in front of me to block me from whatever the sard was going on. I let them do their jobs, but used my wings to rise just slightly, enough to shoot a dart of hot water between their shoulders.

What was happening? Was this a trap? Was the yellow-tailed mer in on everything? Or worse...was this a diversion? Had we been set up to swim all the way across the city only to have a real attack occur somewhere else?

My nostrils flared in fury as I eyed the entire scene with suspicion, ready to attack or swim off, whichever was called for, at the drop of a pin.

A merman with a maroon tail and empty hands shot up out of the group below, stopping twenty feet below us.

I aimed my fingers in his direction, coaxing my magical song louder, letting my ribs vibrate with the music, but not releasing.

"Marw, what's going on?" the maroon-tailed merman asked, his confusion clear as day with his thick brows furrowed as he took in the massive swell of people behind us.

"What the hell are you doing here?" Marw, the yellow-tailed merman exclaimed.

"Me! What are you doing here?"

"This is a scheduled sarding holiday!"

"Got a last-minute order in from Kremos. They had a landslide, have some damaged buildings. Paying double."

Marw's hand went to his chest. "I thought you sarding fools were robbing the place! Making a statement. Sarding hell, Petri!"

I lowered my hand, tension still thrumming through my system. A mistake. This is just a mistake.

My limbic system didn't agree. It was ready for action. Ready for a fight.

Gorgono swam over to the pair and he was questioning the two mer, berating them.

"You didn't sarding check!"

"The city is crawling with guards, everyone on high alert for stuff outside the usual. I saw a group of men! What was I supposed to do? Take them on myself?"

I tuned them out and tried to breathe deeply. The song of the sea surged in my ears, her voice loud and resonant, making my hands tremble and making it difficult for me to comprehend anything outside of her need. She wanted me to use her. My magic wanted me to sing with her, to roll the water across my fingertips and send it rollicking to the shore, sweeping up everything in its path. *We can't.* I spoke to her. But then I decided it might be better to sing.

In a slow melody that was jarring and poorly arranged, I mentally sang, *It was just a mistake, just an accident. Save your power for some other hour. Some true need.*

Though my words fumbled along and my tune was awful, the song inside of me responded with a purr, pleased that I'd attempted to speak her language.

I took deep, slow breaths, humming in my head until my magic also calmed down to a gentle thrum.

I was able to tune back into the conversation just as Gorgono turned to the rest of us, eyes dark, and said, "False alarm."

I closed my eyes and nodded, glad, yet also strangely disappointed. I was scared but also excited to face the rebels because I needed to redeem myself now that I'd claimed my power.

"You're lucky it was false." Gorgono's words made my lids pop open, and I glared at the mayor, who'd returned to my side and was glaring at me as if this false alarm was entirely my fault.

"As are you."

"Yes…well, I didn't need this sort of luck a few weeks ago before you took that crown."

"No. A few weeks ago, your monarch would have slain you if you'd dared speak to her the way you're speaking to me." I let ice cool my gaze as I stared at this man, no longer holding back the fury he made me feel. He pushed too hard—was too disrespectful. And for all I knew, his hatred for me could make him fall in with the rebels. He could already be working with them. But unlike the poor sods who'd attacked my carriage, Gorgono had much to lose if he did. I decided he needed a reminder of that fact.

"I prefer not to operate as Mayi did. I don't feel violence is always warranted. But just because I don't prefer her techniques…don't make the mistake of thinking I won't use them."

I held out my hand, and let the musical voice inside, which had been so eager to do something, have its way. I pushed the notes lower, deeper, darker…until a trident made of black ice formed in my right hand.

Gorgono stared at me, his emerald eyes sharp as my threat registered. He didn't speak, just whirled and swam back the way we'd come, leaving his startled citizens with no explanation.

Despite the fact that he left the fight today, I had a feeling that my confrontations with the defiant mayor had only just begun.

Once the mayor was a pinprick in the distance, flanked by a few city guards, I let my trident melt.

Then I swam up to the floating mob of men, who were still tense and ready for action. I had to both explain… and find a way to redirect all their pent up energy… hopefully into a positive direction.

"Because today was declared a holiday, there was a miscommunication. No one attacked." I made the announcement as I eyed the men, some of whom looked relieved while others seemed disappointed.

"I want to personally thank each of you for your bravery and your willingness to defend your home from harm. This is how it should be. My guards will take down your names...because heroes deserve a celebratory meal, after all. I'll arrange for a few of the local taverns to host you all tonight. Please keep your brawls outside of these fine establishments though. I'd like to pay for your meal, not broken furniture."

Chuckles rippled through the crowd as applause started and stopped in fits. But it seemed to satisfy them enough to disperse and make their way back to the city.

Ugo winked in my direction. "Well. That was epically entertaining. A bit more so than waiting for this tournament to finish."

I sighed. "Perhaps for you. Gorgono's an issue though. I wish he'd just stop testing me."

"He won't. He thinks you're too young, and too... attached to the sky breathers," Paavo contributed.

"Supportive. Great job," Ugo clapped him on the shoulder. "Want to add 'the rebels will keep attacking' too?"

Before they could descend into squabbling, I started back to Gorgono's golden rooftop. But I knew in my heart of hearts that Paavo was right. I'd constantly have to prove myself to people like Gorgono and until I defeated the rebels—I'd constantly have to defend against them as well.

One of Queen Gela's sayings rung through my ears. "A queen who rests easy, rests easy forever."

As I swam, I made myself a promise. I was going to start practicing with my magic every day until I felt confident in my control—despite the price. It was the only way to keep Gorgono and the rebels at bay.

I'd have to figure out the price bit as I went.

The song of my magic reverberated as I came to that conclusion. It hit a high, happy note, warbling agreement.

I put out a hand in front of me and let a tiny thread of song turn a three-inch space in front of my fingertip into a miniature whirlpool that traveled through the sea with me, spinning like a top.

Though I was pleased with my progress, a sudden burst of red-hot frustration seared me. And into my mind popped an image of a random siren with light blue hair. I imagined stabbing him in the gut with a knife and then reaching in and yanking out his innards for his children to see. That vicious image jarred my mind enough to muffle my magic's song and snuff out my whirlpool. Instead, I cringed, my arms coming up to my head as rage rocketed through my skull.

"Majesty?" Ugo swam closer. "You alright?"

I clenched my teeth and nodded as the vision inside my mind shifted to Ugo instead and my black rage directed itself at him.

I struggled another minute, floating in place as my stomach churned and my conscious mind fought back against the irrational blots of fury speckling my soul.

Gradually, it receded like the tide, leaving behind only the detritus of tainted memories and the knowledge that something was horribly, horribly wrong with me.

Or with Watkins.

Was Lizza right?

Was I feeling what Watkins was feeling right now? Some manner of frustration and fury during the tournament? Was it warping through our connection and turning awful? Or was he really that heartless a bastard? Was the awkward sweetness of his personality here in Navagio all an act?

Or was Lizza completely off base? Were the visions unconnected to anything or anyone else? Was I paying the price for my magic and going mad?

I'd have to find out which it was sooner rather than later.

Otherwise, these random emotions—no matter their cause—would drive me insane.

20

I CHEATED.

I wasn't supposed to swim through Navagio and look for the competitors—I was supposed to go and sit for another hour just tapping my royal fingers as I waited for my suitors to return. But I was shaken by everything that had just happened and not ready to see Gorgono again while I felt weak and vulnerable.

So I used a queen's privilege and the fact that no one could outright force me back to the mayor's rooftop. I did what I wanted.

I dawdled behind the rest of the guards and soldiers on our return, eyes diving down to search the streets for any man I might find familiar.

Perhaps I was subconsciously searching for Watkins, wanting to understand what was happening to me, but

I didn't see him. I just swam down over an underwater granary tower made of stacked barrels—Paavo and Ugo and two other guards trailing me, concerned looks on all their faces.

I didn't explain myself, just kept on swimming above Navagio's rooftops, the sun warming my hair even as a cool current slid across my toes.

I dove down once—thinking I saw Valdez slipping down a narrow alleyway.

Ugo exclaimed, "Hey! What! Wait!" as he and Paavo changed course to follow me. I darted between a building made out of the side of a ship, complete with little portholes, and a bubbled glass construction that looked as delicate as any sugar-candy tower our cook in Evaness castle had ever made. But when I peered into the shadowy alleyway, Valdez was gone.

I gave my guards a sheepish shrug and used the moment to swim toward a wider thoroughfare lined with people, waving at a few excited mer children, who tugged anxiously at their parents' hands as they tried to get over to me. I swam down the street for a bit as Ugo scolded me for my impulsiveness.

"Well, waiting on that roof is boring!" I exclaimed. And after the false alarm—I was still brimming with adrenaline and I wanted to shake some of it off. I used my transparent fins like fairy wings, darting up and down in the streets, waving to the friendly onlookers as I searched for my competitors.

When I reached a corner that led from a wide, open shopping lane into a narrow and twisting residential corridor, a woman octopus shifter with a pink tentacled lower half, pointed down the side street and said, "There, Majesty! I saw one of them go in there!"

I thanked her and swam, holding up my purple skirts so they were out of my way, wondering what in the world some of my competitors were doing in the middle of what looked like a residential neighborhood. Perhaps a sewing needle or two might exist over here, but certainly no horseshoes or animal hearts…not unless there was a local hedge witch who resided here.

I swam lower and lowered my feet to the sand, tiptoeing along the wall. I peered into a window to see Humberto's striped face flush in frustration as he spoke with an older woman—one who had the hunched posture of a seamstress.

Humberto's words carried through the window, though they were muffled. "Please. I've tried everywhere. I can't go back empty-handed!"

The old woman, whose hair was a grizzled orange and pink, swam around a table and I caught sight of her teal tail, which had a long, ragged scar on it. "I don't want to help that sky-breathing queen!"

I drew back slightly, closer to the wall, so that she wouldn't be able to see me.

"You aren't helping her, you're helping me," Humberto argued. "I'm not trying to win…I just can't get kicked out. I…need to stick around." His voice caught.

Aww. He's falling for Gita. Dammit all, I need a moment to find out the details from her—

"I'll trade you." The woman offered. "One needle in exchange for—"

"I'm a painter by trade. I can come back and paint tonight. Do up your entire room here."

She snorted. "Paint? No. That won't help me. I want your pants."

Humberto started, drifting backward a few inches, arms flying protectively to his waistband. "My pants?"

"I know a guy who'll buy them second-hand no questions asked."

I slid away from the window in slow motion until I was two feet down the wall and out of sight. Then I made a horrified face for Ugo and Paavo. "Let's go quickly. I *don't* want to find out how this ends."

We shot through the water back to the mayor's roof, where Sahar and Keelan both gave me a talking to for scaring them. The lectures were a welcome distraction from my visions of pantless Humberto.

The herald used his conch shell to announce time warnings to the competitors, so that all of them made it back to Gorgono's rooftop before three. The first bellow shocked us all, but he did them in five-minute intervals, with announcements the final half hour—so by the end we were all either immune to or annoyed by the sound.

Radford and his group swam back a drunken, slovenly mess, having clearly spent their three hours at the tavern. Illia even had a lipstick mark on his collar, which would have pitched me into a rage at his downright disrespect, but to my surprise, Marea shot up out of her seat when she saw him and swam right over.

The silent wife of the mayor reared back and smacked Illia hard across the face, her orange and blue hand flicking so quickly it blurred.

I exchanged a startled glance with Keelan before Sahar leaned down and whispered in my ear. "Remember, I told you on the ride over...Illia is her sister's nephew by marriage?"

I had not remembered that ridiculously banal detail. But I quite enjoyed it right now, as I watched Marea whisper shout Illia into shame.

She might not have stopped either, if the judge with the giant mustache hadn't come forward, his gnarled old hand raised in an effort to defuse the tension as he asked, "Excuse me. But we have to score the results of each of the competitors. Have you managed to procure any of the three items?"

All four of them shook their heads—as I'd expected. The judge clucked his tongue and shook his head as he turned and swam back to his seat, to mark down big fat zeros on his little strip of parchment.

Good. We'd all get what we wanted then—separation—though, based on their glares, I'd made lifelong enemies of the four. Because that was what I needed. More enemies.

The herald lifted his conch shell and announced the names of four competitors who had not been able to find a single item. Polite clapping followed.

Keelan swam over, settling next to me once more, though his mother had forcibly prevented him from swimming out to the quarry. He gave a somber look in my direction as he said, "That right there is a pity clap for those fools."

"Is there such a thing?" I asked, glancing around for Mr. Whelk.

"Of course. It's got a very distinctive sound. An 'I'm sorry you're so stupid' undertone." He took my right hand and arranged it palm up underneath his. Then he made his wrist limp as he weakly clapped his good hand down onto mine. "Hear that? Terrible sound."

I chuckled and then retracted my hand to point at the small room just off the roof. "You know what else will be a terrible sound? Gorgono's yell when he finds Mr. Whelk eating all his food."

Keelan turned to see his pet perched on the refreshment table, head buried in a serving dish of seagrass.

"Shite!" he exclaimed, swimming rapidly over to retrieve his miscreant pet.

The next competitor to arrive back was Watkins, who carried a horseshoe clutched in his hand. The dorsal fin he had even in human form was speckled with something—dirt or mud, I couldn't tell what.

His black eyes were somber until he saw that some of the other men were empty-handed. Then his thick shoulders relaxed.

I gave the shark shifter a huge smile as the judge with the hanging mustache approached.

"I see you got one item. Care to tell us how you got it?"

"I asked around at the taverns. I found a local butcher who specialized in scavenged horse meat to agree to let me go through his trash." He gave a shrug. "He let me, laughing the whole time, before he told me that he typically sold off the metal bits to a smithy. So, I went over there and got this. That's why I only have the one item."

The judge nodded, his whiskers wavering. "Understandable. Quite persistent though. Did you happen to deck the butcher?"

"Of course."

The judge chuckled and nodded. "Well, you might lose a point or two for lack of restraint," – Watkins's face dropped at that—"but I do appreciate your honesty."

The judge took the horseshoe and placed it on the table next to his peers. Then they consulted in low whispers, jotting down notes as they sat in their wicker chairs.

Meanwhile, the herald took to his conch shell and announced to the city all the details of Watkins's adventure, setting off a cheer that rang through the neighborhoods.

Humberto arrived next wearing only his underwear, clutching a needle in his fingers as if it was a sword.

To say the roof was shocked was an understatement. The guards couldn't contain their chuckles and even the whiskered judge had trouble keeping a straight face.

Both Marea and I averted our eyes while Humberto explained his trade to the judges. Sahar sent a servant off to find him some new pants.

The announcement of Humberto's "victory," if it could be called that, got an even louder cheer from the crowd because of its entertainment value.

Valdez arrived next, the pirate trailed by several angry mer and a glaring siren. In his hands, he had three huge signs, which he brought directly over to the judges' table, dumping them unceremoniously on top of the other contestants' items.

"I present all three requested items."

The whiskered judge lifted the first. "These are…tavern signs."

"Yes."

The judge glanced over at the angry citizens, who were prevented from swimming onto the roof by the guards.

"I presume you stole them?" the whiskered judge asked.

"Borrowed." Valdez lifted up the first sign and panned around the roof so everyone could see it. There was a black outline of a winged bird on it, with a large red heart painted behind it. "May I present: The Raven's Heart." He grabbed the second sign, which had a silver needle and a twist of green thread painted on it. "The

Needle's Eye." He showcased the final sign. "Landlubbers." It had a horse and rider on it.

"There's not even a horseshoe here," one of the judges protested.

"Nonsense. Humans don't ride horses without shoes." Valdez was dismissive.

I glanced around at Keelan, who looked amused at this turn of events—perhaps keen to find another troublemaker like himself.

Gorgono only looked annoyed, while Marea still glared at her nephew.

I wondered what the judges thought of Valdez's interpretation. It was certainly clever. But was it what they wanted? And would stealing lose him points?

Personally, I was both amused and a bit admiring. Valdez had interpreted the judges' requirements his own way. And then gone full pirate.

I glanced over to see him watching me. He gave me a saucy wink and I couldn't stifle a small laugh. A large part of me hoped that he'd make it through because I wasn't ready to be done with him. I was attracted to his rule-breaking, to his outright distaste for rules and all the manners of polite society that had dictated my life up to this point.

He was refreshing.

Though definitely no contender for diplomat, I thought wryly as I watched the angry tavern keepers argue with the guards.

Still. His appeal—besides his obvious sensual appeal—was the novelty of his free thinking.

There was a long, whispered discussion between the judges—so long that the herald ended up announcing Valdez's items over the conch shell before they'd even finished. They didn't write anything down before Mateo swam up over the roof, breathing hard.

I glanced over at my silver-haired merman. The only one who competed for me, for the legitimate right to be with me instead of being my dark secret. I noticed, with some surprise, that his silver tail was getting a streak of burnt orange in it, like a true mer's did when they reached the mer age of maturity...a bit later than humans.

Mateo's eyes were strained as he looked at me, like he was trying to communicate a secret, but I had no idea what.

When the head judge swam over to ask him what item he'd retrieved, he handed over a horseshoe.

But it didn't look quite right. It wasn't old and aged and corroded like the horseshoe that Watkins had brought back. It was clean, gleaming even, and had a slightly blue hue to it.

I furrowed my brow, as did the judge. "This looks…new."

Mateo swallowed uncomfortably. Nervously. "Yes, sir. It is."

"Well, don't keep us in suspense. How'd you get it?"

"I…have family on land. I went to a witch. Asked her to do a portal spell."

A gasp went up, since portal spells were notoriously unstable.

"And you had your family pass you this through the portal?" The judge finished off with a question.

Mateo nodded, eyes dropping. "I couldn't get anything else. It wouldn't hold."

The judge nodded. "Alright then, well, let us discuss." He looked over at the herald. "Go ahead and announce this one now, won't you?" Then he placed the gleaming horseshoe on the table while he talked with the other judges in hushed tones.

I watched carefully, on alert. Their faces were serious. We never used portal magic in Evaness. It had been illegal there because of the dangers. Was that why Mateo looked so ashen faced? Had it been traumatic?

Mateo swam stiffly, as if his side was hurting, over to the judges' table.

"Excuse me," he asked in a low voice. "I…promised my family I'd give them back the horseshoe. It's brand new and they really can't afford another just because…"

The whiskered judge nodded. "Alright. Go ahead."

Mateo gave a quick nod and quickly scooped up the curved bit of metal. After that, he didn't look at me as he swam over to the refreshment room and downed a glass of bubble.

Odd. Very odd.

But Felipe returned just then, so I was distracted by his presentation.

Like Valdez, he'd taken an interpretive approach. He appeared with a charm bracelet. From it dangled three small golden charms: all three of the tournament items.

I stiffened as I watched the judges complete another long consultation, this time my nerves scratching at me like sentient thorns. I couldn't let them disqualify Felipe. I wouldn't.

I breathed through my teeth, nerves nearly as bad as when I'd hurtled through the city toward danger.

Two men had interpreted their assignment broadly. That meant the judges had to accept it, right? They couldn't possibly score those two worse than the four who'd found nothing. Could they? Could misinterpretation be considered worse than failure to succeed?

I glanced over at Sahar, gaze scolding because I wasn't sure of all the damned rules. Because I didn't get to make the damned rules.

But my future was on the line. And I realized I wanted both Felipe and Valdez in it.

Sard.

Julian arrived next with his hands full. The siren smiled serenely as he gently arranged all three items neatly onto the judges' table.

Their eyebrows all shot up nearly to their hair.

Julian provided an explanation before they even asked. "One of my colleagues, a fabulous man by the name of Mayer. He has a cabinet of curiosities over near the library. He's working on a compendium of knowledge, trying to write a book that explains and categorizes all the surface detritus. He's calling it, 'Insight into Sand Trodder Objects and their Useful Application to Underwater Life.' Working title. I swam over and asked, and we were able to dig up all of these little treasures!"

I couldn't help clapping. Julian really did know quite a few of these local scientists. There was a whole community of them, trying to study and gain knowledge and contribute useful things to society in their own way.

He glanced over at me and blushed, his bronze cheeks darkening to almost brown, when he saw me beam in his direction and I felt the tinge of affection color my cheeks. I might not have had a visceral connection with him, but I appreciated so much of who he was and what he was trying to do. He made the little girl that I'd been—the struggling, imperfect little human sister trying to shine in a world of sparkling magic—proud.

I was thrilled it seemed like he was going to win this competition handily, cheering along with the crowd as the herald announced his return and the judges calculated his score.

In fact, I was so tickled over Julian that I forgot that several competitors weren't back yet. But the bell in the distance started to chime out three o'clock just as Stavros hurtled over the edge of the roof.

He was breathing hard, his expression darker and his demeanor more somber than I'd ever seen him. The shy siren strode forward with a confidence I hadn't seen from him before and dropped a heart onto the table. Blood still trickled from the ventricles, tainting the water with a metallic scent.

Had he just cut it out of an animal?

A different sort of shock rolled across the rooftop.

This was…unexpected.

The long-whiskered judge asked for his usual explanation.

Stavros replied shortly. “I hunted.”

“And what kind of animal—”

“A seagull,” Stavros answered before the question was finished.

The judges didn’t have time to consult before Taft, the blue-skinned nixe arrived. His mouth was tightly closed as he swam up onto the roof, head bowed.

“You’re late,” the head judge said.

Taft merely nodded.

“Well. Did you find anything?”

Taft held up a small needle.

“Where’d you get it?”

Taft ran his tongue across his teeth and swallowed before he answered in a low voice. “At a tailor shop.”

He tried to keep his lips together, but when he spoke, I spotted a gap between his teeth that hadn’t been there the other day in the carriage. He was missing a tooth.

My first instinct was to think he’d been punched in the mouth for his trouble, but then I thought about his magic. If he could transform his entire body…could he also transform part of it?

I stared at the needle and realized it had a slightly blue sheen.

Just like the horseshoe that Mateo had brought up and been so eager to reclaim.

I glanced around and realized that Mateo was no longer on the roof.

Taft had helped Mateo. Yet again.

I started and grabbed onto my purple skirt to hide the physical reaction of my surprise. Because as Taft swam forward and placed the little blue needle on the table, I realized that my true love was falling deeper and deeper into this stranger's debt.

And I didn't like that.

It was dangerous.

21

The judges deliberated while everyone watched, until, finally, they gave their results to the herald.

"And the winner of the second round of the Okeanos Tournament—a Navagio local himself—Julian of the House Golden Sands!"

Cheers erupted all around, and Stavros and several of the other competitors went over and clapped Julian on the back.

Then he swam over to me and bowed formally to kiss my hand. I clasped onto his fingers as he rose and didn't let go.

Bright, warm pride swelled up inside of me and I was so glad that Julian had won. His scores would be averaged across all the events, of course, but a win put him in a good position to make it through to the final round, from which I'd choose my husbands. He and Felipe (and by extension Keelan) were the only ones who could possibly rest easy during the next round.

Julian threaded his fingers with mine and I was surprised by how comfortable it felt to stand shoulder to shoulder with him to listen to the remainder of the results. It wasn't magical, my fingers didn't sweat in nervous anticipation and my stomach wasn't swarmed by butterflies at his touch, but it was pleasant.

We listened to the scores, with the herald announcing and Sahar recording it all for posterity.

My trepidation grew as neither Felipe or Valdez's names were called out.

Mateo's score was middling, as was the score for nearly all the men who'd found a single item.

But the two men who'd gotten creative weren't announced among those.

I tried not to squeeze Julian's fingers and make him aware of how each additional announcement made me tense.

The judges must have wanted only literal interpretations of their quest, which I thought was foolish. But it was also bad.

Sard.

Why couldn't the tournament allow me to judge?

My eyes darted to Sahar, who was chewing her lip as she waited.

Keelan held Mr. Whelk under his arm and kept his eyes on his pet, his posture betraying his nerves.

He was just as worried as I was.

My eyes traveled over to each of the men in question—the creative thinkers.

I tried to weigh my options. I could save one, but only one from elimination.

Saving Felipe would also save Keelan. And both of them were definite finalists—future husbands if I even dared think that word, which still intimidated me.

But what about the pirate? The man who sank ships and sold stolen goods to creeps like Gorgono, who failed to follow any rules, but who made my soul feel like it had been set aflame?

Could I just let him go when I felt like there was potential still? When I felt like he might possibly be earnest about his desire for me? When I hoped he might change?

Would Felipe's high score from the joust be enough to offset whatever points he was awarded here?

Was there a way I could keep the pirate who intrigued me so much…or should I not take the chance?

My stomach see-sawed as every other name was mentioned, even the four shrimp dicks (though I supposed their dicks would return to normal after today).

Had the judges forgotten? I wanted to whip my head to the side to stare them down, but I forced myself to turn slowly, patiently, though inside I felt anything but patient.

The head judge cleared his throat after the herald finished announcing Taft's score. He stroked his long, dangling mustache before saying, "Two competitors brought us quite interesting items today. Not exactly what we'd requested but they did show some creativity. The question becomes, however, how beneficial is this type of thinking? It's unique. It shows ingenuity. But it can also lead one astray. Instead of following the queen's orders, these thinkers may decide to deliberately misinterpret the instructions they are given. And that can lead to disaster. Or…it can very well save the kingdom."

The judge with the strip of lavender hair, nodded her agreement from her spot in her wicker chair.

Good. That was good. My face started to relax into a smile.

But then the whisker-haired judge glanced over at Gorgono.

The mayor looked between the judge and I and smiled, which I thought was odd, until I saw him reach up and scratch at his chin.

The judge swallowed hard, clearing his throat and giving a quick half-nod of acknowledgement, and that's when I realized that Gorgono was calling the shots with these judges. That neck scratch wasn't simply a scratch—it was a signal.

This tournament wasn't about my competitors's wit at all—but the mayor's. Based on the smarmy look in the mayor's eyes, things were about to go very badly for me.

Pins and needles stabbed me as the judge paused, before saying, "Divergent thinking is one of the pillars of our city. It allows new creations, can inspire others, and can be one of the greatest assets an individual can have. But we've weighed this intellectual asset against the responsibilities of the crown. Creativity is within the realm of the city. But not the monarchy. A queen is supposed to provide predictability. Stability. This sort of bending the rules could lead to unfair interpretations of policies, changes to military orders, things of a catastrophic nature that could undermine the crown and the stability of the kingdom. Therefore, we not only didn't award points to these two competitors, we subtracted them."

I felt like I was plummeting down a cliff—my worst fear realized.

Gorgono kept a straight politician's face, hiding his gloat with the practiced perfection of a master. Still—I seethed. My affection for Keelan was obvious, his mother was my advisor and he'd been at my side all damned afternoon on this roof. And Gorgono stripping Felipe—Keelan's stand-in—of points meant that he intended to deprive me of one of the men I found a powerful ally.

I didn't know if Valdez was an intentional target as well. I didn't know if he knew secrets that Gorgono wanted to keep hidden or if the pirate was simply an unintended casualty.

Either way, this was a nightmare situation. Gorgono was pulling strings that altered my very future.

Oh...he'd get his...

But would I be able to fix this? I'd bound myself to this ancient tournament and its idiotic rules and I didn't know if Gorgono's treachery was reversible.

It had better be.

I glanced across the roof to see how others were taking in the news. The expressions of the two men involved were heart wrenching.

Felipe, who always followed rules, who served me without question, looked ready to retch. He was about to be verbally flogged for his ingenuity.

Valdez's eyes, meanwhile, were livid. The pirate's rage was so visceral I could practically reach out and touch it.

Shite.

Shite.

I looked between the two—torn. And I realized I was more attached to the pirate than I'd ever realized. Far more attached.

This choice was even harder than I'd thought.

I dropped Julian's hand as the herald spoke and walked across the gold bricks, the symbols of each noble house stamped into the metal scraping against my bare feet.

Those bastard judges. That fucker Gorgono. His wife recoiled as I walked past. Marea knew what her husband had done.

Scorn threatened to escape my lips—I wanted to verbally lash all of them until their ears bled.

When I reached Sahar, she could read my mood.

I gestured at the parchment in her hand, where she was tallying the scores from both tournaments, ranking the competitors as the herald made the announcement.

I stood, staring over her shoulder as she added up Valdez's and Felipe's scores. There were twenty men, including the four assholes. Only fifteen would make it through to round three.

I scanned the list as her quill finished, sucking in a breath as I correlated numbers to names.

And when I saw both of their scores, I hissed through my teeth. Both of them were in the bottom five. Radford, due to his score on the joust, would still make it through.

Sarding shite. Couldn't I just trade him out?

I pointed and gave Sahar a meaningful look. If she just scratched out Radford's number…

Sahar looked pale as she whispered up to me, "Scores must be tallied on enchanted parchment. They can't be changed."

"If you try, what happens?"

"Your tongue shrivels."

"Well, I don't really like your voice anyway," I said in a low voice. But my tone was strained from stress, from the fact that I was trying to joke about something that very nearly had me on the edge of angry tears—something I didn't find funny at all.

I wanted to punch Gorgono. Or do worse. My magic rose up, the tune mixing with my rage in a quick, blood-pumping frenzy—tempting me. If I could just freeze the bit of water inside Gorgono's gills, then no one else would know. He'd fall over dead, and none would be the wiser.

Or I could slice him a thousand times, tiny little cuts with knives made of ice, scenting the water for all the shark shifters nearby.

My mind took an even darker turn, that strange oily black rage that I associated with my madness creeping over me again.

Perhaps Watkins was mad as well.

I had to fight not to let my inner demons soar out and do all the things I longed to do.

Instead, I smiled with full teeth and continued questioning Sahar in an effort to find some way out of this disaster besides violence. "Well, do we have to eliminate everyone this round?"

"It's always been done."

"But is it in the official rules?" I stressed the word official in the hopes that it was clear to Sahar I was looking for loopholes before the herald made the final announcement of combined scores and gave the public the names of the men who'd proceed forward in the tournament.

Sahar looked at me with pity. "It is in the rules. There have to be eliminations."

"But how many?" I pressed, glancing at her list again. Felipe was only one behind Radford. If we could keep just one more man on the list, then I could use my exception and save Valdez.

Sahar shook her head like it was hopeless, tying a knot in my gut that was so tight that it ached. "We can't change scores..."

No.

Sard Gorgono.

Sard the rules.

Sahar stared at me, eyes growing wide as an idea came to her. "We can't change scores without changing judges. There was a determination nearly five-hundred years ago that a judge was trying to exert undue influence to get a distant cousin through the tournament. He was replaced."

Yes! But who the hell can I get that won't be influenced by Gorgono. He's got the entire city under his thumb...

That thought set me in a new direction. I knew exactly what I had to do.

Determination sparked me to move, and I snatched the list off of Sahar's lap desk, then strode over to the herald. My fate and future would not be determined by rules made by people long dead. And I'd be damned if it was determined by a bastard like Gorgono. "I'd like to give the final scores out please."

The startled man announced me to the crowd before he handed over his conch shell, reminding me of my first announcement at the start of this tournament. I took a deep breath to steel myself, since the stakes felt higher this time. That day, these men had still been figments of my imagination, not flesh and bone. Now, I knew them. And I wanted to know even more.

"Good afternoon, Navagio! I'm here to read out the rankings of the men after both tournaments." I read slowly, thinking as I did so.

The perfect example came to me when I read off Taft's name.

"You know…I was kidnapped as a baby and raised on land," I diverted into a story. "And the queen of Evaness, whom I thought was my mother, had a few sayings I found annoying.

"One of those was that a bird can't change its feathers. The equivalent down here would probably be that a fish can't change its stripes.

"I find it interesting…that in a city renowned for creative thinking, the tournament results here actually punish those who think creatively."

I waited and let that sink in for the crowd before I turned to Gorgono so that the mayor could see the deadly expression on my face and just how utterly done I was with him sarding me over. This little power battle he had begun was going to end here and now. "Of course, I've found many people under duress attempt to change their stripes."

Gorgono paled and I watched his throat bob as he swallowed hard, realizing that this time, I could publicly call him out for his interference.

I gave him a dark grin, my magic humming an ancient battle tune underneath my skin, before I turned back to face the city and slowly lifted the shell to my lips, intentionally drawing out his agony. "Can the judges come forward please?"

I waited, without looking at them, a technique I'd seen Queen Gela use to great effect in her office. She often had people who'd undermined her join her at the window to look out at the gardens. It made them three times as anxious because they couldn't watch her facial expressions to see where she was going with her questions. It made it harder for them to anticipate her moves.

I could practically feel the water vibrating with their anxiety as they surrounded me.

Ugo and Paavo moved closer behind me, guarding my back as I lifted the shell, and then began a very public interrogation.

"So…one of you is a healer, correct?"

I glanced to the side to see the healer with the single stripe of lavender hair nod in acknowledgment.

"Please state your name for the people of Navagio." I held the shell out to her.

"Orlena," the healer spoke softly.

Bringing the shell back to my own lips for my next question, I asked, "And have you ever used a new spell in your healing?"

"Well, yes, but—"

"Have you ever invented a spell?"

"Yes, but that's not—"

"That's exactly the point," I protested as I pulled the shell back to my own lips. "I believe that these judges are using a double standard. Creative thinking is okay for some but not for others. What is wit but thinking creatively?" I asked the crowd.

I glanced at each of the judges, my eyes hooded in disapproval. "And why…why would judges who live in a town bursting with creativity suddenly shun it?" I let the question linger, waiting as it made its way through the city.

"I can only think of one reason. People of Navagio, I think that these judges might change their position if the mayor here was controlling them—because he dislikes me, because he wants the city's power to be greater than the crown's. Because he wants to handicap my reign and deprive me of people who think like you do—outside the box."

"Here's the rub. I think the mayor here is exerting undue influence on this tournament. Why should men who made an effort score below those who found nothing? Does that make sense at all? I don't think so."

"Let me also take a quick moment to tell you about the men that these judges are trying to cut. Let me tell you why I believe they deserve to continue their quest to become kings. Both Felipe, who competes on behalf of Keelan, and Valdez are quite sweet and charming men trying to do their best in a timed challenge with items that could have been anywhere or everywhere. One of them is actually my guard, who's standing in for another man who was injured. Felipe has one of the greatest moral codes you've ever seen. In fact, he's the one who saved me from that vicious attack before our first competition. He took me in his arms and swam me to safety like a knight in a fairy story." I paused, leaving a moment for the women in the audience to swoon. I hoped they were swooning. My own chest felt tight and tense because I was laying everything on the line right now, trusting that it would all work out. I adjusted my grip on the conch shell, which was necessary because my hands were sweating so much. "On the other hand, Valdez is a pirate. He's cunning, resourceful, potentially a bit ruthless even—as I'm sure the tavern keepers who lost their signs temporarily today can attest. But Valdez has his own code of honor, one that is fiercely protective of those he cares for. He shifted and fought off sharks during our attack, fearless as the best soldiers. Can a rogue like that become a good king? Can a villain in one circumstance transform into a hero in another? I'd like the chance to find out."

Here again, I paused to take a breath, and my gaze automatically drifted over to the men in question because I felt vulnerable. In order to counteract everything that Gorgono had thrown at me, I was publicly putting my feelings for them on display. I had to fight to keep my hands from shaking on the shell I held as I met their eyes. Felipe's blue eyes blazed like dragon fire. Valdez blew me a saucy kiss that made me blush.

Their expressions only reinforced how much I needed this to work—I couldn't let go of them. The very prospect of losing them made me feel like I was tumbling, tripping, about to smash my face into a rock. It was too painful to think about.

I took a long moment to look out over the crowd before I put the shell to my lips again. "Navagio, you have impressed me from the first moment I arrived. You are a city full of unique thinkers. I value that. And because I value you so much, I'm putting my fate into your hands."

Gasps went up behind me on the rooftop, but I ignored them in favor of continuing. I had to get this out now. I had to finish it.

"I'm going to enact an old precedent that allows a corrupt judge to be eliminated. I'm going to eliminate these three judges. And I'm going to allow you all to be the judges instead. Should we keep both of these wonderful men in the running? Should we reward those who made an effort over those who brought back nothing? Should we allow them to stay?"

The judges retreated from my sides, shamed and muttering angrily behind me. I heard Gorgono's protest about rules and replacing the entire panel, but I pressed on. I had the crowd's attention and I needed to keep it. "If you think that two creative men whose smiles warm the sea, two creative men who put actual effort into today—unlike some other contestants—if you think Valdez and Felipe both deserve to stay, and those who did not bring back any items should be eliminated, please swim up twenty feet above the rooftops. I'll have my guards count those who vote in favor. If more than half of you vote to keep them, then that's what I'll do. If not," –my voice cracked—"I understand, and I, your queen, accept your decision."

I passed the shell back to the herald and clasped my hands in front of me because there was absolutely no way I'd be able to wait for the crowd's decision without wringing them.

I listened as my message slowly made its way street by street through the city. Each echo of my own voice was agonizingly painful to listen to—I second-guessed my actions, my words, all of it. Should I just have declared I was keeping both? Should I just have said sard all the rules, I'm queen and I'll do what I want?

I could have…but I'd wanted to wrest control from Gorgono. I'd wanted to show the spiteful bastard that I wouldn't just steal away the ruling he'd concocted, I'd steal the loyalty of his citizens.

Now I felt sick. Had I overplayed my hand? Had I misjudged the people?

The silence was eerie.

Until I saw one mer woman slowly swim up above her roof, on the street just in front of us.

Her three husbands swam up after her.

Then her neighbor on the right did the same.

And another.

Another.

Hope fluttered through my veins. There was movement behind me and suddenly, the two men in question floated beside me, reaching out and clasping my hands.

Together, we watched the city as the people rose up until the jewel-colored rooftops of Navagio were obscured by the crowd.

22

We packed up early, because I refused to stay another minute in Gorgono's house. The servants rushed around in a bit of a frenzy, but I knew that the treatment we'd all receive would be far worse here than sleeping out in our tents again.

Sahar hovered near, coordinating a huge party at the local taverns for all those men who'd swam out to protect Navagio.

"Hope there's enough bubble in all these places to keep the men sated," Sahar gave me an exaggerated look of horror. "I'm glad we're heading out tonight. I can only imagine the current's going to smell of piss and vomit here tomorrow."

"Seconded," Paavo agreed, from where he stood behind me, suspiciously eyeing any of Gorgono's servants who dared walk nearby as they went about their evening duties.

I laughed. "This is true."

"You may be earning the ire of all the wives," Ugo warned me, chewing on his lower lip in mock fear.

Our conversation ceased when Marea swam around the corner, her brightly patterned skin and fin hair making her easy to spot.

She stopped short at the sight of us, her eyes turning to gaze at the trunks and bags being shucked out the door.

She swallowed once, and then slowly made her way forward to me, her right hand clutching at her left elbow in a fearful, submissive sort of posture. When she grew close enough, she spoke, though she didn't directly face me, she faced the hallway so that anyone swimming by might think she was just making her way past. "Careful, Majesty," she whispered in a low tone. "You've made him angry. He's evil when he's angry."

"Marea," I reached out but retracted my hand when she cringed away. "Are you in danger?"

She turned her luminous eyes to mine and blinked once. "No. You are."

And then the mayor's wife swam off in a flurry… leaving only a trail of bubbles and worries behind her.

The moon shone down bright and happy, full as a pearl, while we made camp. This time, the square tents didn't use anchors because the sea floor wasn't nearly as deep or cold, so we spread them out on the soft, fine sand just like humans would spread their tents. The guards insisted on a target formation: an inner ring with the competitors and myself, and an outer ring with all of them and the servants.

The center was where we would gather for our evening meal. The castle mages and Lizza were already in place as I swam over. They were just starting up the purple fires that would cook our dinner of halibut.

Several of the fires were already surrounded by servants or guards who were packed in rather tight, because the inner ring of tents was rather small. One fire was still vacant, however, and I made my way over to it.

Rather than intrude on anyone else's respite, forcing them to be polite around the queen, I settled myself down onto the sand by the solitary lavender fire. I was ready for a calm dinner after the tension that had surrounded our trip to Navagio. I'd have to figure out a way to remove Gorgono from his position sooner rather than later.

But that's a task for another day. Right now, just relax and bask in the fact that you get to keep Valdez, Felipe, and Keelan, I chided myself and sighed and subtly stretched my shoulders with a soft smile.

"We should have stolen a barrel of bubble," Keelan declared as he swam over and joined me on my left, sinking down to sit on the sand with his knees propped up, resting his arms on top of them. Mr. Whelk groaned his agreement as he floated around on his back, showcasing his belly, above his master's head.

"It's not a barrel, but try this," Valdez and Felipe appeared on my other side, their faces both slightly flushed. The pirate passed something akin to a wine-skin (though it looked like it was made of seal skin) over to the younger competitor while the other two sat.

I studied Felipe and the contrast between his graying navy hair and the pink of his cheeks. I'd never seen him drink before, much less hover on the edge of tipsy. It was adorable.

I grew a tiny bit giddy, to see the three of them surround me casually, brushing against me intentionally as they handed across the skin full of bubble.

Keelan took a slug and coughed. "Oh, that's strong stuff."

"Majesty?" Valdez's hazel eyes dared me and sent a tendril of heat spiraling down through my stomach.

That look. That right there. I needed to explore it so much more. I licked my lips as I stared at him for a moment, while my breathing grew shallow.

He gave a playful lift of his brows that said, "Well?"

I snagged the skin from Keelan's hand and took a small sip.

Sarding hell! My tongue and throat lit up like I'd just coated them in lava. I pounded my chest as my eyes watered and I handed the skin over immediately to the next set of contestants to arrive—Julian and Stavros.

"Bastard!" I cursed Valdez, who only laughed.

Julian smirked at me, and the level-headed siren shook his head. "No thank you. You look like you just licked the underside of a barnacle-covered boat."

He tried to push the skin gently back toward me but I insisted.

"Come on, Julian. One night. Loosen up. Just give me one night."

"I'll give you one night," Valdez quipped.

"I'll give you a thousand," Keelan parried, not to be outdone.

"It couldn't hurt," Stavros added softly at Julian's side. "I don't think any of us have ever seen you drink."

"I'll bet he's wild," Felipe commented.

"I'll bet so," Stavros grinned.

"You won, you have to drink!" Keelan pointed out illogically, spurred on to join with the others.

"Drink it!" the other contestants chanted as Julian and Stavros sat and joined our little circle.

Julian sighed and took the bubble skin from me. He tilted his head back and squinted his eyes in disgust before the bubble even touched his lips.

I smiled at the camaraderie amongst this circle of men, waving as Mateo swam clumsily over to join us, Taft trailed him and gave me a grin that was quite distinctive—missing a tooth.

"What are we all doing?" Mateo asked happily before someone shoved the skin into his face with a laugh.

This—this is what I wanted, what I'd secretly hoped the tournament could be. Sitting around the campfire with my competitors teasing one another, all of us relaxed and happy.

Navagio might have been a low point—but look at where it had brought us. I glanced around the circle and my chest grew warm as I saw Stavros poking Julian in the ribs, making him laugh. I saw Valdez tempting Mr. Whelk into a game of tug of war with a bit of knotted silk. Watkins came up behind Keelan and the siren moved over so the shark shifter could sit next to him.

The moment was perfect. Absolutely perfect.

Then Mr. Whelk bit Valdez's finger, making the pink dolphin shifter howl.

I started to laugh along with the others, but movement flickered in the corner of my vision, and I turned to see just what it was, possibly a crab or something, scuttling along.

It wasn't.

The movement along the sand became a ripple as the ground started to shift beneath us. The earth wavered and rippled.

We all struggled to stand and swim up as screams ripped through the campsite and, all of a sudden, thousands of stone fish rose up from the dirt inside the ring of tents.

They were horrid, disgusting looking creatures — covered in yellow pustules that looked like a cross between a wart and vomit. The edges of their fins were scalloped and yellow and their tails swished threateningly. I couldn't see their eyes, but their frowning mouths opened up, and gaping black holes appeared.

The sight sent everyone around me into a panic, sirens screeching, mer yelling — bubbles flying as everyone tried to swim away as quickly as possible. But the knot of people was tangled with stonefish, everyone bumping into one another as they struggled not to touch one of the most poisonous fish in all of the ocean.

Stonefish shot venom out of their back spines, venom that could kill a limb—turn it black as death, or even kill a man if there was enough poison.

Strangely enough, I didn't feel fear. I had the rush of adrenaline making me alert, eyes wide and darting. Inside, there was also a tingle akin to excitement that was whipped up by fury into the shakes—my fingertips trembled.

There was no chance that we'd just stumbled upon a group of stonefish. They were solitary creatures, and it wasn't mating season.

We've been set up.

I didn't have a chance to think beyond that before the crowd around me suddenly tightened like a noose. My betta fish fins were crushed to my spine, and I nearly fell down to the stonefish swarm.

A strong set of arms reached out and yanked me against him. I looked up to see Valdez's face contorted with rage. It was only as the pink-haired shifter struggled to swim us up himself that I saw exactly why our entourage had drawn in upon itself.

Stonefish weren't the only threat.

Only seconds after the stonefish arose, we were surrounded by a thick ring of lionfish. The orange and white striped lionfish had venomous spines protruding from their fins like spider legs that could poison with a touch. Their bright zebra stripes and clown-like spots on their fins were a mockery, because those fish were anything but funny.

Sard.

The ring of lionfish tightened around us, some darting overhead.

Death surrounded us on all sides.

That's when the fear hit me. It must have been delayed by the adrenaline but the fear of dying made my mind go blank for half a second, before I had the wherewithal to shove it back a bit and try to find a way out of this.

Several people shrieked and everyone trembled against one another as they swerved to avoid all of the poisonous creatures.

The eyes of the lionfish shown a dull milky, pale blue and my thoughts were immediately drawn to the witch who'd attacked us on the road to Reef City.

I hadn't seen eyes on the stonefish, but I'd have wagered my crown that they were the same.

"We have to go up faster than they can. They're enchanted to attack," Felipe whispered from nearby, reiterating my own thoughts.

This ambush was magical.

Rebels? Or Gorgono? Both?

It didn't matter right then. What mattered was getting away as quickly as possible.

I searched inside for my song, my own magic, but the screams were loud and jarring as panic overtook rational thought.

I saw someone's arm—I had no idea whose—turn black. Stonefish poison. I twisted my head to try to see but the press of people was too thick. I could only see flailing arms and blots of hair.

Shite.

Guilt mangled my stomach as I imagined torturous things—dead bodies, ruined lives. What was happening right now?

Focus, Avia. Stop this attack. You're the only one who can do something. Humberto's magic wouldn't do any good. Speed magic potions wouldn't help.

I saw Taft transform into a metal shield. Mateo grabbed him and held him up to stop a lionfish that zoomed at him.

Where are my mages? I wondered. *Where the sard is Lizza?*

I heard an explosion that shoved the current and made my head curl to one side as the water rolled forcefully across it.

But I still couldn't see. I had to stop this shite. Now.

I focused again on my magic as Valdez fought to swim me up, higher, faster.

I can try to throw out an ice shield. That could block the lionfish surrounding us. But the damned stonefish were right in the midst of us, trying to swim up around our ankles.

How could I freeze them too, without turning everyone else into ice sculptures?

Cold. What if I didn't freeze everything, just turned it so cold that it was like the depths?

These bastard fish lived close to the surface, they'd slow in lower temperatures. So would everyone else… but the fish were smaller…hopefully they'd slow faster.

My song surged up, the hauntingly beautiful voice singing an angry, wordless tune today, one that shouted, made her voice turn scratchy and deep on her long notes. It was a war song.

I tried to take the reins of the music. I tried to focus it, make it yield to me, but my fury was so strong that I couldn't conduct the notes—I lost the thread when I saw a servant nearby shriek and clutch his leg as it slowly turned from gold to black.

I wanted to scream and vomit and cry but I did none of it. I had to focus.

I had to close my eyes to let the music fill me, which went against every instinct to watch my enemies. Instead, I turned into Valdez's chest, clutching at him, while I called up my magic.

I waited longer this time, let the war song fill my bones and make my eardrums shake with the power of the melody. I appreciated the song of the sea, the beauty of its wrath, before I tried to control it.

When my entire body was filled with the hum of a low note, I lifted my hands like I was conducting the music —and an arctic blast erupted from my palms—creating fifty balls of ice floating in the water, forming right between the packed in crowd, instead of the blast of cold I'd wanted.

Shite. Sard. Shite.

I'd messed up.

But around me, my men grabbed the ice and did exactly as the crowd had against the ship, they grabbed the balls of ice and hurled them at their targets, bellowing curses as they did so.

Watkins grabbed five and hurled them in quick succession at a single lionfish, until I watched the thing float up toward the surface, dead as a doornail.

"More, Avia!" Valdez ordered, wrapping his arm more securely around my waist.

Another blast, and I created more balls of ice. A third. A fourth.

The water chilled with every blast, but I didn't stop even when my limbs grew tired and shaky, or my betta fins ached and felt like they might crack from the cold.

It was us or them.

I kept going even when the voice of the sea started to sound strained, scratchy, as if my connection with her was weakening along with my body. I clenched my teeth and tried to tell myself I was one of those machines I'd seen in Navagio, automated.

But my concentration was interrupted by every scream of horror—my fingers contracting, even though I couldn't grab onto anything because I had to keep on with the magic.

I saw one siren body float up from our group toward the sun, the blackened husk casting a shadow over us.

I had no idea who it was, and I strained my neck to look until a lionfish floated too close overhead.

I didn't strain my neck for the second, the third, the eighth body to float up from our ranks and hover at the top of the water's edge, blocking the light like mottled storm clouds.

Tears streaked down my cheeks as I sent out yet another round of ice projectiles, this set smaller than the last as my energy flagged.

Would it be enough?

Misery and fury rollicked through my system.

Another round.

Another.

More bodies floated up until I worked in a daze of disbelief, shock finally taking over and insulating me—far too late.

Finally, someone—it sounded like Lizza, yelled out, "They're all down!"

Immediately, my limbs went limp, and I clasped Valdez for support, a raw sob making my chest shudder.

But I only allowed myself a few seconds of weakness, because Queen Gela's voice goaded me.

"A queen lends her strength to her people—she remains calm so that they can quell their own panic. A queen must remain confident. Provide direction. And guidance."

As much as I wanted to curl into a ball and cry, I couldn't. Because if I did, I'd prove the rebels, and Gorgono—and anyone else who thought I was unfit —right.

I took a deep breath, thanked the song inside my chest, and slowly let it fade to a hum as I straightened.

Then I swam out of Valdez's arms, and slightly up above the crowd, peering about for lionfish but seeing none. It looked like they really were gone.

Of course, the pirate shadowed my every move, as did my guards, and Watkins. But I didn't look down at them, I stared down at the tear-filled eyes of everyone else.

"It's going to be okay—" I started to say, but then a devastating flash of fury swept over me and I imagined attacking the throats of entire towns, dragging mermen out one by one and slitting their throats.

Through my horrid vision, I saw one more person float up through the crowd, his bronze cheeks turning black, his eyes glazing over as his mint green hair wavered in the current.

I watched in disbelief, as Julian floated up to the surface and his soul faded away.

23

I DON'T REMEMBER what speech I gave, something vague about justice and seeking out those responsible. The words didn't matter, because they were broken up by sobs from the crowd and interrupted so often by my own attempts not to completely erupt.

It was Sahar who helped keep us all together. She and Lizza.

The undead mage and Posey gathered together the soldiers to carefully remove any fish bodies to a safe distance.

Sahar and I led another group up to the top of the waves to collect the bodies. I latched onto Julian's hand as my vision blurred and a cold, open hole formed in my ribs—a feeling of emptiness, the utter loss of all the potential he had, all the good he'd been capable of… even a melting sort of sorrow at the loss of his smile.

I hadn't fallen in love with Julian—not by any means—but the misery of losing him was so intense that it almost felt as if I had.

I pulled him in to hug him, one last goodbye, and was startled to find resistance.

My weeping eyes looked across his body to see Stavros clutching his other hand, blue eyes wet and wide, his eyelashes clumped together by teardrops.

We shared a long look of grief for the man between us. Something happened during that look, something monumental. Stavros had always been shy but clever, one of the men I'd thought had potential, but hadn't yet been able to find that sense of connection. In that moment, I found it. It felt as if our souls united, grief tethering us as we clutched at Julian and unwished the prior hour—we begged the universe to reverse time and undo this truth.

I tried to speak several times, but couldn't, sorrow squeezing my throat so hard I thought I might choke.

Julian—who'd never gotten to reconcile with his family… Julian—who'd never get to perform one of the live surgeries he insisted would revolutionize the world… Julian was gone.

I dropped Julian's cold hand and swam over to Stavros, clutching him instead, wrapping my arms around his waist as I gave into this grief that felt like it was swallowing me whole, as if a whale had opened up his giant maw and gulped, enveloping me in darkness.

Stavros's arms slowly came around me and together we cried until our throats were raw, until the other bodies were gone, all taken away to be prepared for funerary rites. We clutched each other until I felt purged and empty.

That's when I drew back and looked into Stavros's face, his beautiful even features.

"I'm sorry for your loss," I said. "I know you two had become close."

He shook his head disbelievingly. "I… have you ever met someone who was so incredible that you thought they might change the course of your life?"

I blinked, stunned. I had realized they'd formed a friendship, but I hadn't known how deep it had run.

I nodded, because Mateo had been that for me. An instant friend, a partner in crime.

Stavros's gaze drifted back to Julian's and he said gruffly, "For a second, I thought things might be different."

I stared at Stavros for a moment, studying the gentle lines of his face. His eyes studied me softly and gently, before darting down so that his wet lashes brushed his cheeks.

He looked so handsome. He was being utterly vulnerable with me. I felt a connection with him, we were bonded by grief.

But not by attraction.

For a moment, I forgot the world around us—the sadness and rage we'd have to deal with, the fear that would lurk in every shadow going forward. That all faded as frustration with myself came to the forefront.

Why couldn't I be drawn to him the way that I was to Watkins or Valdez? Why couldn't I find his softer nature refreshing and kind? I'd fallen for Mateo. And he was sweet-hearted. Of course, I'd fallen for him first, when I was just a girl, before I'd faced darkness and transformed.

And he'd changed in the mountains. Mateo had grown and evolved. He wasn't quite as innocent anymore. Neither of us were. It was practically a miracle that Mateo and I reconnected the way we did and still fit together with all our jagged edges.

I wanted to fall for Stavros, his innocence and sweet honesty in the face of what was probably his first brush with death.

But someone like me could only corrupt shy Stavros. I couldn't be any good for him.

"This is proof that trying to change is merely a dream, that when you're already on a path…" Stavros trailed off when he realized I was staring at him. His expression slowly changed. One of his hands left my waist and went up to smudge away the tears that still filled his eyes.

"Majesty, when you look at me like that…I can hardly breathe," Stavros whispered softly as his eyes grew hooded.

My breath caught when he said that and my stomach swirled with dark uncertainty, then a fierce determination filled me—to keep him, to make him mine, to finish my plan.

Those feelings didn't even make sense.

And making a move to test out my attraction to him wouldn't be right. Not here or now with death all around us.

I should pull away. I should confess that I'm not drawn to him... but what if I'm cutting him off too soon? What if he's simply being overshadowed by the others? What if he deserves more of a chance? My mind argued with itself.

What if Stavros could be good for me?

What if he could lead me away from this dark depraved path I was on—these visions full of pure unadulterated evil—and help me rediscover my goodness?

I might have to pay a price for my magic, but what if keeping him nearby helped me retain my good sense and keep those tendencies in check?

Could it?

I didn't know—though I did believe now that I was paying a price for my magic, because Watkins hadn't been calling for the slaughter of cities after this attack. He hadn't been a raving lunatic…not like the turbulent, emotional visions that had run through my head.

Those were all me. The darkness and loss of humanity were mine alone.

I should warn Stavros to swim far and fast and never return.

My eyes traced the soft golden curve of his cheek, the strong jaw that was common to all sirens.

Why didn't I feel that pull? My lips parted in frustration, and I sought the courage to tell him the truth or even just find the strength to swim away from him. But battle had weakened me, leaving me wrung out, unable to do more than ponder.

Someone came to collect Julian while Stavros and I remained in each other's arms, staring at each other.

Stavros misread my intentions. His light blue eyes darted down to my mouth. Then he leaned down to me.

He was nervous, and it was adorably charming to watch him swallow hard and reach up and cup my cheek, so charming that I forgot to tell him that it was hopeless.

I tried to will fizzy sparks to light up my belly. But my chest gave off only a peculiar shiver, a warning flinch like I might upon spotting a snake or other unsavory creature.

My chest had been doing that a lot lately, feeling strange things at odd moments. It only proved to me that my mind's urges and whims were just as illogically silly as my heart's had ever been.

For instance, when Stavros's lips approached mine, I felt a sliver of anger.

And when his lips pressed against my own.

Nothing.

Just cold skin sliding along mine, warm breath cascading down my chin. I closed my eyes and waited for the kiss to be over, holding back a sigh of disappointment.

Why? Why did I have to feel this way? Was I broken? Why couldn't I want him?

My fingers dug into the creases of his elbows and I suddenly felt the urge to maim him, to hurt him, to watch him crawl bleeding on the floor of my sandstone palace, dragging himself along the ground like a slug, leaving a thick, wet, red trail behind him.

Desperately, I reached up to his own cheek and caressed it as I deepened the kiss, trying to force passion, intimacy, something to counteract my magic's violent vision.

I nipped at his lip and turned our kiss into an open-mouthed exploration, pretending I was still the sweet girl in the ballroom back in Evaness. I tried to fabricate affection, even just the dullest of sparks.

Instead, I felt panic, revulsion, even hate slide across my brain.

Sard it.

I was so utterly warped and twisted that I couldn't find it in me to be attracted to a soft, gentle man.

No, I wanted someone dark and dangerous, someone who could be just as cruel beneath the surface as I was.

Stavros pulled back, blinking slowly and I bit my lip in regret as I studied his eyes.

"I'm sorry." I shook my head and took his hand, almost as if I was pleading with him to forgive me. "I wish I could fall in love with you..."

Stavros yanked away from me, his confused expression morphing into one I'd never seen on his handsome face. His features slowly hardened as his jaw ticked and he reached for a black ring I'd never noticed on his left hand. As he twisted it, he muttered, "Oh, but you can."

EPILOGUE

RAJ

MY CHEST EXPLODED in pain for a second, as if a boulder was trying to break through. I gasped and grabbed Avia's purple skirt as a vice squeezed my heart so tightly that my toes curled.

Then, just as quickly as it had begun, the pain stopped and instead, this utterly bizarre softness filled me as if I was a dandelion and someone had just set their lips to my soul and now it was scattered, swaying gently in a summer breeze, trusting this unseen, unknown force to carry it just where it was meant to go.

The wind inside of me whipped up harder and stronger…just like it used to smack across the sands in Cheryn, shifting them, moving them, reshaping them…

I blinked, startled, unsure how to react, when Avia's face came into focus. Her pale skin, soft oval face, those violet eyes framed by thick lashes. Her brows were lowered in concern as she stared at me, trying to understand what had just happened, why I'd stiffened.

"Stavros?" she whispered, leaning forward, putting that soft hand upon my arm. Her touch was magnetic, immediately all of my cells realigned to point directly at her.

I flipped my hand over and linked our fingers as the heart in my chest gave a longing, plaintive thud.

Somehow...the wish she made had rebounded.

My heart was affected.

My mouth opened and I gaped in wonder as the shadows inside my spirit dissolved like it was dawn, the sun cresting over the horizon and bathing me in light.

I found myself madly, wildly, magically in love.

No.

NO.

NO.

AFTERWORD

Thank you so much for reading! I can't wait to continue this story and bring you with me all over the kingdom of Okeanos! There are lots of secrets yet to unveil!!

Please consider telling someone about this little series. Your personal recommendations and reviews make all the difference in the world. Without your help, I couldn't keep doing what I do. I'm grateful every day that I get to write beautiful words for you!

XOXO!

ACKNOWLEDGMENTS

A huge thanks to Rob, Thais, Lysanne, Raven and Ivy. Thais really saved my butt on this one, so I owe her lots of cookies.

Thanks to my editor Lorie and my cover designer, Carol Marquess at Marquess Designs, and my amazing ARC readers.

A special thank you to Jennifer for saying she couldn't wait for this book. Her words came on a hard day and I really needed them.

ALSO BY ANN DENTON

Choose from books on the following pages based on your current reading mood.

The standalone or the first book in each series are listed by mood. The darkest reads appear first and grow progressively more light-hearted so it makes it easy to find just what you're looking for next. I also tried to add some basic mood info at the bottom of each series page for you.

Feral Princess Series
(Completed Trilogy)

A hot, dark shifter omegaverse with dub con, a steamy alpha, a loving beta, and a sassy omega who thought she was going to be an alpha female. She was sooo wrong, but when she's claimed by the pack alpha, make no mistake, she has something to say about it.

Defiant - Book 1

Mood - #DARK #DIRTY #ALPHA

Stalked and Plucked Series
(Series of Standalones)

A fast-burn, contemporary MF romance series with very morally gray men who stalk their ladies before claiming them. The series follows a group of college girls who are best friends.

Chaining Daisy - Book 1

Mood - #HOT #HOLYHELL #NEWKINKUNLOCKED

Pinnacle Series
(Completed Duet)

A medium-burn paranormal romance about a girl who gets herself sent to a reform academy on purpose, so she can recruit criminally-minded guys to pull off the magical heist of the century. (Reverse Harem)

Magical Academy for Delinquents #MAD - Book 1

Mood - #BADASS #FUN #SEXY GAMES

Lotto Love Series
(Completed Duet)

A medium-burn, contemporary romantic comedy reverse harem about winning the lotto and doing whatever the hell you want with it, even if that means holding a Bachelorette-style competition for an entire harem of hotties.

Lotto Men - Book 1

Mood- #LOL #BLUSHING #NO WAY

Ruby - Jewels Cafe Series
(Standalone)

A medium-burn, fated mates reverse harem with an angel on her last strike, some nerds and a tech demon determined to help her, and Christmas miracles.

Ruby

Mood - #SWEET #AWWW #GIGGLES

Dark Temptations Series

(Incomplete)

A fast-burn monster reverse harem in an alternate reality where monsters rule the earth. A human woman is captured and auctioned off to the Four Terrors who will haunt her nightmares and her dreams alike. Cowrite with Katie May.

Ravaged by Monsters - Book 1

Mood - #DARK #FATED LOVE #WILD SEXY TIMES

Broken Howl

(Standalone)

A female omega rejects her mates so she can escape her abuser. She's sent to an island for rejects but her mates refuse to let her go…

Cowrite with Katie May.

Broken Howl

Mood - #CRYING #HEALING #FIGHTING

Darkest Queen Series
(Incomplete)

The devil is a woman. And this is the story about she fell from Heaven only to rise as God's greatest enemy... (A reverse harem spinoff of the Darkest Flames series) Cowrite with Katie May.

For Whom the Bell Tolls - Book 1

Mood - #FURY #SOUL-DEEP CONNECTIONS #BATTLE OF WILLS

Darkest Flames Series
(Completed Trilogy with a novella)

A medium-burn paranormal romance about a girl who tries a love spell on the hot guy at school and accidentally summons demons instead. It contains psychotic, alpha males, and student/teacher relationships. (Reverse Harem)
Cowrite with Katie May.

Demon Kissed - Book 1

Mood - #OOPS #NAUGHTY LAUGHTER #FORBIDDEN HEAT

Demon's Joy

(Standalone)

Santa's daughter has to save Christmas from demons! And all she's got to help her are five funny reindeer. (A reverse harem spinoff of the Darkest Flames series) Cowrite with Katie May.

Demon's Joy

Mood - #SILLY #HOLIDAY CHEER #YUM

Mage Shifter War Series
(Completed Duet)

A medium-burn paranormal mafia romance. A fae princess is taken captive by three shifter criminals.
(Reverse Harem)
Cowritten with Elle Middaugh.

Fae Captive - Book 1

Mood - #BONNIE&CLYDE #BADASS #HOT

Hammer Time
(Standalone)

A medium-burn paranormal comedy featuring Thor's daughter and a quest to save demigods from prison. Expect lots of ancient deities and potty humor.
(Reverse Harem)
Cowritten with M.J. Marstens.

Hammer Time

Mood- #PUNTASTIC #NOYOUDIDN'T #SNORT

CONNECT AND GET SNEAK PEEKS

Do you want to read exclusive point of views from different characters, make predictions and claim your book boyfriends with other readers, see my inspiration for these books, and hang with fellow RH lovers? Then join my Facebook Reader Group! I promise you'll love it!

Join Ann Denton's Reader Group

Facebook.com/groups/AnnDentonReaderGroup

ABOUT ME

I'm a shy lady who has always been obsessed with reading and travel and live theater. I've lived in four states and currently reside in Oklahoma, hence the nickname from my writer friends: Annie Oakie.

I have two of the world's cutest children, a crazy dog, and an amazing husband that I drive somewhat insane when I stop in the middle of the hallway, halfway through putting laundry away, picturing a scene.

Printed in Dunstable, United Kingdom

64652209R00231